Be swept away by Phillipa Ashley . . .

'Gorgeously romantic, with plenty of twists to
keep me turning the pages'
Holly Martin

'Escapist and uplifting'
Woman & Home

'Deliciously entertaining'
Liz Fenwick

'The ultimate summer reading escape!'
***Yours* magazine**

'Enjoyable and uplifting'
Jo Thomas

'A feel-good read for summer'
The Sun

'Warm and funny and feel-good. The best sort of holiday read'
Katie Fforde

'Romantic and life-affirming'
Woman's Weekly

'Sparkling and festive'
Milly Johnson

Phillipa Ashley writes warm, funny romantic fiction for a variety of world-famous international publishers.

After studying English at Oxford, she worked as a copywriter and journalist. Her first novel, *Decent Exposure*, won the RNA New Writers Award and was made into a TV movie called *12 Men of Christmas* starring Kristin Chenoweth and Josh Hopkins. As Pippa Croft, she also wrote the Oxford Blue series – *The First Time We Met*, *The Second Time I Saw You* and *Third Time Lucky*.

Phillipa lives in a Staffordshire village and has an engineer husband and scientist daughter who indulge her arty whims. She runs a holiday-let business in the Lake District, but a big part of her heart belongs to Cornwall. She visits the county several times a year for 'research purposes', an arduous task that involves sampling cream teas, swimming in wild Cornish coves and following actors around film shoots in a campervan. Her hobbies include watching *Poldark*, Earl Grey tea, Prosecco-tasting and falling off surfboards in front of the RNLI lifeguards.

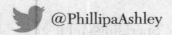 @PhillipaAshley

Just Say Yes

Phillipa Ashley

REVIEW

First published in 2008 by Little Black Dress
An imprint of HEADLINE PUBLISHING GROUP

This paperback edition published in 2023 by Headline Review

Cataloguing in Publication Data is available from the British Library

ISBN 978 1 0354 0136 9

Typeset in Transitional 511 BT by Avon DataSet Ltd, Alcester,
Warwickshire

Printed and bound in Great Britain by Clays Ltd, Elcograf S.p.A.

HEADLINE PUBLISHING GROUP
An Hachette UK Company
Carmelite House
50 Victoria Embankment
London EC4Y 0DZ

www.headline.co.uk
www.hachette.co.uk

For Valerie and John Sizer

Acknowledgements

This book was a terrible struggle to write . . . no, I can't lie, it was great fun from the first word to the last. Here's my chance to thank some of the people who made it such a pleasure, especially Claire Baldwin and Cat Cobain at Headline and my fantastic agent Broo Doherty. I'm also indebted to Rosy Thornton, Annette, Julie Haggar, Izabella Gawarecka, Duntay, Ania, Liz Fenwick, Janice Hume, Catherine Jones, Lorelei Mathias, Barbara Whale, and to Sue Jackson and Lynne Logan at Heart of the Lakes.

Most of all, to John and Charlotte. ILY x

Prologue

'Well, are they *there*?'

'Fiona, is the Pope Catholic? Of course they're here.'

The phone subsided into silence as Lucy Gibson did a left into the anonymous north London street. She could have sworn she heard actual cogs whirring in Fiona's mind before her mobile crackled into life again.

'OK. This calls for guerilla tactics,' said Fiona as Lucy narrowly avoided a nun on a bicycle. 'Have you got a paper bag in the car?'

'I think there's an old Monsoon carrier bag in the boot. But I'm driving right now and besides, what should I do with it? Cut holes for eyes and wear it over my head? I think I've got my manicure set in the glove box and—'

'Actually, I was thinking you could breathe into it to stop you from hyperventilating.'

'I – am – not – hyperventilating!' said Lucy as the nun wobbled precariously along the gutter.

'No. Of course not. Stupid of me to detect a slight hint of apprehension. I'll go away.'

'Fi, I know you're trying to help. Stay on the line until

I get to the flat. I'm nearly there now and – Oh. My. God.'

'What?'

'Fiona, there are *hundreds* of them.'

'You mean actual hundreds or about seven?'

'Ten. At least.'

There was another silence, but this time no cogs whirred, from which Lucy concluded that Fiona must think the situation was hopeless.

'Lucy, are you sure you're OK? Chin up. Maybe this won't be as bad as you expect.'

Lucy suspected it more likely that Elvis was alive and well and working as a manicurist in Shepherd's Bush but she thought the better of telling Fiona because right now, her best friend appeared to be one of the few people on the planet who didn't want to cut out her heart with a rusty knife.

'Maybe. Thanks for being here,' she said.

'No problem, hon.'

As Lucy pulled into the space in front of her flat, she knew that Elvis was well and truly dead and that it was going to be at least as bad as she expected. A pack of long-range lenses and furry microphones all swung in her direction like the velociraptors in *Jurassic Park*. As she reached for the door handle, a thought struck her. She had another choice: she didn't *have* to get out of the car at all. She could head straight down the street and right out of London as far as a tank of unleaded would take her. If she wanted to, she could run away from all of this right now.

But she wouldn't run away because she was still

convinced, despite what seven million people had said, that she hadn't done anything *wrong* and that, actually, she had done the *right* thing and one day, maybe when she was pushing up daisies or had been recycled into mulch, everyone (including Nick) would realise it and forgive her.

Before she could change her mind, she flicked the lock, took a deep breath and pushed open the door.

'*Lucy!*'

'Miss Gibson!'

'Over here, love!'

'Let's have a big smile for *The Sport*!'

'Can you just give me a moment?' she asked, barely able to hear herself above the shouting and whirr of camera drives.

'Is it true you're in talks with Max Clifford?' shouted a man.

'Er . . . no, I don't think so.'

A girl in a huge scarf thrust a microphone under her nose and Lucy had a horrible feeling she was going to sneeze. She hoped not; it always made her eyes water and she didn't want them to think she was crying.

'Are you seeing someone else? Is that why you did it?' shrieked a woman in a pink beret.

'There's no one else,' said Lucy, head down, making for the steps that led up to her flat.

'Did you know Nick Laurentis has checked into rehab?'

Lucy ground to a halt in the middle of the pavement.

Nick was in *rehab*? Surely she hadn't driven him to drink and drugs in just one week? She knew he was terribly hurt, shattered even, but in therapy? It couldn't be true.

'Your mum's said to be devastated by your decision, Lucy. How does that make you feel?'

Lucy was sure her mum definitely wouldn't have said anything of the sort, not in public, anyway. 'No comment,' she said firmly, lifting her chin and focusing on her navy blue front door. The crowd gathered ahead of her, barring her way. 'Can you let me get to my front door, please? I've got a hungry Siamese kitten in need of its dinner,' she said.

It wasn't quite true, but close enough. Fiona was coming round later with Hengist who was slightly larger than a kitten but always starving. Yet even that went against the grain. Lucy had A Thing about lying. It wasn't that she was against it, per se, not if it was to spare someone's feelings or avoid a parking ticket. She just wasn't very good at it. While some people had fibbing down to a fine art, Lucy turned scarlet, got flustered and protested even more suspiciously than Lady Macbeth.

One of the reporters frantically scribbled in her notebook. 'Is there one "s" or two in Siamese?'

'Three,' said a photographer with a purple Mohican hairstyle. 'Do you own this flat, then, Miss Gibson? How much is it worth? Did your boyfriend pay for it?'

'He's not my boyfriend.'

'Have you split up for good, then?' the pack bayed in unison and Lucy finally gave up.

'Do you think it's because of your cellulite?'

'Is that a Prada handbag or Primark?'

'Miss Gibson, is it true that you've had sex with a warlock?'

'Excuse me!' she declared, lowering her head and pushing people out of the way with her handbag (FCUK, actually, not that it was any of their business). As she reached the steps, there was a clatter followed by a shriek and then some scuffling.

'Who left that bleedin' wheelie bin there?'

'Mind my camera, you dickhead! That lens cost over a grand.'

She took her chance as the reporters scrambled over a pile of used nappies and takeaway tins spilling out of the bin. One guy was wiping something nasty from his hand and cursing. Racing up the steps, she shoved her key in the lock with shaking fingers. It jiggled a bit, clicked then opened. The dark and dingy hall that led to her flat looked like the opening to a magic cavern. Behind her, the press were still arguing and cursing around the bin. Excellent. Served them right.

'Ha-ooof.'

The breath whooshed from her chest and the welcome mat rushed up to meet her face. Someone had moved the hedgehog boot scraper in front of the door.

'Oh yes, there is a God!'

'Quick! We'll make a bloody mint out of this one.'

'Get off, you oaf! Don't you know who I am?'

A hairy hand, poking out of a black sleeve, reached down for hers and pulled her roughly to her feet. 'Quick. Get in here.'

Then she was safe inside, her back to the door.

'OK?'

'Yes. Thanks,' she panted, brushing some dirt from her knees. When she looked up, her rescuer was smiling benignly down at her from behind his neat little goatee.

'Charlie. Forgive me for asking, but why are you wearing a nun's habit?'

'Oh – this. I'll explain later. Now, I need to lock my bike up before that pack of wolves nicks it.'

Suddenly, Lucy had an insane urge to giggle. She knew it must be nerves and adrenaline and the shock of having been chased into her flat and rescued by her neighbour, a six-foot-tall nun. She also knew that if she didn't laugh, she might cry because only a week ago, she'd been able to walk into her own front door without running the gauntlet. Just a few months ago, life had been normal but that was before a tall, dark, handsome stranger had chased her down the street with a bagel.

Chapter One

It had been a murky November day, six months before, when Lucy had first joined the queue at Love Bites, the sandwich bar around the corner from Able & Lawson, the City law firm where she worked as a marketing assistant. She'd offered to get Letitia, the senior partner, a hummus pitta because Letitia was not only very nice but also very pregnant.

As soon as she walked into Love Bites that day, Lucy noticed that it had a new attraction beyond its collection of home-baked muffins, *tarte aux fraises* and sticky brownies. There was a new guy behind the counter who was busy creating a tower bagel for the girl who worked in the travel agents on the floor below. It was a beautiful bagel, oozing relish and overflowing with red salami and creamy mozzarella. Lucy eyed the bagel with envy, and then checked out its maker: a mouthwatering proposition himself.

He was tall and broad-shouldered with a definite touch of the Mediterranean about him. Everything from his olive-green apron to his caramel skin was edible. His hands were tanned and strong, yet the way they handled that bagel, he might have been a sculptor. Not that she'd ever known any sculptors but that was how she imagined the hands of an artist might be: long, slender and very gifted. His badge said, 'Hi, I'm Nick and I'm ready to serve you', which, she had to admit, was less romantic.

'And what can I do you for, lovely laydee?' she half expected him to say, but of course he hadn't. What he actually said was, 'Next, please.'

'A hummus and salad on wholemeal pitta, no cucumber,' she replied, snapping out of her fantasy and trying to act cool. Nick stood by patiently, his hands poised over the chopping board as she scanned the menu behind the counter. 'And a chicken salad on granary, please, no butter or mayonnaise,' she added.

'You don't need to diet.' OK, he hadn't said that either, but nodded, smiled and murmured: 'Coming up, madam' without a trace of irony.

The next time she'd wanted a sandwich, she'd been strangely drawn to Love Bites, even though, to be honest, the prices were cheaper and the choice wider at the usual office haunt. And so, she found herself queuing again, as Nick 'Ready to Serve Her' chopped and spread and filled and stuffed.

'How can I 'elp you, babe?' said Marvin, the shop owner, as Lucy stood dreamily by the counter. Nick seemed to have disappeared into the kitchen. Perhaps he's fetching some more baguettes, she thought, trying to hide her disappointment.

'Philadelphia and grapes on granary, please,' she muttered, her cheeks reddening. Minutes later, clutching her lunch, she rushed out of the shop, not even bothering to take her fifty-pence change.

She *really* wouldn't have gone into Love Bites again, but Letitia had begged her to fetch a slice of carrot cake with frosting that 'simply couldn't be had anywhere else in London'.

'I do hope you don't mind, Lucy,' Letitia had said, rubbing her back as she hovered by the water cooler in the office. 'I know it's my hormones and I really should *not* be eating for two, but the thought of anything else makes me want to throw up.'

'It's fine,' said Lucy, crossing her fingers behind her back. 'I was going in there anyway. Their tower bagels are irresistible.'

She managed to stroll out of the office, before reaching the pavement and almost skipping down the street and around the corner. It was Friday and there was already a queue snaking out of the door and in front of the window. Lucy joined it, hoping to catch a glimpse of Nick. There, through the clear spots left by the 'o' and 'v' of the etched logo, she thought she could see him, assembling a sub roll. What seemed like hours later, she was inside the shop, mentally tossing a coin to see whether it would be Nick or Marvin who made up her lunch.

'Next!' called Marvin as she got to the front of the queue.

'Um . . . er . . .'

'Difficult decision?' offered Nick, already splitting a bap for the customer behind her.

'Yes, I'm dithering a bit, aren't I?'

'Yeah. You are,' grunted a bloke in the queue.

'You have my turn,' she said, in what she considered

to be a flash of spontaneous genius. The man tutted in exasperation and stepped in front as she hung out by the chiller cabinet, pretending to study the menu. When Nick had finished the bap, he smiled and invited her to take her turn.

'Carrot cake, please,' she said, feeling strangely shy. 'And a tower bagel.'

'Large or extra large?'

'Do you do medium?' she asked daringly.

He winked. 'For you, yes.'

A few minutes later, she'd paid her money and hurried out of the shop, already wondering what on earth had possessed a sane, intelligent woman to hang around a bagel bar specifically in the hope of having her lunch made up by a complete stranger. She'd almost reached the office when she heard a shout behind her.

'Hey!'

She knew better than to turn round when people shouted in the street. You always felt such a plonker when you realised it wasn't you.

'Hey you! Bagel Girl!'

Bagel Girl? Still she kept her eyes forward. It was lunchtime, lots of girls must have bagels right now and she didn't want to draw attention to herself.

'Oi! Tower bagel and carrot cake fan. Stop this minute!'

She had no choice. Not after he'd been so specific. If she didn't turn round and answer, he'd be telling everyone she didn't want mayo or butter and then the whole street would know she was watching her weight. Well, they could have spotted that anyway but—

'You . . . forgot . . . your . . . bagel . . .' panted Nick, stopping a few feet away and holding out a paper bag.

Her face was glowing like a beefsteak tomato. 'Have I dragged you away from your work?'

He smiled. 'That's OK. Anything to get out into the fresh air. Marvin told me to come after you. He can spot a potential regular when he sees one.'

'Right. Of course.' Her heart began to sink. So, Nick had been ordered by his boss to chase her down the street. Perhaps Marvin was thinking of launching a loyalty card scheme.

'You work for Able & Lawson, the solicitors, don't you?' he asked.

'Yes, but how do you know that?'

'Marvin saw you when he dropped off some menus last week. He said you were watering a big plant in reception.'

'Someone has to do it. No one else in our office seems to have an affinity with foliage.'

'So you're the plant-care consultant, are you? Very high-powered.'

Lucy saw the twinkle in his eyes and grinned. 'Yes, that's me. Also tea maker, sandwich jockey and, in my spare time, marketing assistant.'

He gave a low whistle. 'Sounds important. Especially the sandwich jockey.'

'Oh, it's vital. Able & Lawson simply couldn't manage without me.' Even as she joked, she felt the irony of her words. She was sure that, come the next round of belt-tightening, Able & Lawson could manage without her.

No amount of late nights, watering plants or being helpful could stop that. Times were tough and marketing assistants, while very useful, did not bring in the massive contracts required to keep afloat a City solicitors'.

'I won't be working in a sandwich shop for ever, you know,' said Nick suddenly.

'But I may be working at Able & Lawson for ever,' she said. Then added, 'It doesn't matter if you do work in a sandwich shop. We all need to eat.'

'No, you don't understand. I want to run my own catering business. I used to be a biochemist but I hated it so I resigned my job and took this one to get hands-on experience of the trade. I've got some savings and when I get the opportunity, I'm going to be my own boss.'

She smiled at his earnestness and Nick must have caught her expression because he laughed awkwardly. 'Hey! Why am I telling you this? You must be bored sick. Look, I have to get back because Marvin doesn't deserve a backslider like me. But before I go, tell me you'll come round to mine for dinner? I can promise you something more interesting than a sandwich.'

'I'm not sure,' Lucy heard herself saying. But why was she even hesitating? The hunky Bagel Boy was asking her out, for goodness' sake. Then again, she didn't know the guy and her instinct kicked in. However gorgeous he was, maybe going round to his place on a first date wasn't such a great idea.

Nick looked downcast.

'OK. Why don't we go and see a film? Then perhaps we can grab a pizza afterwards. My treat,' said Lucy.

'Well, I'm not sure. I invited you. I don't want you paying.'

'It's fine. After all, I am a marketing assistant. I can run to a pizza and we can go Dutch on the film tickets.'

He chewed his lip for a moment before nodding and grinning. 'Done. Pick you up here at seven tomorrow night?'

'OK.'

They both hovered for a while in the middle of the pavement, causing shoppers to push past them and a skateboarder to weave dangerously close.

'I'd better be getting back to work,' said Lucy eventually.

'Me too.'

'Bye then, Nick.'

'Bye, Bagel Girl and . . . what is your name, by the way?'

'It's Lucy. Lucy Gibson.'

He held out a hand. Lucy took it, even though she knew she'd get covered in flour.

'Sorry,' he said with that disarming grin. 'It's those farmhouse baps. I'm Nick Laurentis, by the way.'

'Hello, Nick Laurentis, Bagel Boy.'

Nick laughed, then she thought she saw him hesitate as she lingered, still holding her hand. 'Lucy, I have to confess. Marvin didn't ask me to chase after you at all. That was all my own idea but I didn't want you to know how mad I really am.'

Before she could reply, he was gone, melting into the crowd like carrot cake frosting on a hot day. When Lucy got back to the office, she watched a grateful Letitia wolf down the cake, yet she was barely able to touch the bagel Nick had made for her. Worse, as she drove home from the station that night, the tiny flutters in her stomach told her that she was excited and a little scared. Nick had an air of danger about him, of risk, if that were possible for someone who was armed only with a butter knife.

Yet, he did have an *edge*. She'd seen the fire in his eyes when he'd told her he was going to make something of himself. She really believed he would have a great future. And what had she got to lose? What had either of them got to lose? He was gorgeous, he fancied her; they both wanted fun. He was just a slightly crazy guy who she was going to the movies with.

Or then again, maybe not, thought Lucy, as she stamped around on the steps of the Odeon the next evening. As the autumn rain rebounded off the pavements, she watched as laughing couples and groups of friends dashed into the cinema. Nick was now well over an hour late and her sense of humour was rapidly disappearing down the drain too. She could no longer deny it. It *had* been too good to be true and she ought to have known it. A gorgeous guy like Nick? Asking her out on the spur of the moment? He'd got cold feet, not that she was going to find out. Shaking her head, she ventured down the steps to have one last scan for Bagel Boy.

Spotting a Costa down the street, she headed for the door. She wondered if Nick really was a scumbag. There could be a perfectly reasonable explanation for his non-appearance. He might have had an accident, or maybe his mobile battery was dead, or he had been urgently commandeered by MI5 to make their sandwiches. Wake up and smell the coffee, she told herself as she pushed open the door. He was never going to show anyway.

Chapter Two

Dohhh! Can you ever forgive me, Bagel Girl?
Please accept this small gift from your very
humble (and hopelessly inept)
sandwich maker. I'll call you.

Nick

xxxxx

PS I can explain everything

The card delivered to the Able & Lawson reception the following Monday morning came attached to a large pot plant. It had nondescript green-grey leaves but its main attraction was unmistakable: a proud red spike, about nine inches tall.

'If you don't mind me asking, what on earth is that?' asked Letitia as a red-faced Lucy carried the plant, complete with ribbon-bedecked pot, into the office.

'It's a *Vriesia splendens*. A Flaming Torch,' said Lucy, placing the pot carefully on top of her filing cabinet. There wasn't room for it; the small *Impatiens* her mother had given her would have to be moved.

'This chap is seriously in love,' said Letitia, reading the card. 'Either that or he's had a blow to the head.'

'Actually, I think he's overcome with guilt.'

Letitia settled herself in her black padded office chair and patted her bump. 'I appreciate the gesture but couldn't he have sent something a little less practical? A dozen red roses maybe? Even carnations, if he's truly strapped for cash.'

Lucy was almost certain that Letitia had never been strapped for cash in her life. Her idea of slumming it was buying a pair of knickers in the Janet Reger sale.

'I suppose so, but maybe he thought I looked like a Flaming Torch kind of girl,' said Lucy. And actually, she would much rather have the plant than some grand gesture. The note was a little OTT, but it was so disarming, she couldn't help but almost forgive him.

'On the other hand, five kisses is promising,' said Letitia. 'Has he phoned you with a suitable fairy story yet?'

Right on cue, Lucy's mobile warbled out with the theme tune to *Lost* and she disappeared into the corridor. Five minutes later she was back.

'Well?' asked Letitia, midway through an organic muesli bar.

Lucy didn't want to repeat her conversation because she knew what Letitia would think and probably say. She didn't want to examine Nick's alibi herself too closely. His explanation hadn't been totally convincing and she was seriously wondering whether he deserved the benefit of the doubt or not.

'He says he got the cinemas mixed up,' she said, rolling her eyes.

'Oh, Lucy. Don't tell me you're going to fall for that.'

'Of course not! I'm not that gullible, Letty.' Lucy gave her best attempt at a scornful laugh. 'I'm not going to be taken for a ride that easily by some guy. It was a pathetic excuse, but on the other hand, he's only been in London a few months and it's easily done. And he did say he waited ages outside the Odeon Swiss Cottage in the pouring rain. Maybe I should cut him some slack.'

'Doesn't the man run to a mobile as well as weird plants?'

'He says the battery was dead.' Lucy slapped her forehead. 'Doh! Blokes. What are they like, eh? They'd forget their brains if they had any.'

And besides, it wasn't Nick's brains she was interested in, she thought to herself, thinking of his chocolate-brown eyes and talented hands.

Letitia smiled benignly. 'I admire you, Lucy,' she said. 'I used to be trusting like you, but I've toughened up now. I've had to; otherwise people take advantage of your sweet nature.' She pulled an apple from her bag and opened a well-thumbed copy of *The Little Book of Labour*. 'If you aren't too busy, is there absolutely any chance of a teeny weeny glass of wheatgrass juice from that new Nectar place that's opened?'

Fiona had been even less impressed with Nick's floral tribute when she popped round to the flat the following Saturday to join Lucy on her latest fitness campaign: power walking round Kentish Town. Fiona was a bestselling crime writer, and probably the most unromantic person Lucy had ever known. She was also serially suspicious and not just because she spent her whole life thinking up ingenious and horrible crimes.

After four years of marriage, her husband had run off with a glamour model and a large chunk of Fiona's royalties. Since then, Fiona had vowed only to date men with an IQ that was smaller than their chest measurement. 'That way, they'll be too thick to fleece me,' her logic ran.

Lucy pulled on her trainers, hearing heavy breathing way before Fiona buzzed the door. There was panting, too, and the sound of a tail thumping on the banisters, which could only mean one thing: Fiona had decided to bring Hengist with her.

'A pot plant. What is wrong with men these days?' declared Fiona at the sight of Nick's Flaming Torch. Lucy had decided to bring it home with her and leave her mum's Busy Lizzy on the cabinet.

Lucy zipped up her tracksuit top as they stepped out into the chilly autumn air. 'It's fine. You know I love plants.'

Fiona was following a 'Get Fit with Your Dog' programme but, so far, Lucy hadn't known either of them to get much further than the lamppost at the top of the road. The problem was not so much Fiona's allergy to physical exertion but Hengist's fetish for street furniture. Today he headed straight for the street sign opposite the flat and refused to budge. Being a Great Dane, he usually got his way.

Fiona tugged in vain at his lead. It was like a flea trying to tug a juggernaut.

'Do you think they use superglue on those lamp-posts?' asked Lucy, trying not to laugh.

'Buggered if I know. Hengist, you villain. Hee-eel!'

'Let me try,' said Lucy, taking his lead. At that moment, Hengist spotted the Chihuahua from the tanning salon and took off at warp speed. 'Whoa!' cried Lucy, as her arm was nearly wrenched out of its socket.

Fiona jogged alongside. 'Still, this Nick guy' – *puff* – 'leaving you in the lurch and' – *huff* – 'sending a plant. It's not promising. Don't tell me you're' – *puff* – 'seeing him again?'

Hengist ground to a halt with a clatter of claws.

'Y-yes. T-tonight, as a matter of fact. We're having a m-meal at m-my place,' panted Lucy. 'N-not that it's r-really any of your business, Fiona,' she added, just to show Fiona she was in control of the situation.

Fiona stopped to lean on a post box. 'On your head be it,' she said. 'And Hengist, will you *please* leave that poor man's leg alone!'

To stand a girl up once, Lucy decided later that evening, was suspicious but excusable. To do it twice in a row was definitely shittiness of the highest order. Despite her resolve not to invite Nick round to her flat on a first date, he'd somehow managed to get her to anyway. She was well aware of what a charmer he was and had determined not to be taken in. On the other hand . . . Nick was by far the sexiest guy she'd ever met; and even if she didn't know him that well, did it really matter? Why should she play things safe? Why shouldn't she take a risk for a change?

Eight o'clock came and went and there was still no sign of him. Lucy certainly wasn't going to call him so she spent the time pacing the flat, plumping up cushions, then hastily trashing them again so that the place didn't look too tidy. She didn't want him to think she was a control freak. But what if it had some sort of subliminal 'odour' which she'd become used to? Then again, Fiona would have told her about that. Fiona had a very sensitive nose, even better than Hengist's.

By nine, her Jamie's idiot-proof chicken casserole was a rock-hard mess and the bottle of French wine that had been chilling in the fridge was half-empty.

'That's it,' she declared as the hands on the kitchen clock crawled past ten. 'You had your chance, Bagel Boy, and you blew it.'

Tipping the chicken on top of a pile of wilted salad, she headed for the bathroom. As she splashed cold water on her face, she ran through all the reasons why Nick seemed to have his mobile switched off, why he hadn't even called, why he'd let her down *again*. She liked to think of herself as a tolerant person, but if there was one thing she wouldn't stand for, it was lying, and what else could Nick be doing other than deceiving her? Why else would he make promises, send flowers, and stand her up twice unless he had something to hide? As she lifted her head, she saw her face in the bathroom mirror and her expression hardened. No man, not even one as lush as Nick Laurentis, was going to stand her up twice and think he could get away with it.

Back in the sitting room, she was about to turn on the TV when a rogue thought struck her. Was she overreacting a tiny bit here? Letting what had happened with her mum and dad turn her into a bitter and twisted old crone before she'd even hit thirty – which wouldn't have been surprising, considering her one experience of True Love. The truth was, she'd seen enough disappointment during her teenage years to last her a lifetime. Lucy's dad had been a charmer like Nick and, having swept her mum off her feet (according to her mum, anyway), he'd proceeded to sweep several other women up in the same way.

By the time Lucy was twelve, she and her mum had left home to live with her gran four times after her dad's 'moments'. Those moments had all involved another woman, none of whom had been old enough to be Lucy's mother, and, each time, he'd returned, contrite, begging to be allowed back. Each time, he'd wooed her mum back with flowers and tearful promises – wooed Lucy back, too, with trips to Disneyland and (Oh God, she was so easily bought then) a designer coat she'd been desperate for. Come to think of it, maybe that was where her allergy to lying had come from: seeing her dad do it so well and so often had given her a phobia about it.

By the age of fourteen, she was almost as seasoned to disappointment as her mother, and probably a lot more hardened. She already knew, then, that there was no way she was *ever* going to put up with what her mum had in her own relationships, no matter how charming and cheeky the guy was – no matter how much she wanted to kiss him, feel those sexy hands on her body . . .

No way.

Flicking on the TV, she resisted the urge to check her

mobile one last time. She tugged open the fridge and reached for the bottle of wine. She poured another glass, grabbed a bottle of Evian for the inevitable three in the morning rehydration call, and headed for her TV with a *Lost* box set. Sawyer got naked in this episode and, for the purposes of lust, Lucy had A Thing about bad boys. Scumbags were a different matter.

Chapter Three

'Lucy!'
'Bleurgh . . .'

As she peered over the top of the duvet, Lucy's first thought was that someone was trying to break into her bedroom. They appeared to be doing it by lobbing bricks at the window and next they would probably get a ladder and crawl through the hole with an axe and have their evil way before stealing her complete *Sex and the City* box set. She scrabbled about on the bedside table for her watch, saw the time, and lay back on the pillow with a groan. Another assault on the window had her jumping out of bed, stubbing her toe on the exercise bike and pulling up the blind so hard it clattered against the window.

Her eyes adjusted slowly. Too slowly. *It couldn't be.* He wouldn't dare. A man was standing at the bottom of the steps to the flat with a rose.

'Morning!' he called cheerfully.

Lucy blinked. 'Nick?'

'Yes. Who did you think it would be?'

'What are you doing down there?'

'Hoping to say it with flowers?'

'Shhhh! You'll wake up the neighbours!' she said, crossing her fingers and praying that Charlie, who lived below, had enjoyed a hard night and was dead to the world.

'So am I forgiven?'

No, actually, she thought, he wasn't. Not even if he did have a great body and a cheeky smile and more flowers. She wasn't going to forgive him unless he had a very good excuse for last night's no-show. Closing the window, she pulled on a wrap, debating whether to go down and let him in. She waited a few minutes before padding slowly down the stairs. He deserved to be kept waiting. It was only a shame it wasn't tipping down outside.

'Sorr-ry,' he mouthed as she unlocked the door and poked her head round the jamb.

'And you actually expect me to let you in?'

His face fell. 'Well, I was kind of hoping. I know you must be surprised to see me—'

'Surprised isn't the word I'd use.'

'Pissed off, then.'

'You're getting warmer.'

He nodded. 'I don't blame you, but I do have an explanation.'

'Involving what? Alien abductions? A multiple pile-up on the North Circular?'

At this last suggestion, he heaved a sigh. 'Now, I'm afraid, *you're* getting warmer.'

His last comment had her interested enough to open the door a little wider. Nick tugged at an imaginary forelock and held out the rose. 'I really am most dreadfully sorry, Miss Lucy, but if you let me in, I can try and explain myself.'

He managed to sound both contrite and sexy and, to her annoyance, Lucy felt her resolve thawing a fraction of a degree. She reminded herself that, ultimately, she was in control of the situation. There would be no harm in letting him say his piece, surely. If she didn't buy what he had to say, she could still kick him out. She also realised she was clutching the front of her wrap tighter.

'We'd better go upstairs and this had better be good.'

'Lucy, I can promise you it will not only be good, but it will also be true.'

She raised an eyebrow, determined not to be taken in by his charm.

'Yeah? Don't make promises you can't keep.'

Once in her flat, Nick flopped down on her sofa and laid the rose on the coffee table.

'I owe you an apology – again,' he said as she perched on the edge of a chair, trying to keep her distance from him. 'I know you'll find this hard to believe, but I was actually on my way here last night, when I got a call from my sister. Harriet is as ditzy as they come and she'd crashed into a lamppost in her car.'

She was taken aback. This wasn't what she'd expected at all. She could hardly go all righteous on him now if he was telling the truth. 'Oh. Is she OK? I hope it's not serious?'

'No. It's not serious. She'll be fine. It turned out to be just a few cuts and bruises, in fact, but she's still pretty shaken up. The paramedics were there when I arrived and they insisted she be checked out in hospital. I spent until two this morning in A&E with her, surrounded by winos and druggies.'

Lucy resisted the urge to sympathise just yet.

'By the time I realised I'd left my mobile in her car, it had been carted off to the garage and after that, well, I didn't dare phone you in case I woke you up,' he went on. 'I really do feel awful. I can only imagine what you were thinking about me.'

Lucy didn't bother telling him what she'd been thinking. She was too busy wondering if his story was true. It certainly seemed genuine, and it was a fairly major tale to make up. And one she could check up on, if she really wanted to. Besides, while the accident was awful for Nick's sister, at least it meant that he hadn't stood her up.

'I don't like being messed about by anyone, Nick, but it's fine. I mean, not the bit about your sister crashing the car, but the not phoning,' she said at last.

'Are you sure? Because I would have been completely pissed off if I were you. I bet you were thinking I was an unreliable, lying git of the first order.'

She gave him a rueful smile. 'Now why on earth would I think that?'

He rolled his eyes. 'Hmm. Come to think of it, you did seem less than welcoming when you opened the door . . .'

'It is six thirty on a Sunday morning. I don't do mornings that well or being stood up,' she said.

His stomach rumbled like a mini train. 'God. Sorry. What am I like?'

He looked so embarrassed, Lucy bit back a smile. 'I don't suppose you've had breakfast?'

'Nothing more than several gallons of disgusting hospital coffee and, now you come to mention it, I am fairly ravenous.'

She hesitated before making her next offer, knowing what it might lead to. 'Well, I could do you some toast, if you like. I've even got some Marmite somewhere.'

'Thanks for the offer, but I don't really fancy toast, and I'm, er, not a big fan of Marmite,' he said, pushing himself to his feet. He pulled her to her feet and rested his fingers lightly on her upper arms. 'In fact, if I was forced to choose, I'd say I'd prefer something sweeter and more substantial.'

'Then you should head back to the deli,' replied Lucy, removing his hands from her arms. His skin was warm under her touch and every sensible brain cell told her he was a presumptuous, cheeky sod who didn't deserve a piece of toast, let alone anything else from her. The trouble was, other parts of her were saying she'd like to give him much more.

He held his arms out, palms upwards. 'OK. Just say the word and I'll be out of here for good. It's your decision.'

Lucy felt the heat rising to her face. All she had to do was show him the door and he'd be out of her life. But why should she? He'd made a couple of mistakes and there seemed to be perfectly reasonable explanations for both. Why should she push him away? Why should she throw out the best-looking guy she'd seen for years?

'Of course, it's the last thing I want,' he added.

It was the last thing she wanted, too. She was bored sick of being a good girl and was ready for some good old-fashioned fun.

'I'm not sure if I'm making a big mistake here, Nick . . .'

If he'd fed her a cheesy line, she'd have thrown him out on the spot, but he just replied softly, 'Maybe it's time we both took a chance?'

She wasn't sure who moved first but in a moment, they were both leaning forward and his hands were cradling her face. She was amazed by how thick his lashes were, how full his lips, the caramel-latte tone of his skin. He reminded her of some old movie star her grandmother used to have a crush on. Someone called Rock or Dirk, she thought, and she squashed down a giggle. The next thing she knew, he was sweeping her into his arms. Well, not sweeping, exactly, but he did manage to pick her up and he did a good job of hiding the grunt. Then they were lying on the sofa and Nick was sliding off her camisole.

'Close your eyes,' he whispered.

'Why?'

'Just do it, Bagel Girl.'

'Ohh . . .'

She guessed the velvety sensation she could feel was the rose being drawn over her bare stomach and between her cleavage.

'Nick . . .'

'Hmmm.'

She wriggled beneath him as the petals tickled her. 'Ouch!'

'Thorns. Sorry.'

His fingers slipped inside her pyjama shorts and began to slide them down. By then she'd forgotten what she was going to say and, besides, Nick was doing something utterly delicious to her nipples with his tongue.

By the time they surfaced, the aroma of roast beef was drifting into her bedroom from Charlie's flat. Outside, she could hear laughter and chat ringing out from the pub beer garden down the street. Rumpled and crumpled, sated and sheened in the afterglow of a marathon sex session, Lucy fumbled on the bedside table for her watch.

'Whattimeisit?' Nick's voice was muffled by the duvet.

'Just after two.'

There was a pause, then the duvet was thrown off and Nick jumped out of bed, stark naked and waggling.

Lucy giggled. 'What's the matter?'

'I'm late! Where are my bloody boxers?'

The expression on his face was so different to the laid-back, slightly mad guy who'd sent her to heaven with a rose and his tongue that Lucy was taken aback.

'Jesus!'

In the middle of pulling on his jeans, he'd tripped over Lucy's exercise bike and got tangled up in a pile of shoes and handbags on the floor. 'Christ, I'm going to be late. Where's my T-shirt, for fuck's sake?' he shouted, trying to unwind a beaded bag from his ankle.

'Hey! Chill out.'

'*Chill out?* I should've been out of here half an hour ago.'

Lucy grabbed her wrap. Suddenly, being naked in front of Nick didn't seem like so much fun. He hadn't seemed like he was in a hurry when he was making love to her. Not after the first time, anyway, she thought with a blush.

'Here's your top,' she said, rescuing it from the carpet and holding it out. Snatching it from her hand, he pulled it over his head.

'That's OK, it's a pleasure,' said Lucy sarcastically.

Nick snapped round and for a moment, she could hardly believe the fury in his eyes. Then the anger disappeared and he raked his fingers through his hair in exasperation. He shot her a little-boy-lost look and said: 'Sorry, I'm a real control freak, aren't I? I've no right to be acting like this.'

'Your trainers are in the sitting room,' she replied coldly, still reeling from his scary outburst.

He kissed her nose. 'I'm a total bastard. Really.'

She flinched away but the way he'd said it managed to make being a bastard sound almost sexy. Almost, but not quite. Planting a hasty kiss on her mouth, he grabbed his trainers and pulled them on. Lucy waited, trying to stay calm, hoping there would be a further explanation for his weird behaviour, but Nick was intent on gathering up his belongings from a variety of locations around the flat.

'Have you seen my wallet?' he asked.

Lucy spotted it under a half-empty packet of condoms and her pyjama shorts; both tossed carelessly on to the sofa.

'I think it's here,' she said, holding it out.

Grabbing the wallet, he shoved it into his jeans pocket. 'Sorry, but I have to go. I've got an appointment.'

'On a Sunday?'

'It's an – oh, I may as well tell you the truth.' He grabbed her shoulders, his eyes bright. 'You'll have to know some time, if we're going to carry on seeing each other.'

Lucy's heart started racing. Here it comes, she thought. He's married. Or a member of a cult. She could feel his fingers digging into her flesh, almost hurting but not quite.

'I, Nick Laurentis, am going to be rich and famous!'

So. Not a cult. Not married. Just delusional. Delusional, she could live with. He could be cured, and gently helped to see that ordinary mortals, even expert sandwich wranglers, did not become superstars in their Sunday lunchtimes. Not unless they managed to be snapped handing Victoria Beckham a large baguette.

'Right. Sorry to be dim, but can you run that one by me again? Did you just say you were rushing off to be rich and famous?'

His expression, as he pulled open the door to the landing, was one of total determination. 'Yeah. That's what I said. Rich and famous. I'll see you this evening. I'll explain everything then.'

Chapter Four

Later, the Heart FM chart show had just finished and Lucy was seriously wondering whether to accept Charlie's invitation to a read-through for an all-male production of *The Sound of Music*, when the door to the flat buzzed. She hesitated for a nanosecond, grinned, and then pressed 'talk'. 'If that's someone wanting to throw bricks at my window and ravish me, I'm sorry, but I've already been ravished very thoroughly today.'

There was a pause. 'Have you been at the hookah pipe again, Lucy?'

'Charlie! Sorry, I didn't think . . .'

'It was me? Clearly. Are you coming to this SoM bash, or do I have to put my nun's outfit back in the wardrobe?'

'Oh, Charlie, I'm sorry. I thought I'd wait a bit longer, just in case . . . a friend turns up.'

'A *friend*? Lucy, I think I detect the fragrant odour of a teeny weeny fib here.'

'There's no odour and I am expecting a friend. Hopefully.'

'You don't sound terribly sure to me. I'd go out, if I were you, and play hard to get.'

'And that strategy has worked for you so far?' said Lucy, thinking of the times she'd had to salvage the wreckage that was Charlie after a failed love affair.

'Hmm. I suppose you do have a point. I hope this friend puts in an appearance soon but I'd advise you not to make a "habit" of waiting in for people.'

'Ha ha,' said Lucy. 'You will still go to the show?'

'Well, I'm all dressed up now and one doesn't get to wear a wimple every day, so I'm bloody well going.'

When Charlie had gone with an audible kiss and another warning, Lucy flopped down on the sofa, her heart sinking. So far, Nick had her waiting by the phone, outside the cinema and by her own intercom. Her neighbour, her sort-of-boss and her best friend had all told her to steer clear of him which, naturally, had only made her want him more. She thought she knew why, too. Nick offered a rollercoaster ride and while she knew it might be scary and uncomfortable, it promised to be exciting.

'Lucy!'

She shot off the sofa and pulled open the door to find Nick there, dressed in a suit and tie. His hair was slicked back like a merchant banker and he was carrying a laptop case.

'Who let you in downstairs?' she asked.

'Would you believe me if I said a nun with a beard?'

'Of course. Who else?'

Five minutes later, he'd abandoned the suit and they were in bed. Yes, the sex was definitely the high point of the rollercoaster ride, she thought later. Making love to Nick was pure unadulterated pleasure. It was like being able to eat a huge plate of profiteroles without worrying about the calories. Or spending a whole month's salary on shoes without the cost ever appearing on your credit card statement.

'So?' asked Lucy, playfully pinning Nick down on her bed. 'You can't get away now. Where have you been?' she said, laughing.

'Converting sinners,' he said, with a grin and a waggle.

'Tell the truth!' she cried, laughing, yet feeling an uneasy stir in the pit of her stomach again. Freeing himself, he shuffled up the bed and touched her cheek gently. 'I've been to an audition. No, let's qualify that: a final audition.'

'For a job?'

'You're getting warm.'

'A part in a film?' she asked slightly sarcastically.

'Warmer, but still not red-hot.'

She frowned. 'Now you're teasing me.'

His expression became more serious and he wasn't waggling any more, which Lucy thought was rather a shame.

'I've just been to the final round of auditions for *Hot Shots*. It's a new reality series for wannabe entre-preneurs made by an independent company. There are ten of us in contention and every week we have to complete a series of arduous tasks.'

Lucy had a vision of Nick crawling through a pit of scorpions and shuddered.

'You don't have to catch and kill your own python or anything?'

He laughed out loud. 'Much harder than that, I suspect. We have business tasks to complete – it's all top secret at the moment, but I guess we'll be setting up mock-companies, cold calling, selling things, and all kinds of weird stuff. There are no snakes involved except Denby Sweetman. He's the judge.'

Lucy's eyes widened. Sir Denby was rarely out of the newspapers and not just the business pages. He had a reputation for being tough as old boots and very outspoken. Lucy had always wondered if this was a front and that, in reality, he liked doing the dusting while his Amazonian wife stood over him with a carpet beater.

'Isn't he a real bastard?'

'A hard-nosed git? Yeah, but I like a challenge.' Nick grinned. 'And I'm going to get one. Sir Denby recommends one person to be booted out every week. The winner – get this – gets a quarter of a million to invest in the enterprise of his choice plus the full backing of Sir Denby for a year.'

'Or *her* choice,' said Lucy, in the interests of equality.

Nick pulled a face, 'No, *his* choice. Because it's going to be me.'

Lucy could feel the excitement fizzing through him; he was almost trembling with adrenaline. He took her hand. 'I also have a confession to make that I'm not proud of.'

Lucy had the strangest feeling she was about to plunge down to Earth very quickly. 'Go on,' she said, pulling her hand out of his.

He took a deep breath. 'Don't hate me for this, but . . . I didn't get the wrong cinema last week. I got a recall for the programme at the last minute. You see, I was the last to be chosen and I couldn't pass up the opportunity. I was on my way out of the house when they called. After that, they took my mobile, and by the time I got home, it was three in the morning.'

She blew out a breath. 'Why didn't you tell me all of this at the time?'

'I thought you'd think I was mad or making up the whole story. The mix-up over cinemas seemed more plausible.'

Actually, Nick, the truth is always more plausible, she thought as he began to open his mouth, but she shook her head. 'Please. Don't say you're sorry. I've heard that one. Just tell me this. Were you with your sister last Saturday night? Did the accident actually happen, or did you make that one up, too?'

'Sadly, the accident is all too true.'

'I don't like being lied to, not even a little white lie.'

'I know and it won't happen again. I promise,' he said as she still hesitated, but he couldn't disguise the little-boy excitement in his eyes. 'So, what do you think about the TV show? I haven't even been home and told my family yet.'

Lucy couldn't help but be carried along by his enthusiasm. She'd have to have a heart of stone not to be pleased for him and it might even be a whole lot of fun to be part of it. 'It's a lot to take in, Nick; I'm gob-smacked, in fact. If you win, it means you could set up your events management business, make a fortune, change your life, save the world . . .' she teased.

'I know. I can be king of the world,' he declared, but his eyes were still gleaming with happiness. 'How do you fancy going down the pub to celebrate?'

Still reeling from his announcements, Lucy managed a smile. Inside she was fizzing almost as much as he was. Nick a reality TV star. Her boyfriend: famous. Except, he wasn't her boyfriend. They hadn't even been out on a date yet, technically speaking. He was just a guy from a deli she had slept with.

'Why not? It's not every day you get the chance to be rich and famous and humiliated in public.'

'I hope it won't come to that too often,' he said with a wink. 'Come on. Let's go.'

Later, as they lay in bed after returning from the pub, he kissed her and whispered, 'From now on there will be no secrets. I'm determined to make it all up to you.'

Over the next few weeks, she had to admit, he was as good as his word. Despite frequent trips to the studios, he still managed to find time to take her out. Nothing fancy, of course, which was how she liked it. Just fun stuff. A picnic in the park complete with bubbly and what seemed to be the entire stock of Marvin's deli. A visit to some obscure cinema in the sticks just to track down the film she'd missed. A night at a club where Nick had managed to get VIP tickets from 'a bloke' at the studios. Then one night, as she lay in his arms in bed, he'd stroked her hair and whispered. 'Lucy . . .'

'Yes, Nick?'

'I know we haven't known each other long but I want you to be part of this adventure. Support me, help me through it, have mad passionate sex with me when I get chucked out in the first round.'

'You won't,' declared Lucy, and she meant it. She had a funny feeling that Nick was going to achieve everything he'd said he would – and more.

Chapter Five

A month later, Nick had resigned his job in the sandwich bar and moved into a massive mansion in Notting Hill which had been rented by the TV studio. During the week, he was locked away preparing and carrying out the tasks set by the programme makers. Then, each Friday night, the candidates would gather in Sir Denby's study and have their performances analysed, ridiculed and derided. Then one of them would be 'let go'.

Unlike most reality shows, the victors were allowed home for part of the week. Nick suspected the studio couldn't afford the staff to keep them there every night. Lucy's theory was that the contestants were being secretly watched by the crew while they were 'at large', as Sir Denby put it.

'That's just your suspicious nature,' laughed Nick as she told him of her theory one Friday evening. He'd got into the habit of visiting his family for dinner before heading over to Lucy's flat where he'd spend the night. That was all he had time for apart from the odd phone call and Lucy tried very hard to understand. After all, she kept reminding herself, they still barely knew each other.

She understood that the show had to come first, even though it took its toll on him. After the first sacking, he'd virtually crawled into her flat.

'This isn't going to be easy,' he'd said as they'd lain in bed at five in the morning, too fired up to sleep, eating bacon sandwiches.

'No. I never expected it to be.'

'But I need to do this. All my life I've felt I've been waiting for this chance. It's like I've been sleepwalking through everything until now. As if I've never lived up to what I promised.'

'You don't have to live up to anything,' mumbled Lucy through a mouthful of bacon sandwich. 'No one expects you to take over the planet.'

He smiled and touched her cheek. 'Ah, Lucy. You are so sweet. You have no idea. Did you know what my dad gave me for my twenty-first birthday?'

'A train set?'

'The telephone number of an old school friend of his who ran a food-processing factory. They made frozen chips.'

'Happy Birthday to you . . .' she sang, thinking he was joking.

'Yeah. He told me if I hadn't made it on to the board by the time I was thirty, I'd never get anywhere, so I went for the interview and, despite trying very hard to come across as a complete idiot, I got a job as junior manager in the lab.'

'Maybe your dad was just trying to look after you,' she said, thinking of what she'd received from her dad on her own twenty-first birthday. It had been a card asking her to contact him. She'd thrown it in the bin. She and her mother hadn't spoken to him for three years and after her lack of response to the card, she guessed he'd given up. He'd brought it on himself – as she'd told herself a thousand times.

'But he must have meant well. Lots of fathers don't bother with their kids at all.'

He shook his head. 'I wish he hadn't bothered with me. He almost ruined my life. I stayed in that bloody factory for nearly six years until I'd had enough. One day, while we were having a meeting to work out how to reduce the size of the crinkle cut range by ten per cent without the customers noticing, I finally saw sense. I mean, what kind of existence is that?'

The kind that a lot of people have to lead if they're lucky, thought Lucy. 'It could be worse,' she said a little impatiently. 'You might have had to work in the factory, making the chips. It's not glamorous, but it's real life.'

Nick shook his head. 'I don't want real life. I want more. Much more.'

'I know,' she said, laying her plate on the duvet and stroking the hairs on his arm. It was useless trying to persuade him that she'd have respected him even if he wasn't aiming for the top; maybe even more.

He let out a laugh. 'I told them to shove their chips where the sun doesn't shine and I left. The next week I was working in the sandwich bar and Dad threatened to disinherit me.'

'Now I know you're joking. Threatening you with disinheritance sounds like something from a Victorian novel.'

'My father *is* like someone from Victorian times. He meant what he said. He told me I'd humiliated him and I wouldn't get any more help until I'd seen sense and got a proper job again.'

'But surely your mum and dad are proud of you now?'

'Oh, the old man's come round a bit recently, but he still thinks I'm a fool. This is my last chance, Lucy. It has to work. I *have* to win.'

His face was taut with tension. No matter that he'd had a comfortable, even privileged upbringing. Lucy could see it would never be enough and, in one way, she genuinely admired his passion. You had to reach for your dream whatever it was. Maybe she shouldn't be settling for her marketing assistant's role. Maybe she should fire herself up and go for what she really wanted. Whatever that was.

'Nick? Are you still here?' she asked, seeing him staring into space.

'Hell, yes. Hey – I know it's early and I should get some sleep, but . . .'

She reached for him and the last thing she heard was the plate thudding on to the floor. That was one of the last times they had a chance to make love because, after that, even their weekends seemed to be taken up with *Hot Shots* business. Lucy went along to the studio to see a couple of the rehearsals but their meetings became hurriedly snatched as the excitement built and the press attention mounted.

She'd understood when he hadn't been able to turn up for her birthday dinner. Instead, he'd arrived at the office mid-morning in a rickshaw while the TV crew snatched a breakfast in Love Bites. Letitia had been highly amused but Mr Lawson had said he hoped 'her fame would not get in the way of efficient working practices'.

Then there were the papers. Halfway through the *Hot Shots* run, Nick's face began to appear in the national press. Lucy thanked her lucky stars she was neither gorgeous, thin, fat, nor weird enough to attract more than the attention of a few local newspapers back in her home town. Being ignored was fine by her. Nobody from the nationals phoned her up, so she tried to get on with her job. As long as no one bothered her mum or delved into her past, she convinced herself she was OK.

Week by agonising week came and went and, somehow, Nick survived as the *Hot Shots* final approached its climax. The pressure grew and then one day everything exploded. It had all started when Nick had wanted her to go along to a party but Lucy had needed to visit her mum who'd had a minor operation. When she'd said no, he'd got so annoyed that he'd grabbed a vase she'd been left by her gran and hurled it through the air in frustration. It was an ugly glass thing that she hadn't realised how much she'd liked until she'd seen it flying through the air and smashing against the fridge. The moment he'd done it, he'd started to apologise, but it was too late. He bent down and started to gather the pieces together.

'Leave it!' she snapped, but he continued picking up the glass shards as if she hadn't spoken.

'Nick, stop this minute.'

'I'm really—'

'No, you're not sorry! You wouldn't have done it if you were.'

He let the glass slide from his hand back on to the tiles before standing up.

'I want you to go.'

'Luce, don't be silly.'

'Get out!' she shrieked.

His mouth twitched and his face darkened, then he shrugged. 'Fine. If that's what you really want.'

She heard him collect his jacket, open the door and thump down the stairs. She was shaking with adrenaline but was too angry to cry so she set to, clearing up the mess. It was dark before she heard footsteps on the stairs again.

'Bugger off!' she said, as the door buzzed.

There was a short silence, followed by a small voice. 'Are you sure you mean that, darling?'

She didn't know whether to be relieved or disappointed to hear Charlie's voice on the other side of the door.

'Sorry, Charlie, I thought you were someone else,' she said, letting him in. He kissed her cheek. 'Excuse me for prying, but I was just wondering if the frolicking was getting a teeny bit out of hand. I heard a racket earlier then I saw Nick racing out of here like a scalded cat. I don't like to pry but I had to see how you were.'

Lucy tried a grin. 'It's OK. Just a lovers' tiff.'

'Are you sure?'

She thought of the glass vase now wrapped in paper in the bin and finally had to bite back the tears. 'Yes. I'm sure.'

'Do you want me to make you a cup of tea, anyway?'

She and Charlie had demolished a packet of Ginger Nuts when the door buzzed briefly again. Lucy set her mug down on the table.

'Lucy, it's me,' came Nick's low voice.

'Are you going to answer that?' asked Charlie as she stayed in her seat, wondering whether to let him in.

'I'm not sure.'

'Do you want me to open it?'

She shook her head. 'No. I'll do it.'

'Lucy! Are you in there? I've got something for you,' she heard Nick call as she reached the door. He was standing in the corridor, clutching a brown paper bag in his hands, his face flushed. 'I've been round every flea market and junk shop in north London,' he said breathlessly. 'And I know this isn't quite the same, but it's the best I could do at short notice. I am really, really sorry for losing my temper.'

'I'll be going then, Lucy, love,' said Charlie, picking up his messenger bag from the kitchen floor as Nick shuffled in.

'Hello, Nick. Nice to meet you again.'

A shadow of embarrassment crossed Nick's face. 'Hello, mate. Sorry about the noise.'

Charlie smiled graciously. 'What's fine with Lucy is fine by me. I'll be here if you need me,' he whispered, brushing his lips across Lucy's face. 'Farewell for now.'

After he'd left, Lucy took the paper bag from Nick but didn't open it.

'Aren't you going to look inside?' he said, sounding disappointed.

'Maybe later.'

'It's almost the same,' he murmured. 'Not quite, but I did my best.'

'It's the thought that counts, my gran would probably have said.'

'I should never have blown up in that way.' He held out the bag. 'I'm in uncharted territory here, Lucy. The pressure's making me freak out but taking all the crap out on you is unforgivable. Look, why don't you let me make you some supper?'

Lucy stared at the worried expression on his face, knowing that part of her was enjoying seeing him suffer.

'Or we can just open a bottle of wine and sit and talk things through,' he offered when she didn't answer.

'Right now, I think I'd rather just have sex.'

The relief on his face was almost comical, then she felt the rasp of stubble against her skin as he kissed her, tentatively and hopefully. Already she was thinking of them being in bed together, relishing their passionate 'making up', and forgetting everything in the heat of the moment.

'Sex it is, then,' he whispered as they headed for her room.

The next morning at work, a huge bouquet of roses arrived, impressing even Letitia. But they hadn't impressed Fiona. When Lucy had told her about Nick's behaviour later that week, her friend had snorted in derision.

'You're just jealous because you're on your own,' Lucy had retorted, finally stung by Fiona's jibes. To which

Fiona had replied: 'I'd rather die alone and be eaten by Hengist than put up with Mr Sodding Wonderful.'

After that, Lucy had stormed out of Fiona's flat.

The weeks stretched out and there was still no phone call from Fiona, no exploratory text or test-the-water email. Lucy began to worry. They'd had spats before, of course, even rows that had ended in one of them walking out, but nothing that had ever lasted this long.

But she wasn't going to be the one to make the first move. No way.

Chapter Six

One Saturday morning Lucy was dawdling her way round Tesco's. Nick was doing a photo shoot and had promised he'd make it to the flat for dinner. She was fairly sure he meant it and was just loading some Häagen-Dazs into her basket when she heard a voice from the pet supplies aisle.

'Luce, is that you?'

Peering round the end of a dog chew display, Lucy saw the unmistakable profile of Fiona. They had to meet one day soon, and maybe Tesco's was as good a place as any. At least it was public so they could hardly start chucking tins of Pedigree Chum at each other.

'Lucy, it *is* you, isn't it?'

'Hi, Fiona.'

It was too late to hide, even if she'd really wanted to. Fiona had abandoned her trolley and was headed towards her. They stopped about a foot from each other, like gun slingers at the OK Corral.

'I knew it was you,' she said as Lucy clutched the handles of her basket defiantly. Fiona was staring at her and frowning and Lucy guessed what was coming next. 'What on earth have you done to your hair?'

'I thought it was time for a change,' said Lucy firmly.

Fiona's silence said everything.

'Stop looking at me like that. This is my natural colour, Fi!'

'No need to explain yourself to me.'

'I'm not.'

'Fine, then,' said Fiona with a sniff.

Privately, Lucy admitted that her new hair style must come as a surprise to Fiona. She'd had it jet black with aubergine highlights for a year until changing it to a nondescript brown bob.

Fiona narrowed her eyes suspiciously. 'I suppose it was his idea.'

'No, it was not his idea!' hissed Lucy indignantly.

Two pensioners turned and tutted so Lucy beckoned Fiona deeper into the dog food aisle and lowered her voice. 'It was *not* Nick's idea, actually. I decided to dye it. I thought it was more appropriate for work.'

Fiona still looked doubtful.

Lucy was worried they really would end up hurling canned goods at each other if one of them didn't back down, and she'd genuinely missed Fiona, not to mention Hengist. Her little flat didn't seem the same without the stray dog hairs and wet-dog smell.

'Oh, sod it!' said Fiona, suddenly hugging her. 'I've missed you, Luce. I've hated us falling out, but I just hate seeing you with a guy who doesn't deserve you. I suppose I'm the one who should be holding out the olive branch, or should it be dog chews?'

Lucy sighed with relief. 'Dog chews, definitely. Shall we go for a double espresso?'

Fiona pulled a face. 'Sod the coffee. Is there anywhere to get a decent G&T around here?'

Lucy deposited her ice cream haul in the frozen pea section while Fiona abandoned her trolley, and they headed for the TexMex Diner on the retail park. Over a plate of nachos and the screeching of a toddler's birthday party, they sat down to make an awkward peace. Fiona kept taking bird-like sips of her G&T, by which Lucy guessed she must be feeling nervous. 'It's no use me lying. You know I think Nick Laurentis is an unreliable, sex-mad selfish git who'll break your heart.'

'Say what you really think, Fi.'

'I am. That's why we're friends. Someone has to save you from yourself.'

'And what is myself?' asked Lucy, slurping her strawberry daiquiri as though it were going out of fashion.

'A gullible, trusting, loved-up idiot.'

'I'm not loved up.'

'Sexed-up, then.'

'Our relationship is based on a lot more than sex.'

'Yeah?'

'Yeah, and – not that it's any of your business – even if it was just based on sex, is that so wrong?'

'No. I think a relationship based on sex is an excellent idea and I'd try it myself if I could find some buff young guy to be shallow with. But it's only right if both partners have the same expectations.'

'How do you know we don't?' said Lucy quietly.

'Just a hunch.'

'So you think I'm expecting more from this arrangement than Nick is?'

'I'm not sure, but I'd hate to see him using you, Luce. I mean, how often does he take you out? How often has he let you down?'

'OK, I'll admit he's been a tiny bit unreliable at times but, Fi, we have such a great time when we're together and you're forgetting, this is his chance of a lifetime. I mean, a lot of guys wouldn't want to be saddled with a relationship at all. I'm perfectly happy to go along with it and soon it will all be over anyway, and then we can get back to real life.'

'What if he wins?'

Lucy hesitated. Hadn't she turned that scenario over in her head a hundred times? She had no idea what would happen if Nick did win, other than that their lives would be even more manic and bizarre than they were now.

'We'll deal with it,' she said firmly.

'And if he loses?' said Fiona from over the top of her glass.

Ah, that was even more difficult, thought Lucy. Nick wouldn't hear talk of defeat or negative thinking these days. She didn't want to be the one to pick up the pieces if he got voted out, but she'd have to, of course. She'd have no choice.

'I'll handle it. Now listen, Fi. I won't discuss Nick any further. Tell me what you've been up to in the past six weeks? How many victims have you killed off this week and have you managed to get that Welsh guy from the health club to show you his lotus position yet?'

Later, as Lucy finally reached home, she couldn't help feeling uncomfortable over her conversation with Fiona.

She wasn't sure what she wanted from her relationship with Nick other than a chance to find out. Nick had swept her off her feet and she'd been enjoying the whole drama too much to stop and analyse it. Why shouldn't she just enjoy herself? After all, Nick was never boring, utterly gorgeous and startlingly creative in bed. Yet, other times, when he was stressed or just couldn't get what he wanted quickly enough, he would just lose it and blow up. The problem was that she hadn't really got to know him before this whole bizarre TV thing kicked off. She couldn't tell whether he was volatile because of the extraordinary situation he was in, or whether he was like that anyway. She still felt she didn't know the real Nick.

But did that really matter?

Did she even know the real *her* any more? Fiona had been spot-on about one thing. It *had* been Nick's idea to change her striking colour to something more 'mainstream'. Just in case I do win, he'd said, and the papers wanted to take pictures of her. That prospect had filled her with horror but she could see some logic in the hair thing. Her boss at Able & Lawson was always giving her funny looks. Maybe it was time she went for something a little more 'corporate'.

As she dumped her bags on the passenger seat of her car, Lucy caught sight of her reflection in the rear-view mirror and wasn't sure she recognised the person staring back.

Later, as she laid the table in her little sitting room with a proper cloth and candles and even a vase with a rose in it, she couldn't dispel the feeling of unease. Even as she opened the pesto, got the pasta out of the packet and shaved the parmesan, she wondered if he would turn up. Then the door buzzed and he was there: half an hour late, looking devastatingly gorgeous and bearing champagne and a white lily.

'Hello, my gorgeous Bagel Girl,' he murmured while gently stroking her cheek with his hand. 'You know, there are times when I think that all I really need is you.'

Then he'd led her to the bedroom as the pasta boiled dry in the saucepan. As his head disappeared beneath the sheet, Lucy could almost believe him.

Chapter Seven

'And now, the moment we've been waiting for, for twelve long weeks. The moment when dreams come true for one of you. This is your opportunity of a lifetime! Your ticket to fame and fortune! Your chance, possibly your one and only chance in your entire life, to be a Hot Shot . . .'

Lucy gripped the edge of her seat as if for dear life as dazzling Gerry Brigham, the presenter of *Hot Shots*, introduced the Grand Final. The day had come, at last. The day they'd never thought would happen, the day Nick had worked so hard for and that they'd both dreamed of. It was here after four long months. Just minutes separated him from his dream.

'Where does that man get his tan from – B&Q?' hissed Fiona, who was sitting beside Lucy in the audience.

'Fiona, shut up!'

Nick and his rival, Layla, sat opposite each other around a mock boardroom table. Sir Denby sat at the head of it, flanked by two of his assistants. Layla looked terribly serious. Nick was smiling but underneath, Lucy knew the truth. He'd thrown up in his dressing room as Lucy had wished him good luck.

'In a few moments,' squealed Gerry, 'we are going to know the identity of the woman – or man – who will walk away with a £250,000 investment in his or her business. Who will get the backing, the acumen, of Sir Denby Sweetman, the entrepreneur you all love to hate!'

Boos rang out from the audience. Sir Denby grimaced. In front of her, Lucy could tell Nick's family were feeling the tension as much as she was. Lucy had only met Hattie, his sister, twice before, once at Nick's flat one Sunday evening, and once for a snatched meal in a restaurant. She'd never met his parents until tonight. They were all sitting in a row below in front of her. Hattie with her hands over her eyes; his mother twisting a handkerchief between her fingers; his father stiff-backed and impassive. Lucy's own stomach was on the spin cycle.

'And this is supposed to be entertainment,' murmured Fiona in her ear. 'It's about as much fun as the reading of a will.'

On the screen at the side of the studio, the camera cut from Nick to his rival, back to Nick, then back to Sir Denby. Nick's face was weird. Like she'd never seen him before. Pale and still, almost as if he'd gone into some other place. It wasn't like him. It wasn't Nick. Meanwhile, Fiona was squeezing her hand so tightly that Lucy could feel her rings gouging into her fingers.

'So, Sir Denby, the time has come. Have you reached a decision by which one of these two candidates will get the glory – and who will go home with nothing?'

Sir Denby glanced from Nick to his rival before turning to the audience. 'Yes, Gerry, I have.'

'So, will it be Layla, the financial manager, who, if we believe the press, says she'd sell her own mother to win?'

Laughter and gasps erupted from the audience.

'Or Mr Popularity, Nick Laurentis, who gave up a promising career in a sandwich bar to have his chance at fame and fortune?'

There were giggles from the audience. Lucy heard the girl in front of her murmur. 'He's fit. Don't know what he's doing with that mousy girlfriend.'

'Don't do it, Fi,' warned Lucy as Fiona's eyes narrowed dangerously. 'Put her in a book instead.'

'As a victim,' said Fiona. 'Horribly mangled.'

'Shhh.'

The presenter had paused. The audience seemed to collectively hold its breath. Nick was staring straight ahead. Lucy really thought she might pass out with the tension.

'Sir Denby, can you please give us your decision?' said Gerry.

Sir Denby's face was solemn. 'It's been an almost impossible task, but I've made my choice.'

Lucy's hands flew to her face. Like Hattie, she just couldn't bear to watch any more.

'Before I announce my decision, I want to say a few words about each of the candidates. First, Layla Knightley.'

Layla, clad in a purple power suit and six-inch heels, snapped to attention and fixed Sir Denby with a look Lucy could only describe as withering. She squared her shoulders, every inch the supremely confident entrepreneur. Nick looked like a rabbit caught in a headlight. Layla was the wolf about to devour him.

'Layla, you've astonished me. You've completed all the tasks. You're a capable, talented, ruthless business-woman and I've no doubt you'd sell your own mother if you thought you could make a profit out of her.'

Layla gave a megawatt grin.

'She thinks he's joking,' said Fiona.

'Now on to Nick Laurentis.'

Nick sat up straighter and managed a smile but Lucy knew that he must be at breaking point. Yet she was proud of the way he met Sir Denby's eyes. No matter what happened, she was so proud of him.

'Yes, Sir Denby.'

'Nick, I've had my doubts about you.'

Boos rang out. Nick's face fell a little but he recovered fast.

'At one time I thought you were a lightweight, that you didn't have the bottle to see this through. You've come a long way and you've got here on sheer balls at times. I admire you. In fact, I can see a lot of myself in you at your age.' He hesitated. 'But I'm still not sure you've got the cool head needed to run your own business and be a real Hot Shot.'

Lucy's heart sank to her boots. She felt Fiona grip her hand. Nick's dream seemed to be slipping away as Sir Denby hesitated, glancing from one candidate to the other, ready to bring down the axe on one of them and shatter their dream to smithereens. That axe looked like falling on Nick, and Lucy didn't know how she was ever going to pick up the pieces.

Sir Denby smiled benignly at Layla. 'Layla, I said earlier that you'd sell your own mother to win this competition.'

Layla laughed again, confident now that she'd got the vote as Sir Denby continued.

'But I didn't know you'd sell yourself.'

There were gasps. Gerry held up a hand and a deep hush descended on the studio. Gerry perked up. Every ear strained to hear what was coming next. 'It's come to my attention that during the course of filming, you attempted to seduce both my PA and the producer of this show and I won't give my backing to someone I don't trust as far as I could throw her. For that reason, Nick Laurentis, you are the Hot Shot!'

Layla gave a shriek before launching herself, hands outstretched, at Sir Denby's throat. Three technicians and a bouncer had to hold her back and carry her kicking and screaming from the studio. Nick seemed rooted to the spot, totally shell shocked.

The studio erupted like a volcano.

A mighty blast of cheering, clapping and stamping exploded, seeming to make the very building tremble. People jumped to their feet, screaming and whistling. Fiona threw her arms round Lucy and hugged her until she could hardly breathe. Hattie hugged Nick's mum and even his father got to his feet and applauded.

As for Nick, Lucy couldn't see him for people slapping him on the back. For some reason, an ex-*Hollyoaks* actress and a Page Three model were also hugging him.

'For crying out loud, where did those two come

from?' shrieked Fiona as Nick's head disappeared between a humungous pair of boobs.

Lucy didn't know and didn't care. All she knew was that Nick had won! Nick was a Hot Shot! Nick was made for *life*! Nick was—

'Get a move on, love, we want you on stage!' shouted a floor manager, grabbing her arm.

'Ow!'

A microphone was suddenly slapped in her face. 'Wahhhhey! Lucy, pet! What do you think of your Nick, then? Isn't he a megastar?' shrieked Gerry.

'It's wonderf—'

'Aren't you just so proud of him, petal? How were you feeling, waiting for the verdict? Wetting your knickers, I'll bet.'

'Well, not quite, but it was nerve-wrack—'

'Wow! That's great. Just amazing! Hey, Nick! We've got your Lucy here to see you!'

On stage, Nick had managed to break free of the actress and the model and was searching the audience, his face anxious, as Lucy was led down the steps, wondering why the floor seemed to have been replaced with jelly.

He broke into a huge grin as Gerry propelled Lucy on to the stage.

'Awwww . . . will you look at that, folks?' said Gerry as Nick rushed forward and Lucy found herself wrapped in a bone-crushing bear hug. They didn't have to say anything. He just looked into her eyes, shook his head in amazement, and then kissed her.

'What a guy! Gets the cash, clinches the deal and gets

the girl, too! I'd like to be a fly on the wall of the Laurentis house tonight. Woo-hooo!'

The clapping and cheering started again as they carried on kissing. Then, softly, Nick broke away. He stood facing her, still holding both her hands, and suddenly he was serious.

Gerry leapt forward, beaming.

'So, Nick, what do you have to say? What comes next?'

Nick didn't glance away. His eyes were glued to Lucy's and he was looking so serious that she felt a tiny frisson run up and down her spine.

'What comes next?' he echoed.

He turned briefly to Gerry, his voice quiet. 'Gerry, winning *Hot Shots* is a fantastic opportunity. It's what I've lived and breathed for the past four months. It's what I've always wanted, but there's something missing.'

The breath caught in Lucy's throat. What something else could there possibly be? Was he going to say he loved her live on television? It darted into her head that she hoped he wouldn't. Not here. Not in front of everyone.

'Winning *Hot Shots* means more to me than almost anything else in my life, but there's someone else who has come to mean even more. That someone is the woman standing in front of me now.'

Gerry and the audience uttered a collective 'ahh'. Lucy didn't know where to look. It was flattering, it was . . . lovely, but she so wished Nick had waited to tell her in private. She'd hoped to share this intimate moment together, not with zillions of others. She felt the heat rising to her cheeks.

Then, still holding her right hand in his, Nick sank to his knees. Lucy thought she was going to faint. No. No, he couldn't. He wouldn't.

'Lucy . . .' he murmured, looking up into her eyes.

She shook her head gently. Her legs were about to give way. Maybe that would be best, then they might carry her off, away from the millions of eyes watching, waiting, expecting . . .

'Lucy Gibson, will you do me the honour . . .'

Oh, Nick.

'. . . of being my wife?'

The studio erupted. 'Wooo-hooo!'

'Way to go, mate!'

She had to look away. Up and away from Nick's expectant gaze. A few feet away, Gerry was dancing a jig of delight. Over his shoulder, she could even see a smile tilting the corners of Sir Denby's jowls. When she glanced down again, Nick was still staring up at her, smiling.

The studio subsided into an eerie silence. Lucy could hear the whirr of air-conditioning; she even caught the wail of a siren somewhere in the outside world. The perspiration was trickling down her spine, a lump had formed in her throat, blocking the air and making it hard to breathe.

This was supposed to be the happiest moment of her life. The moment when the best just got even better. Nick had done his bit; he'd delivered what the audience wanted and now it was her turn. A shiver danced its way up her spine. Her hand in Nick's was trembling as the seconds ticked by, each like a lifetime.

Nick's lips moved. He mouthed one word: 'Well?'

Her mouth opened but didn't form words.

'Lucy? Did you hear what I said?'

She nodded slowly.

'And?'

'Come on, love! Put the lad out of his misery!' came a shout from the audience.

'Yeah, get on with it, love. We wanna get to the pub.'

Everyone laughed.

'Give her a break, she's in shock. It's not every day you see a man sign his life away in public,' said Gerry. Even Nick smiled, but the expectation was still there in his eyes.

Lucy felt like a sideshow at the fair or an exhibit at the zoo. She and Nick were performers now and this happy ending, this perfect moment, was what everyone was demanding. What everyone needed. Everyone, it seemed, except her.

'*Lucy?*'

'I – I can't . . .'

His smile slipped.

'I – I'm sorry. I mean, I can't do this. Not like this . . .'

What could she say, when every word she uttered, every tiny expression on her face, was being beamed live to millions of viewers? People were sitting on their sofas at home; in the pub; in the Chinese takeaway; at the gym . . . all watching her. All waiting to see what her answer might be. They wanted that answer to be 'yes'. Nick wanted a lifelong commitment. One she knew she wasn't

ready for, not by a long, long way . . . and not right now.
The blood rushed in her ears, her heart pounded, Nick
started getting to his feet, his face a mix of anger and
anguish.

'I can't do this . . .' whispered Lucy through dry lips.
'I'm just not ready for this, Nick, I'm so sorry.'

Then she wrenched her hand out of his and fled from
the stage.

Chapter Eight

As Lucy stumbled off the set, a floor manager grabbed her arm. 'Hey, wait. Where the hell do you think you're going?'

Ripping off her microphone, she tossed it to the floor, tears almost blinding her eyes. 'I don't know. Home. Out. Anywhere . . .'

Gerry appeared, his orange face beaded with perspiration. 'Come back, love! Say you were overwhelmed. Tell them it was a dodgy green room sandwich or something, anything, I don't care, just get back in there.'

A make-up woman tried to dab his face with her brush but he batted her away. 'Not now! I've got more important things to worry about than a shiny schnozzle. Look, Lisa, Lucy, whatever your name is. This is Nick's big moment. *Your* big moment. Everyone out there is baying for blood – and it's yours. Come back now and you can still be a hero.'

'There'll be cash in it,' said the producer. 'The sponsors will cough up. The ratings will go through the roof.'

'Come now while the commercials are on. Crystal here will do your face.'

Crystal aimed her brush at Lucy but she flinched away. 'I can't change my mind and it's none of your business. No one's business except mine and Nick's.'

Gerry shook his head. 'Wrong. You made it your business when Nick signed up for *Hot Shots*. You're public property now, love, and it's too late to go back.'

Lucy felt icy cold even though the studio was as overheated as an old people's home. She realised Gerry was right; Nick had made himself public property and, by being his girlfriend, she'd bought into the drama, too.

'We've got the main sponsor on the line,' said the producer. 'There's an extra ten per cent if she agrees to marry him live in the second half.'

'Don't bother.'

Lucy twisted round to find Nick standing feet away, his face hard as stone.

'She won't change her mind, will you, Lucy?'

'Nick. Let's talk about this but, please, not in front of strangers.'

'Over here,' he said roughly, grabbing her arm and yanking her towards some curtains. It was hardly private but the curtains hid them from most of the technicians' prying eyes.

'What is wrong with you?' he demanded. 'I get a once-in-a-lifetime deal, I propose to you in front of millions, and you blow me off! What more do you want?'

Not more, but less, she wanted to tell him, but it was hopeless. He'd never understand that all she wanted was normality. She didn't understand it herself. Maybe she was a selfish cow. Or maybe it just wasn't *right*. At no time had he ever got within a million miles of mentioning marriage, or, come to think of it, 'commitment'. And she hadn't expected it. What had just happened was so totally out of the blue.

'For God's sake, all you had to do was say yes!' he hissed.

Anger rose within her. 'Don't speak to me like that. It's not that simple, Nick. You've just put me in an impossible position! How did you expect me to react?'

Heads craned to look at them.

'Keep your voice down,' snarled Nick.

'I'm not ready for this,' said Lucy, trying to keep her voice calm, yet shaking inside. 'Not to be put on the spot in front of the whole world.'

'Just the UK, don't flatter yourself.'

'I don't deserve that.'

'And I don't deserve to be humiliated on national TV, Lucy. I thought you loved me.'

Her heart almost stopped. He'd never said that word. He'd never come close. She didn't know how to reply. Did it make a difference, the 'L' word? It was supposed to make all the difference, wasn't it?

'Nick, I don't feel that I *know* you. Not really, not nearly enough.'

He curled his lip in contempt. 'Our lack of acquaintance has never stopped you before, has it? I don't recall you saying that when you're moaning in ecstasy and begging me for more. You couldn't wait to get your knickers off, could you? And now, when I'm offering you a chance that, let's face it, Lucy, you'll never get again, you say you don't know me well enough.'

Lucy's heart was pounding. A cocktail of indignation

and hurt was pulsing through her veins. She was sorry for the hurt she'd caused Nick but his fury at her refusal was beyond fair. 'We can't talk about something this important here. It's not the right place or time to make a decision that's going to last a lifetime. Not in front of millions of strangers. Getting married isn't part of the *Hot Shots* game plan, Nick, no matter how much you think you need to give the people a perfect ending.'

As soon as the words left her lips, she knew she'd made the situation even worse. Nick almost spat out his reply. 'A game? Is that what you think this is? Maybe you're afraid of commitment, Lucy? Scared you can't cope? Maybe it's you that's the player.'

'I didn't mean that you were a player!'

'Really? That's what it sounded like to me.'

He was right. It did sound like that and worse, she realised, what if she did think that he was playing a game? Using this occasion to maximise his moment?

'This is going nowhere. I'm leaving now.'

Nick's face was dark with fury as Lucy felt her adrenaline ebbing away. Then an orange hand ripped the curtain aside.

'Here are the lovebirds!' shrieked Gerry. 'Have you made up, then, or were you having a bit of a quickie behind the curtains?'

Nick's face suddenly crumpled and Lucy saw mascara running down his cheeks. Oh my God, she had made a grown man cry. What kind of an evil witch did that make her? Did he *really* want to marry her?

'Oh dear. Looks like the iron lady's not for turning,' said Gerry as a sob wracked Nick's body.

'Oh, just piss off, you ghoul!' cried Lucy, forgetting that Gerry had his microphone in his hand. She was sure she could still hear the boos of the audience as she raced out of the studio, through the foyer and into the nearest taxi.

Chapter Nine

And that was why, a week later, Lucy was still unable to go anywhere or do anything without a pack of newshounds chasing her. She was public enemy number one: The Wicked Stepmother crossed with Cruella de Vil. One tabloid dug up an old flame from college who claimed Lucy had broken his heart and caused him to seek refuge in junk food, which was why he now weighed twenty-five stone. A weekly magazine ran a poll asking if Nick was better off without her and ninety-three per cent of the readers had said yes.

One story (in the red tops) had a picture of her with a caption saying: '*A haggard-looking Lucy Gibson, 28, emerges from her London pied-à-terre with a mystery man just days after rejecting her devastated boyfriend live on TV.*'

In fact, she'd been emerging from her flat with Charlie en route for the Thai takeaway at the corner of the street. Unfortunately, notoriety had gone to his head and he'd suddenly morphed into Pete Doherty and aimed a finger in the direction of the cameras. And, actually, she was only twenty-seven-and-a-half but, admittedly, the past few weeks might have made her look older.

It was bad enough that the press had intruded into her home life but they'd also turned up at Able & Lawson, the world's stuffiest law firm. They hadn't dared get inside, although she'd been bombarded with emails and the receptionist had had to screen every call so she'd hardly got any work done all week. Letitia, back at work after the birth of baby Crispin, had been sympathetic and even ambled down to the shop to fetch Lucy a ginseng tea. However, Lucy knew she couldn't go on like this; sooner or later she was bound to be summoned to the upper echelons to explain herself.

Towards the end of the week, things seemed to have been dying down a little and she'd breathed a sigh of relief – until that story of Nick and the rehab centre which had brought the paparazzi buzzing round her door like a pack of flies.

Worst of all, there was the guilt, the worry, not about herself, but about Nick. His words, spat out in anger and hurt, had lodged deep in her heart.

'A game? Is that what you think this is? Maybe you're afraid of commitment, Lucy? Scared you can't cope? Maybe it's you that's the player.'

Maybe he was right. She'd only had two serious boyfriends since university. One had lasted three years and was now saving turtles in Mexico; the other had emigrated to Australia. The twenty-five-stone ex didn't count.

She'd tried to contact Nick every day since she'd run away from the studio but he'd ignored every call. The answering machine at his flat was permanently on and she gave up leaving messages after day five. The previous night, after she'd fallen over on her doorstep and crawled inside, fighting back the tears, she'd found the courage to phone Nick's parents, hoping he was there. She'd only got Hattie who, as Lucy might have expected, was furious.

'How could you do that to him?' she shrieked.

Lucy tried to stay calm. As Nick's sister, Hattie was bound to be upset but Lucy refused to shoulder the blame for something she hadn't caused. She took a deep breath.

'Hattie, I'm sure you must know that whatever happened is between me and Nick. Is he there? Can I speak to him?'

'Yes, he's here, and no, I'm afraid he doesn't want to talk to you.'

'Can you ask him? Please, Harriet?'

'He's already told us he won't speak to you,' squeaked Harriet.

'Well, can you at least let me know if he's OK? This story about the rehab centre . . . is it true?'

'No, it's not – but that's no thanks to you. He's in pieces because of what you've done.' Harriet slammed down the phone, leaving Lucy feeling angry and hurt. 'I won't be made to feel guilty!' she cried aloud to the empty room, but inside, a tiny voice was niggling at her that she was angry with Nick precisely because she *did* feel guilty.

Later that night Fiona turned up. Lucy had already indulged in generous helpings of Baileys and then she and Fiona hit a bottle of gin while Hengist hit a king-size bag of Bonio biscuits. Lucy had rolled into bed around two in the morning. Fiona was in the spare room where Lucy had managed to wedge a foldaway bed between the computer and the end of the wall. There was just about room for Fiona, but as for Hengist, he'd just have to sleep on Fiona's feet. And her legs – and probably her stomach.

In the morning, bleary-eyed and dry-mouthed, Lucy headed for the kitchen. Hengist's chain was rattling against the china dish he was using as a dog bowl as she walked in. His tail thudded against the bin, slobber spraying from his mouth on to the fridge door. Hengist was a kitchen-sized dog, thought Lucy. Or more likely, she had a dog-sized kitchen. Fiona was sitting at the tiny café table at one end of the galley kitchen. Crunching on a piece of toast she scanned a newspaper, frowning.

'And how are you today, Britain's Most Wanted?' asked Fiona as Lucy slunk over to the sink. The cafetiere was still half-full, still hot to the touch. Grabbing a mug from the drainer, Lucy filled it to the top with coffee. 'OK-ish. No, fine, considering. How did you and Hengist sleep?'

Fiona wrinkled her nose. 'OK, but I should have brought his charcoal tablets. Tikka masala has never agreed with him.'

'Good job we didn't order the Vindaloo, then,' said Lucy, sipping her coffee. It was strong enough to wake a mummy from the tomb. Emptying the last few drops of milk, she threw the carton in the bin. Inside, she could see the *Mirror* and the *Daily Mail*, crumpled up on top of an empty bottle of Bombay Sapphire, a couple of cans of slimline tonic and a takeaway tray.

She knew then that she'd made the papers again. She'd nurtured a tiny flame of hope, for a brief moment, that Johnny Depp was running for President or Victoria Beckham had gone Goth. At least that would have kept her off the front pages.

'Hope we didn't disturb your beauty sleep, but Hengist was a bit restless in the night,' said Fiona through a mouthful of toast. 'I had to take him out for his constitutional, first thing.'

'You mean you actually went *outside*?' said Lucy.

'Yeah. Why not?'

'I just thought they might have been waiting.'

'Not for me,' said Fiona. 'It's you they want, and if they had dared to come near me, I'd have had no hesitation in letting Hengist have 'em.'

'And he'd have licked them to death?'

'One word from me and he turns into the Hound of the Baskervilles.' On cue, Hengist flopped down on his rug, laid his head on his over-sized paws and let out a sigh like a small earth tremor.

'Truly terrifying,' said Lucy, pulling out a chair opposite Fiona. Lucy knew it couldn't be put off any longer.

'Sorry,' said Fiona when her mouth was empty. Pushing the newspaper towards Lucy, she smiled ruefully. 'It's not that bad, really, you know. I mean, it's only an inside spread.'

'What do you mean, Fi?' said Lucy, turning the newspaper the right way up with trembling fingers.

'Well, it's only your bum. Not the . . .'

Lucy felt slightly sick.

'I mean, you're not on the front this time and they haven't shown your face,' said Fiona cheerily.

Slowly, Lucy turned back the pages of the newspaper. Relief at the story about David Beckham on page two and the editorial about educational standards slipping on page three was followed by shock on page four and horror on five. Fi was right. They hadn't shown her face.

She read the headline again which wasn't difficult because it was a screamer, with letters two inches high:

NICK-ERLESS!

She closed her eyes and swallowed hard.

'I'll get the Rescue Remedy,' said Fiona.

'No. No, it's OK. Actually, it's not OK, but I'll be OK.'

Fiona patted her hand. 'It could have been worse. You might have been wearing granny pants.'

'Fiona, it couldn't be worse. I wish I had worn granny pants. I could have. I only had two clean pairs left and I chose . . . that thing.'

'Frost French Floozies, are they?' said Fiona. 'Looks like the current range.'

'Elle McPherson, if you must know, Fi. I bought them for—'

'Nick?'

Lucy nodded then risked another peek at the newspaper. Looking at the picture of her bottom spread across the crease of the page was like watching one of those cosmetic surgery shows on TV. You didn't want to open your eyes as the surgeon was stretching some poor woman's skin over her eyeball, but somehow, you just had to know the full horror. Lucy squinted at the photograph again and her stomach lurched.

Yes, it was just as horrific as the first time.

'Hmm, you know something,' said Fiona, 'it may say "nickerless" but that's not strictly *accurate*, is it? Maybe you could sue, because you did have knickers on, just not very big ones.' She wrinkled her nose. 'Then again, I suppose that doesn't matter to them. I suppose the pun was just too good to resist. I must admit, if I'd been the sub-editor, I'd have found it hard to resist myself.'

'Thanks very much.'

'On the other hand, there is something appealingly vulnerable about your expression.'

'But what if Nick sees it? What will he think of me?'

'Do you care what he thinks?'

'Course I care!' There was no hesitation. Of course she cared what he thought. She cared very much about Nick, she . . . she stopped short at the word love and that was the problem. The issue that had turned her life upside-down in a matter of weeks or rather, in a matter of about thirty seconds, to be accurate.

Fiona pushed a bowl of Rice Krispies towards her but Lucy didn't touch them. 'I never wanted to hurt him, Fiona. I was horrified when I thought he'd had to go into rehab . . .'

Fiona snorted. 'Rehab! Just because he gets a little knock back?'

'In front of ten million people.'

'Ten point six, actually,' said Fiona. 'Says here on page four, look.'

Lucy felt a warm, wet and heavy presence on her knee. Two huge brown eyes stared dolefully up at her.

'See, Hengist loves you,' said Fiona proudly.

Lucy looked at Hengist. 'You too, boy,' she whispered, patting the dog's huge head. He gave a tiny growl of pleasure.

The Rice Krispies were uneaten and soggy when they heard Lucy's phone ringing.

'Not already,' she groaned.

'Shall I answer it?' Fiona asked as Lucy hunted for her mobile.

'No. If there's any music to be faced, I'll face it.'

She found the phone on top of her collection of *Cosmo* centrefolds in her room, and her face brightened as she set eyes on the display. 'Hello, Mum.'

Five minutes later she was back in the kitchen, shaking her head. 'That's it. That's the last straw. I don't mind what they do to me but they can leave my mum alone. Gah!' she cried, dropping the phone on the worktop.

'Hey, calm down,' said Fiona. 'Tell Aunty Fi what's happened now.'

'I know you think I'm being paranoid, but you don't know what lengths they'll go to. You wouldn't believe it. One of them has been hiding out in my mum's coal bunker.'

'I thought your mum had a gas fire.'

'She does now, but she kept the bunker to store her gardening tools and one of them – a great big Australian bloke – jumped out on her and took a picture. Mum said she nearly had a heart attack.' Lucy collapsed into a chair.

'Was he naked or something?'

'No. He had some kind of funny hat thing, though, according to Mum.'

'With corks on it?' Fiona erupted into a huge guffaw.

'Fiona, it's not funny. He jumped out when Mum went to peg some washing out and asked her if commitment issues ran in the family.'

'That's below the belt. Especially with your dad's track record and all that. They haven't managed to track him down, have they?'

'No. Not yet, but he's been mentioned. Some columnist was asking if that's why he walked out. They didn't bother to say that he'd had God knows how many affairs, just that he'd left us and we'd refused ever to speak to him again.'

'How the hell did they find that out?'

'It said they'd spoken to a close family friend.'

'Some bloody friend!' declared Fiona.

'Mum thinks it might have been that Brenda Thingy from the horticultural society. She never did like the fact that Mum's sweet peas beat hers in the last Grimeton Show.'

'This Brenda sounds like a deeply vengeful woman.'

'I know, I know, Fi. It's ridiculous. I'm paranoid after all this, but what can you do?'

'Has Nick spoken to the press yet?' said Fiona gently.

'No. he's refused to comment, which I'm grateful for,' she added.

'Have you spoken to him yet?'

Lucy sighed. 'I've tried a couple of times but only got the answer phone. I spoke to his sister, Hattie, and she said he never wanted to talk to me again.'

The phone rang again. The screen showed a London

number and Lucy pressed it to her ear cautiously. 'Hello?'

'Is that Lucy Gibson?'

'Yes . . .'

'You're live on Sleaze FM, the station that leaves nothing to the imagination! Tell us, Lucy, what was Nick Laurentis like in bed? Is it true you made him get down on all fours and howl like a wolf?'

Lucy stabbed the red button, breathless with shock. 'Sleaze FM. No idea how they got my mobile number.' She caught sight of the time on the radio. 'Oh flip. I've got to get into work. Can you let yourself out?'

'Sure,' said Fiona, 'Call me any time if you need me, but not for the next hour. I'm doing some research on lethal substances with a very well-built toxicologist. I could almost break my IQ rule for him. Almost.'

As Lucy was hunting for a clean blouse, the phone range again. She didn't recognise the number.

'Is that Lucinda Gibson?' asked the caller.

'It's Lucy. Can't you even get my name right?'

There was a pause. 'Ah. Yes. Lucy, it's Hugo Lawson Senior. From Able & Lawson. Your um . . . boss.'

Lucy sank down on the bed, one shoe on and one off, her mind processing the voice on the end of the line. Hugo Lawson Senior, who was seventy-squillion (as opposed to Hugo Lawson Junior who was a veritable babe magnet at sixty-two). 'I am sooo sorry, Mr Lawson. I didn't mean to be rude, only I thought you were one of them,' she gushed.

'Them?'

'A tabloid hack.'

'Oh. Well, I never read the tabloids,' said Mr Lawson.

'Only the *FT*. However, this morning my attention *has* been drawn to a number of publications of a more scurrilous nature. Miss Pettigrew happened to catch sight of your um . . . image in one such newspaper while on her way to work on the Tube. She deemed it necessary to purchase several copies with the petty cash.'

Lucy could imagine Miss Pettigrew, the management team PA, bearing a neatly folded pile of 'scurrilous publications' into Mr Lawson's oak-lined office.

'I believe several young men were making observations about your photograph on the Piccadilly line this morning. I have to say, Lucy, that it would have been preferable if the name of the firm had not found its way into the article.' She heard rustling on the end of the line. 'Ah, here's the paragraph in question: "*Love-rat Lucy Gibson must be used to taking down briefs in her job with a firm of City solicitors. But her bosses at Able & Lawson probably didn't have anything quite as scanty as THIS PAIR in mind.*"'

Lucy wanted the floor to open up.

'I am so sorry, Mr Lawson.'

'It's wholly inaccurate, of course. I've never asked you to take down any briefs. You're only the marketing assistant, but you get my drift . . .'

'I apologise. I mean, it won't happen again. These tabloid reporters are scumbags!'

'Quite – and that is why I'm calling.'

Lucy's stomach began to churn a little. This sounded ominous.

'I've been chatting to your line manager, Letitia, and

she tells me that it has been difficult for you to perform your duties as we – and, doubtless, you – would wish to. Therefore, we thought it might be appropriate if . . .'

. . . *you sacked me?* thought Lucy, feeling sick.

'Are you still there?' asked Mr Lawson.

'Yes. I'm still here.'

'We have discussed the matter and thought it prudent for you to take your annual leave now. I believe you have two weeks owing and perhaps, if you concur with us, as I'm sure you will, considering all the circumstances . . .'

Lucy now knew why Letitia's blood pressure had risen when she'd had a meeting with Mr Lawson Senior.

'We were hoping that you might consider adding a spell of extra leave on to your holiday to give time for this . . . this extraordinary situation to resolve itself. A month would appear to be an appropriate timescale.'

'A whole month? But that means I won't be back until the summer! Are you sure?'

'It seems like a prudent course of action, Lucinda, yes. I'm afraid we can't have this kind of attention drawn to a firm with a reputation such as ours.'

'Whatever you say, Mr Lawson. Probably best for everyone, in the um . . . extraordinary circumstances. Thank you for being so understanding.'

'Capital. We'll hopefully see you in a month, when, I trust, any unpleasantness will be behind you. I mean, when this is all over. Goodbye.'

Fiona appeared in the doorway. 'Well?'

'That was my boss. He wants me to take some leave and put any unpleasantness behind me. Fi, I don't think this incident has helped my prospects of making

Assistant Marketing Manager rather than Marketing Assistant.'

'Is there a difference?'

'About three grand a year and someone else gets to fetch your sandwiches,' said Lucy lightly, but inside she had a distinct feeling of unease. Bringing the firm into disrepute was hardly a great career move, even though it wasn't, technically, her fault. Hugo Lawson might sound bumbling but she guessed he could be as ruthless as Sir Denby himself if he sensed an opportunity to save money. Right now, however, she had to make the best of a bad situation.

'I think I need to get away somewhere where people are not,' she said as Fiona piled crockery in the sink.

Fiona turned, plate in hand. 'You mean—'

'Would you mind? Just for a few weeks. I'll contribute to expenses,' said Lucy, pulling off her office heels.

Fiona shook her head. 'Don't be silly. I could do with getting out of London and doing some actual writing and it would be fun to have company. I've only managed fifteen thousand words of *Murder at the Mall* and I've a deadline looming. Besides, I fancy a taste of sea air and buff surfer boys.'

'Oh, God! No men! Will you believe me if I say I never want to get within ten feet of another man as long as I live?'

'Maybe today but not for ever. It might not be all over with Nick yet, Lucy.'

Lucy was touched. Fiona had never had a good word for Nick before, but now she was trying hard to be helpful.

'For a writer of fiction, you're a hopeless liar, Fi.'

'But an enthusiastic one. Look, let me go home and make a few calls while you pack. I'll pick you up later.'

Lucy nodded and went through into the bedroom. Standing in front of her dressing table, she caught sight of herself in the mirror and was shocked by the woman who frowned back, pale and forlorn and mousy-haired. She studied herself for a few more moments, then grabbed her purse and headed back to the kitchen where Fiona was clipping Hengist's lead into his collar, ready to leave.

'Fiona. Can you do me a favour?'

'Sure, hon.'

'Pop into Superdrug for me. There's something I need to do.'

Chapter Ten

'So run it by me *again*, Josh. Just who is this woman demanding we drop everything and get the cottage ready for her?' asked Sara Pentire, shaking up the duvet so hard that she knocked a china vase from the bedside table.

Josh Standring was too late to save it from rolling on to the patchwork rug by the bed. He was reluctant to touch anything in the bedroom, afraid of getting muddy fingerprints on the pristine white sheets that Sara had expertly tucked under the mattress. Yet he thought the vase deserved rescuing, so he picked it up carefully.

'Her name's Fiona Bentley-Black,' he said, holding out the little vase.

Sara wrinkled her nose at it before dumping it back on the table. 'The crime writer?'

'Is she? She needs the cottage in a hurry, that's all I know. If Mrs Sennen hadn't had a fall, she'd have taken care of everything as usual.' He raked a hand through his hair in embarrassment. 'Sara, I'd have done it myself but I have to get the paddock fence finished. I don't like to see you doing my dirty work.'

Sara shrugged. 'Some notice would've been nice rather than phoning up at ten o'clock and asking us to get the place ready for her.' Josh smiled. Sara hated people being disorganised and it was always a surprise to him that she was interested in him. Live and let live, that was his philosophy in life these days. In fact, even having a philosophy at all sounded way too close to an actual plan.

'And she's got a friend with her?' said Sara, smoothing an imaginary wrinkle from the cover. 'Mrs Sennen said she phoned again and asked her to make up the spare room.'

'Right,' said Josh, already itching to be outside again. He'd almost finished repairing the fence around the paddock where one of the cottage owners kept a few rare-breed sheep. He'd only popped into the house to see Sara and thank her for stepping in at the last moment.

'Thanks, Sara. I know this isn't your scene.'

Giving the pillow a final thud, she slotted it into place on the bed. 'Josh, it's not a problem. Just chill out, I've cleaned up the best I can but this place hasn't been used in months, by the look of it.'

The house looked immaculate to Josh, but then he was hardly a domestic goddess.

'And I've made the beds, the double and the single, so this Fiona can bring any combo of friends she likes. Is she gay?'

Josh smiled softly. Not from what he'd gathered from his few meetings with Fiona. She'd almost pinned him against the worktop in her kitchen before he'd convinced her she wasn't his type.

'No idea,' he said, adding, 'Tresco Creek attracts all kinds of people, you should know that.'

Sara stopped midway to adjusting a heart-shaped tapestry cushion so that it was exactly in the centre of the pillow. 'Some more tasty than others,' she said, her gaze travelling to Josh's chest.

He glanced down and gave a rueful smile. He should have known, in hindsight, that it was a mistake to wander into the bedroom of the cottage, stripped to the waist. Even as Sara flicked a tongue over her lips, he guessed that the fence was going to have to wait a while.

'Sweetheart, I'm filthy,' he warned as she took a step towards him.

'So is what I have in mind.'

She entwined her arms around his neck and touched the tip of her tongue to his bare chest, grimacing slightly at the bitterness.

'I warned you.'

'I don't care.'

'This is Fiona's cottage,' murmured Josh. His fingers slipped inside the back of her white shorts, finding her skin deliciously warm. He was no longer worried about leaving dirty marks. He lowered his mouth to her ear. 'I don't suppose she'd be too pleased to know the hired help was having sex in her bedroom.'

'What Fiona Thingy doesn't know won't hurt her, and you won't get anything dirty,' said Sara, releasing him, only to whip back the rug off the floor. The next thing Josh felt were wooden boards beneath his naked backside and Sara sliding on top of him.

*

An hour later he was back in the paddock, swinging a sledgehammer, almost wishing he hadn't sucumbed so easily. Almost, but not quite. If there was one thing he was sure of in this uncertain world, it was that he loved sex. He loved women, and until he'd met Sara a couple of years before, he'd wasted no time in indulging himself.

Josh had been one of those lucky blokes who bulked up young. At eighteen, he'd had the body of a man of twenty-five and he'd known it. Despite what the social workers and, occasionally, Marnie, had told him, his 'reputation' hadn't put off the girls. In fact, it had acted like a magnet. Local girls and holidaymakers alike had flocked round him but nowhere had his pull been stronger than with the girls who arrived in Porthstow, regular as clockwork, at the end of every June.

Girls from places like Surrey and Cheshire. From universities like Durham, Oxford and Cambridge. Places that would have probably ejected him from their manicured cloisters and halls if they'd caught him climbing up their ivy. Girls who were blond, raven-haired, brunette and auburn. All with lithe bodies, shiny hair and glossy accents.

They had one thing in common: when they heard about his 'challenging' background, seen him in a wetsuit and discovered that 'Oh gosh, you actually do *manual labour*?' they turned to shiny, well-groomed mush. Forget their Ph.D.s in Anglo-Saxon poetry, their M.Sc.s in the sex life of the potato, or whatever the hell they were into, all they really wanted was to get his boxers off.

So he didn't bother to tell them the whole story. How, after he'd stopped being quite such a bad boy, he'd worked his balls off to get a place at the local college and then done a part-time degree in business studies. How he'd worked as a community development officer for a while before he'd had to go back to Tresco Farm because, for the first time in his life, Marnie needed him more than he'd needed her.

Those glossy girls just wanted a taste of bad boy for the summer and Josh had no problem with giving them exactly what they wanted. Over and over again.

But as thirty loomed like a dark cloud on the horizon and his foster mum, Marnie, had struggled her way out of the world, Josh had had a shock. He'd grown tired of his diet of summer sex and, against all his better judgement, had started to want something more.

When Sara had turned up at the sailing club one summer, very cute and extremely capable, he'd thought he'd sensed someone he wanted to have more than a fling with. After two years of sharing skin and breakfast, he knew she wanted to move into the farmhouse and he was seriously thinking about inviting her to. *Seriously*.

'Shit!'

Midway to bringing the hammer down on the final fence post, a blast of pain tore through his shoulder. He cursed himself, knowing he should have worn the harness when he'd been windsurfing the day before. Maybe he deserved it, mixing it in a Force Five on the entrance to the estuary. Or maybe, he thought in disgust, he was just getting soft.

The post, already halfway into the earth, accused him. 'Bugger it,' he declared. He picked up the hammer, took a deep breath, and brought it crashing down on the post-head. It sank into the ground and Josh straightened up, waiting for the wave of pain to pass. It did but it took a minute. Then he grabbed a two-litre bottle from the ground, drank half and stood back to check his handiwork. The fence would do, he decided, it would stop the sheep from roaming, keep the cottage visitors happy. That was all that it needed to do.

Beyond the fence, the far side of the paddock and the cliff edge that marked one boundary of Tresco Farm, the sea glittered. Today it was inky-blue topped with white caps and sun sparkles but Josh had seen it black, grey, green and turquoise, depending on its mood and the weather.

Wiping the sweat off his forehead with the back of his arm, he studied the sky. That morning it had started off postcard-blue, the kind of day that drew day trippers and weekenders from London and the Midlands like wasps round a jam jar. As he'd grabbed a sandwich at lunch, he'd heard snatches of the news on Radio Cornwall. Bank Holiday tailbacks and pile-ups were jamming the motorways and the A roads as the public vied to grab their piece of the sun and sky and sea.

Josh didn't blame them. And if he sometimes wished, for the sake of his overdraft, that Tresco Farm was not so far off the beaten track, there were far more times that he was glad you had to look hard to discover it.

And now, though the sky on the horizon was still blue at past five o'clock Josh could almost smell the change in the atmosphere. He hadn't lived in Tresco Creek for nigh-on twenty years, give or take a few lapses, without knowing what that heaviness in the air meant. He turned. Already there were clouds billowing up like anvils behind the cluster of whitewashed cottages which included Fiona's bolt hole, Creekside Cottage.

The water gone, he rolled out the final reel of fencing, secured it with a hammer and nails, and picked his T-shirt up from the ground. Good thing the job was finished. He reckoned he might not have had another chance for days now. He hoped Fiona and her friend would make it before the storm broke.

Chapter Eleven

'Y ou can come out now, Luce.'
　'Are you sure?'
'I'm sure.'
'And you're absolutely certain none of them are out there?'
'Absolutely certain.'
There was a pause while Lucy considered just how certain Fiona really was. She certainly *sounded* confident enough and after all, she was, in theory, an expert on this sort of thing. It had taken a very long time to get to Tresco Creek, which Lucy found comforting. The more miles she could put between her and the newspapers, the better. In fact, it had taken so long that Lucy had fallen asleep somewhere around Exeter. As she'd dropped off, she'd been convinced she was naked, and being chased down the M4 by the press, all throwing bagels at her.
'And you're sure that it's safe here?'
'Lucy Gibson, I, Fiona Bentley-Black, swear on my next advance and Hengist's life, that no photographer or journalist is lying in wait for you up here.'
'OK, then.'

If Fiona had staked her word on Hengist, thought Lucy, then she must be sure. Peering through the mud-spattered windows of the Land Rover, she suppressed a gasp of surprise. It was no longer raining as it had been most of the way from London. In fact, there was blue sky peeping out from between the clouds. 'Enough to patch a sailor's shirt,' her dad would have said. Enough to clothe a whole fleet of sailors, thought Lucy, staring at the sky which seemed to go on for ever. Or maybe, that was just because it met the sea on the horizon and blended with it as the sun sank low in the sky.

Lucy jumped down from the Land Rover into the cool evening air. She thought she could smell woodsmoke but there couldn't be any because it was too warm for anyone to want a fire today. Yet there was a definite freshness to the air, and a stiff breeze blowing from the sea set the goose bumps rippling on her arms.

'Do you want me to fetch your bucket and spade?' asked Fiona, clearly amused at her reaction.

'No. But it's beautiful here.'

'You wait until the electric gets cut off while you're watching *Desperate Housewives* or the roof is leaking because the slates are loose.'

Lucy didn't care. Creekside Cottage seemed idyllic to her. It was the end property of a row of six that faced outwards across a field with . . . she squinted against the setting sun, yup, a field with sheep in it, cute sheep with little heart-shaped faces.

'Woof!'

'Oh God, not bloody sheep,' muttered Fiona as Hengist barked joyfully from the back of the Land Rover.

'Is that bad?'

'Only if they manage to come face to face,' said Fiona, opening the tailgate. Lucy could have sworn the Land Rover suspension groaned in relief as the dog leapt on to the grass.

'Stay-yy, boy!' ordered Fiona.

Hengist sniffed at a tub of geraniums, the sheep forgotten.

'I'll get the bags,' said Fiona, grinning. 'Chin up. You can relax now. I'll fetch the booze in a while when we've settled in.'

'Thanks, Fi, I really am grateful, you know. I'll never forget what you've done for me. I'll remember you in my will, if I make one. I'll even leave you my *Oklahoma!* programme.'

'Is that the one Charlie got signed by the London cast including Hugh Jackman?'

'The very one.'

'Then you're more grateful than I thought but before you bequeath me all your worldly goods, wait until you see inside the cottage.'

Even if the cottage had been a derelict shed on a tip, Lucy would have been more than grateful. In fact, it seemed to have dropped straight from the pages of a National Trust handbook, right down to the green front door, the trellised porch and the tub of scarlet geraniums. There was even a wonky gate that squeaked as Fiona pushed it open.

'Bugger. This thing's knackered. I'll have to get it fixed,' said Fiona, wrestling with the lock. Then, suddenly, the lock clicked, Fiona hissed a triumphant 'yes!' and they were inside. The door opened into the hall where a small window let in a glimmer of blue light. The smell of damp was faint but unmistakable, even over the tang of ozone and seaweed.

'Needs a fire lighting and, of course, the storage heaters have been off all winter. Normally, I'd have got it aired but, of course, I couldn't let anyone know we were coming. You'll be fine with a drop of gin inside you,' said Fiona, throwing her bag on to the couch.

Lucy hovered in the doorway, taking in the room.

'I'll fetch some wood in from the shed while it's light. We might need a fire later when the sun goes down.'

'Want any help?'

'Nah. I like playing Girl Guide and Hengist needs a run round the garden. Why don't you put the kettle on?'

Once Fiona had left, Lucy pushed open a latched door which she guessed led into the little back kitchen. She flicked a switch and blinked as the strip light flickered into life before filling the kettle with water and popping it back on its stand, waiting for the faint hiss that told her it was doing its stuff.

Outside, she could make out Fiona at the end of the garden, stooping low over what must be the log store. No reporters had leapt out and grabbed her friend yet and Lucy smiled. She really had become totally paranoid lately and now it was time, if not to relax, to get things into perspective. To 'sort yourself out, love', as her mother had put it, and to decide what to do about Nick, if anything could be done.

While the kettle boiled, she headed back to the sitting room to try and make herself useful. Table lamp,

TV, heating: that's what she always did on dark evenings when she got home from work; put on the light and TV for company.

And waited for Nick.

She hunted in the usual places for the control unit, down the side of a large velour armchair, among a pile of fading copies of *Horse and Hound*, on top of the oak bookcase. On the shelves she had at least a year's supply of reading material. *Blood on My Hands* by Fiona Bentley-Black, *Hanging by a Thread* by Fiona Bentley-Black, *Dying to Meet You* by Fiona Bentley-Black, etc. She certainly wasn't going to be bored while Fiona churned out her latest bestseller. She finally spotted the remote control, gathering dust on top of the last remaining log in the basket by the hearth. Even though the cottage must have been empty for months, there was still a soft undernote of woodsmoke beneath the damp.

Checking that the programme was some innocuous wildlife documentary and not news, current affairs or *Jeremy Kyle*, she turned down the sound and returned to the kitchen. Through the window, she saw Fiona throw down the axe and gather up some wood in her arms. Lucy was at the back door in a moment, holding it open.

'That was hard work. I hope we've got some bloody firelighters. I mean, I meant to ask the maintenance guys to make sure we've got some but—'

'Bit short notice?'

'A bit. They said they'd arrange for the cottage to be cleaned and make the beds up, which was good of them. Mrs Sennen, the housekeeper, is very good at that sort of thing.'

'Fi, I can't just mope around here like this. Can I do anything to help? You look worn out after all the driving.'

'Thanks!'

'You know what I mean.'

'OK, you're right, I'm knackered. Why don't you make a decent cup of tea while I get this fire going.'

'Coming up.'

Minutes later, Lucy was carrying two steaming mugs into the sitting room as Fiona set a match to a neat pyramid of wood, newspaper and firelighters. She glanced up at Lucy, her eyes bright. 'You know, I'd make a brilliant pyromaniac,' she said wistfully, watching the blue and orange flames curling round the wood. 'Shame I'm not getting any younger; most pyromaniacs are under sixteen, you know.' She pushed herself to her feet with a groan.

'You're not even thirty-five yet, Fiona. Still time to set the world on fire.'

Fiona flopped down in a chair with a sigh, took a sip of the tea then pulled a face.

'That bad?' said Lucy.

'The tea's fine. I just remembered the gin's still in the boot of the car,' groaned Fiona, already halfway to her feet.

'I'll get it.'

Fiona looked doubtful. 'Are you sure you're up to it?'

'Absolutely. If I can't manage to get outside to the car, then there's no hope for me, is there? I'll end up hiding here, surrounded by decaying rubbish with all my meals delivered by the local takeaway.'

'Which is four miles away.'

'Four!'

'Yup. There's a post office in the village and a pub, but that's it. Nearest form of civilisation is in Porthstow, down the coast. If you can call three thousand public school kids, tourists and surfers civilised.'

'Hand over the keys,' said Lucy. 'I really need a drink after that.'

Fiona dug in her pocket and held out a bunch of keys. 'Thanks, Luce.'

Lucy was struck by a pang of guilt at her friend's weary face. If it wasn't for Fiona, she might still have been trapped inside her flat in London, scared to answer the door or even open the curtains in case a photographer was waiting to get a shot of her, preferably looking minging, which wouldn't have been difficult considering the state she'd been in recently.

The sun had slipped below the horizon now and a few stars were already pricking the indigo sky. The light from the porch windows spilled out as far as the Land Rover. Her breath misted the air as she unlocked the 4×4's rear door and tugged it open. There was a faint smell of wild thyme in the air. Behind her, she knew, was the narrow lane that led to the cottage and the woods. Apart from the wind, she suddenly realised that all else was silent. *Almost* silent. A faint hoot from behind the cottage made her jump. She was, finally, ready to believe that there really was no one lying in wait with a long-range lens. The tailgate light glowed reassuringly and she quickly spotted the neck of a bottle of Bombay Sapphire.

'Hey!'

Her head jerked up and her heart took off at warp speed as a voice emerged from the darkness.

'Luce, can you manage the wine as well – in the Waitrose bag.'

As Lucy's pulse returned to normal, she shook her head and smiled in relief. She really had been getting paranoid.

Later, as they were sitting in front of the fire, Lucy could almost believe that she and Fiona were just here having a girly weekend. The fire smelled tangy and sweet, reminding her of the early days at home. After her dad had finally left, her mum had had a gas fire installed because it was so much easier for a woman on her own.

'Stinks a bit, doesn't it?' said Fiona, waving her glass in the direction of the hearth. 'But I love it.'

Lucy could feel the warmth against her cheeks. 'It's great.'

Fiona gave a tiny burp. 'Well, excuse me, but I need the little girl's room then I'll get us a top-up. God, I hope there's some loo roll in the cabinet otherwise it's the magazine rack.'

'I don't fancy ending up with *Horse and Hound* printed on my bum,' said Lucy with an unexpected giggle.

'What are you laughing at?'

'I don't know.'

By the time Fiona had returned from the Land Rover with a second bottle of wine, Lucy wasn't laughing any more. It was probably the effect of the wine, it might have been tiredness, but she realised she was crying.

'Tissue?' said Fi, holding out a box.

'It's the wine,' said Lucy. 'And the gin. And I'm tired. That's all.'

'Yeah?'

'Yes. Actually, no. No, it's not the wine. It's just that I can't help wondering – I can't help thinking ... I've caused so much trouble, I've hurt Nick and his family so much.'

'You did what you thought was right, Lucy. Marriage is too big a commitment to be taken lightly. You have to believe that you did the right thing for him and for yourself.'

She had believed it, had been so certain she was doing the right thing, but now, for the first time, that resolve was softening like melting icing on a cake. She wiped her eyes.

'But Fiona, what if I was wrong? Wouldn't it have been so much easier if I'd just said yes?'

Chapter Twelve

Easier but not right. That had been Lucy's first thought as she'd woken up the next morning in the boxroom of Creekside Cottage, to rain drumming on the roof and wind lashing the creeper against the panes.

She was almost sure saying no to Nick had been the right thing to do for his sake as well as hers. As for fleeing the aftermath by running off to Cornwall, well, it was only for a month until the heat died down. She'd soon be back home, back to . . . well, back to whatever. She didn't want to think about that right now.

In the morning light, she saw her mobile lying on the rickety table by the bed and wondered if she should try and contact Nick again or whether it was better to give him some space. Or was that a cop-out?

She didn't know what to do. Whichever way she jumped was wrong.

She listened for the sound of Fiona moving about but it was becoming difficult to hear anything above the noise of the gathering storm. At least nothing was leaking yet. Above her a patch of damp was visible on the sloping ceiling and a cobweb nestled between the beams. The room had a faint odour that reminded her of her gran's place when she'd been little. Mothballs, maybe, but did moths actually have balls, she wondered.

Although it was only eight thirty, she was surprised Fiona hadn't been woken up by Hengist. Perhaps they'd already gone out for a walk or maybe the heavy night and long drive had finally knocked them both out. Right now, being knocked out for a couple of weeks would be a huge relief, rather than having to face up to what had happened.

Deciding that she needed a coffee, Lucy pulled a fleece over her camisole top and knickers and ventured out. The wooden boards felt strangely comforting under her bare feet as she padded out on to the landing. The stairs creaked as she made her way downstairs, through the tiny hallway and into the kitchen. There was still no sound from Fiona's room and she now knew why. Propped up against the coffee jar was a note:

Luce,
Hope your hangover isn't too bad. Mine's a bitch but worth it. Gone with The Hound to semi-civilisation a.k.a Porthstow, to try and track down some Lucozade Sport and a wireless card for the laptop and/or email my agent from the local library if it hasn't been closed for sheep dipping or whatever. I'll be back by lunchtime with more supplies and possibly Pinot Grigio. I may be some time . . .
Hugs
Fi x

PS I'm expecting the proofs of *Wax Murderer* from my publisher. Post usually arrives around ten-ish so can you sign for them?

Lucy glanced out of the window at the grey sky and dripping bushes. She could barely see the end of the garden, the rain was hammering down so fiercely. Fiona was going to get soaked. Then again, there was an upside. It would have to be a very determined reporter – and a very wet one – who would track her down to Creekside Cottage.

The coffee was black and bitter but she found a left-over doughnut they'd bought at a garage en route to the cottage. Back upstairs, armed with a yellowing copy of the *Porthstow Mercury*, Lucy had just sunk her teeth into the doughnut when she heard the noise. Even above the deluge, the banging was loud and clear. She froze, a large bite of sugar and jam melting in her mouth. There was no way she was answering. They'd soon get bored and go away.

The hammering started again.

The boxroom overlooked the back of the house so Lucy couldn't check who it was. Then she remembered Fiona's note. Well, it was a bit early, but you might expect a few surprises down here. Doughnut abandoned, Lucy walked back down the creaky stairs. Through the bottle glass in the door, she could see the postman's dark jacket. His hood was pulled right over his head and she didn't blame him, poor man. He must be drenched.

Pulling open the door, she gave him an encouraging

smile, then her face fell. She could clearly see the camera poking out from under his coat.

'Bugger off,' she said, starting to close the door.

'I'm sorry?' said the man.

'I said bugger off.'

'Right. I suppose that's fairly clear, if verging on the blunt side.'

Lucy was unrepentant. 'Yes, well, I don't like to be rude but you lot have driven me to it. How's this, then? Bugger off, *please*.'

Rain dripped off his hood and thunder rumbled overhead. He looked absolutely freezing and despite the hood, his face was spattered with moisture and mud. Lucy suppressed a giggle.

'What's so funny?'

She snorted in derision. 'You are. Your outfit. Did you honestly think I'd be fooled by that get-up? You haven't even made an effort, have you?' She was really warming up now and she had nothing to lose, not even her knickers. Let him plaster her all over his paper if he wanted to. 'And by the way,' she said. 'Your Cornish accent's rubbish.'

'Maybe that's because I was born in Peckham, but I suppose you're entitled to your opinion.'

'No? You don't say? Gee, I'd never have guessed. Shame your lens is showing.'

The man glanced down at the camera. 'Ah. This. Doing a spot of bird watching.'

Lucy snorted. 'Can't you think of anything more original than that?'

'No, because it's true.'

'Yes. Of course it is. I suppose you collect stamps and hang round restored railways noting down engine numbers. I bet you even volunteer at the local youth club.'

'Well, now you come to mention it . . .'

'Somehow, I think not.'

He pulled his hood off and Lucy did a double take. He didn't look like any of the photographers or reporters who'd hung about outside her flat. It wasn't an unpleasant face – in fact, he was startlingly good looking; all razor cheekbones and cool blue eyes. But the *Prison Break* buzz cut gave him such a hard, uncompromising edge that she felt her bravado rapidly ebbing away. What if he wasn't a paparazzo? What if he'd escaped from somewhere? Wasn't there a jail on Exmoor – or was that Dartmoor?

Tiny beads of rainwater glistened in his thick eyelashes. He attempted a smile which managed to make him seem more threatening than ever. 'So, are you going to be sensible and let me in, or are you going to make me stand out here in the rain all day?'

She curled a lip in what she hoped was defiance. 'I think, on balance, I'm going to be stupid and let you get wet.'

Then she slammed the door on him and locked it.

After his encounter with the mad girl who'd moved into Creekside Cottage, Josh headed to the club to help Sara out with a novice windsurfing course. Even before he got there to find no one had turned up, he'd known it would be a wash-out. Only a nutcase, or him, would want to go out on a day like this. Now he and Sara were watching the rain and wind whipping up white caps on the estuary and Josh had made the mistake of mentioning what had happened.

'She did *what*?' said Sara.

'Slammed the door in my face,' said Josh, scrolling through the weather reports on Windguru.com.

'And this is Fiona?'

'No, this is the friend.'

'Doesn't sound very friendly. What does she look like?'

'Hell, I don't know. Average. Tall-ish,' he said, closing the browser on the computer.

'As tall as me?' she asked.

He thought for a moment. 'A bit taller, I guess.'

'Slim? Fat?'

Josh knew he had to close down this discussion quickly. He guessed what Sara was fishing for. She was a hundred per cent beach babe, fit and tanned. He'd often told her so, and yet it still didn't seem to satisfy her. Lately, she'd wanted constant reassurance that she was attractive. She needn't have worried. From what he'd seen of her, the mad girl was fair-skinned and curvy in a way Sara would have derided.

'How old is she?'

'Same as us, I guess. Difficult to tell.'

Sara nodded. 'From London?'

'I suppose so, she had one of those non-accents.'

'So average, no accent, medium height, but mad as a hatter.'

'She had unusual hair,' he said, suddenly recalling the girl's black hair curling over her shoulders. He had to kill a smile as he remembered her expression: she'd acted as if he was an axe murderer or a Peeping Tom – or maybe the law.

Sara's eyes lit up. 'How do you mean, "unusual"? Spiky? Punk? Goth? Pink?'

'Dark, I suppose,' said Josh, jumping down from the desk and lacing his arms in front of him in an effort to ease his aching shoulder. Maybe it was a good job the course had been rained off, for the sake of his back. Someone had to save him from himself.

Sara pressed on. 'Dark as in black or as in brown? I need detail.'

He scratched his chin thoughtfully. 'OK. Let me see. Her hair was black like the paint job on the Wilsons' Sunseeker, maybe with some kind of purply thing happening like the sails on the Mirage dinghy Dave Hollins just bought off Esme Trerice. And her skin was a sort of creamy-white – you know, I think it was exactly the colour of the leather upholstery in that French couple's Beneteau thirty-six-footer and . . .'

Sara's mouth gaped open.

'Well, you did ask me.'

'Not to take the piss!'

He lifted her chin and planted a quiet kiss on her mouth. 'Would I? Sara, I really have no idea what she looked like and, frankly, I don't give a toss. Now, I have to get back. I need to fix the dishwasher in Porthcurno Cottage before the guests arrive, and maybe Fiona will be at Creekside to let me fix her heating.'

She nodded as he picked up his keys from the in-tray. 'So, shall I see you later? There's a gig at the Smugglers tonight . . .'

He smiled and hesitated just long enough to sow a seed of doubt in her mind. 'Why not? Pick you up around seven?'

'Cool.'

He was halfway out of the door when he turned back. 'Sara?'

'Yes?'

'That mad girl at Fiona Thingy's place?'

Her eyes lit up and for a moment he had second thoughts about teasing her. 'Yes?' she said eagerly.

'She had jam round her mouth.'

Leaving a kiss on her indignant face, Josh strode out of the office, across the slipway to his pick-up. He wasted no time in driving back to Tresco Farm. The high season was nearly here and as usual, he had a list of jobs as long as his arm to get on with. Ten minutes later, he was pulling up in the courtyard. A joyful bark from inside told him that Tally, at least, was pleased to see him.

'Don't have to ask how you are, do I, girl?'

In response, Tally leapt to her feet and padded over, tail thumping against the Aga in excitement. Crouching down, Josh ruffled her ears and tickled her belly as she rolled on to her back in pleasure.

'Sorry, girl, I don't have time for a walk,' he said as the dog jumped up and raced for the back door. 'Later.'

Outside, the rain was easing. Josh could see the row of cottages opposite and, beyond that, he could almost make out the sea now, grey against a grey sky. The cottages never ceased to inspire him with wonder. That they belonged to him at all, he still found hard to believe.

From his background, with all that he'd got up to in

his youth, even in his wildest dreams, he could never have imagined running a business and owning property. If it hadn't been for Marnie Trewellan, his foster mother, Josh had no idea where he'd be now. Probably the same place his brother Luke was – on the streets. But Luke had had the same chances and Josh had tried hard enough to find him and give him a share of what was rightfully his. What could Josh do if he'd chosen a different path? And now wasn't the time to be wringing his hands over Luke. He had work to do.

'See you later,' said Josh, gathering up his tool kit from the kitchen worktop. Tally laid her head on her paws in misery.

'It won't work,' he said, seeing her soulful eyes.

Tally flattened herself on to the quarry tiles and Josh shook his head.

'Why do you do this to me every time? Come on, then – but don't leave hairs on the bed.'

At that, the dog leapt to her feet, paws slithering on the quarry tiles, and stood panting by the stable door that led out on to the yard. Outside, a peep of blue sky was now peering down between ragged clouds. Josh set off through the yard. Once pigs and hens had been kept here, but now it was gravelled and provided extra parking for the guests of the cottages. Tally sniffed around the walls. Josh turned to look at the house, all dour grey stone, with roses and some purple plant running wild around the doors and windows.

He knew he ought to cut the climbers back or they'd block out the light, maybe destroy the mortar, but he was way too busy trying to keep the rental cottages in good repair. Tresco Farmhouse had managed for three hundred years; it could wait a while longer.

A hundred metres away from the farm stood the four former farm workers' cottages which included Fiona's place, Creekside. He knew Fiona had persuaded Marnie to sell her the property years ago while Josh had been away at college, struggling to get a degree in business. The other three cottages belonged to him.

They rented out well enough, considering Tresco Creek was off the beaten track. Seaspray was empty right now but Porthcurno had guests arriving later. With Mrs Sennen still laid up with a sprained wrist, it fell to Josh to clean and prepare the cottage for the next guests. He also needed to repair the dishwasher, although he'd rather be carve gybing in a Force Five, flying over the water of the estuary. He smiled. Getting it wrong, more like, and catapulting into the creek, salt water shooting into his mouth, eyes, nose . . .

'Work, Tally!' called Josh, and the dog came to heel and trotted after him towards the cottages.

Chapter Thirteen

Lucy turned on the shower in the bathroom and hoped that the trickle of hot water dribbling out of the faintly mildewed head might someday be powerful enough to wash in. She fiddled with the controls and then the water suddenly whooshed down, icy cold. After a shriek and some hasty adjustments, it heated up. At least in here she was safe from reporters.

She'd decided that the scary guy with the camera had to have been from the press and wondered if he was from some local paper, hoping to make his name out of snapping her in her knickers. She had no idea how he'd found out she was here unless he'd been tipped off by the people who maintained the cottages. If so, why would Fiona have told them who she was? Above the hiss of the shower, Lucy heard the cottage door open and the familiar sound of Hengist's bark. There was a clattering of claws on stairs.

'Fiona?' she called.

'Hi!' Fiona called back. 'Shower working OK?'

'Fine,' lied Lucy, hastily turning off the shower as the hot water ran out unexpectedly.

'I'll make some coffee. I managed to get some almond

croissants. There's a posh new patisserie opened in Porthstow,' called Fiona.

'OK. Thanks. I'll be down in a minute,' said Lucy.

Wrapping herself in a towel, Lucy brushed her teeth and checked her face in the cracked mirror above the sink. She still looked pale but definitely not 'haggard'. Maybe a few weeks of fresh air and sun would help with the outside but her inner paleness would take longer to go. She wondered how Nick was coping. Gathering up her pyjamas and wash bag, Lucy lifted the latch.

'Oh my God!'

A black Labrador was slurping her bare leg but that was the least of her worries. The fake postman was standing on the landing, holding a wrench.

'How the hell did you get in here?' cried Lucy.

'Fiona let me in,' said the man, with chilling calm.

'Fiona?'

He spoke slowly, as if she was an especially dim *Big Brother* housemate. 'Yes. The woman who owns this cottage.'

Involuntarily, Lucy raised her hand which was armed with a particularly noxious bottle of lavender bath soak.

'Fiona asked me to come over to fix the central heating pump,' said the man, eyeing the bath soak with a mix of amusement and alarm.

Then Lucy noticed the canvas tool bag further along the landing, spilling an array of deadly weapons such as pliers and screwdrivers on to the floorboards. The door to the airing cupboard was also open, which was quite a large clue to the fact that he was telling the truth.

'If you came to fix the heating, why didn't you say so

earlier when I answered the door?' Lucy asked, reluctantly lowering the bath soak.

'You hardly gave me the chance.'

'I thought you were a postman . . .'

'A postman? Why would you think I was a postman?'

'Fiona was expecting a package . . . oh, it doesn't matter. And after I realised you weren't a postman, I thought you might be a reporter.'

He scratched his chin. 'Right. OK. That makes everything crystal clear. Of course. Why would I be a reporter?'

How could she explain? She'd come down here precisely to disappear, it was no use blurting out the whole charade to the first stranger she met. 'You had a camera and—'

'She's exhausted after the journey,' cried Fiona thudding up the stairs after Hengist. 'Hengist! Will you please leave poor Tally alone?'

Hengist had squeezed past the man and was giving the Labrador's tail a thorough sniff.

'Tally, lie down!'

Trotting to his side, Tally dropped to the floorboards and laid her nose on her paws. Hengist gave a mournful howl but kept his distance. Some use he was, thought Lucy in disgust. Then again, she hardly blamed him, confronted by six feet of thug.

'Lucy,' said Fiona, 'this is Josh Standring. He's come to mend the central heating.'

Lucy clutched her towel tighter. Josh seemed unconcerned, as if he was introduced to wet girls in towels every day of the week.

'Pleased to meet you,' he said sarcastically, holding out his free hand.

Lucy kept hold of the bath soak. 'So you're the um . . . plumber.'

'Plumber, electrician, builder, cleaner. Even do a bit of bird watching and youth-club work in my spare time.'

Lucy swallowed and felt her cheeks growing warm, remembering her taunts to him on the doorstep. Now she came to think of it he was, she grudgingly admitted, *far* too good looking to be a reporter. Most of the reporters who'd swarmed round her doorstep had been flabby specimens smelling of cigarettes, or in need of a decent body spray. This guy looked like a PT instructor in the marines. But he didn't look like a bird watcher either.

'Actually, Josh owns Tresco Farmhouse,' cut in Fiona. 'Apart from Creekside, the rest of the cottages are part of his holiday rental business. It really is very good of him to drop by and help out.'

'It's no trouble,' said Josh, throwing Fiona a smile that was barely more than a grimace. Lucy could tell he was desperate for them to leave him alone to get on with the job. As she was desperate to leave too, that was absolutely fine.

'Of course,' she said, finding it difficult to make small talk half naked. 'Um . . . sorry about earlier by the way . . .'

'Don't mention it.'

'I'd better get dressed.'

'And I'd better get the central heating fixed. You look cold.'

Lucy hoped the towel was stopping him from seeing just how cold she was. 'I'll get you both a coffee,' said Fiona hastily.

'Thanks, Fi. Um . . . excuse me,' said Lucy, realising that Josh and his wrench stood between her and the safety of the boxroom.

'Of course.' He flattened himself against the wall. As she passed, his mouth twitched and Lucy thought he might be laughing at her but she couldn't be sure. Scuttling into the boxroom, her cheeks burning, she closed and latched the door. As she sank on to the bed, she heard Fiona twittering. 'You'll have to make allowances for Lucy. She's from London and she's not been well.'

Some time later, dressed in jeans and a sweatshirt, she headed downstairs to the kitchen where she found not only Fiona, but also Josh and a petite blond-haired girl drinking out of mugs. As she walked in, their faces turned in her direction and the conversation stopped. Anyone would think that the Bride of Dracula had just entered the room, she thought. She tried the smile she used when trying to get the partners to approve the budget for a marketing campaign.

'Hi, everyone.'

Josh nodded curtly and took a slurp of his coffee. The blonde smirked. So that had gone well . . .

'Feeling better?' asked Fiona brightly, holding out a mug.

'Yes, thanks. Much.'

'Good. Lucy, meet Sara Pentire, from the sailing club,' said Fiona. 'She's Josh's girlfriend.'

'Hi,' said Lucy, holding out her hand, determined to make up for not shaking Josh's earlier, even if she had had a good excuse, clutching her towel and bath soak.

Sara smiled but didn't take her hand. 'No need for formality here, Lucy. Tresco Creek is a laid-back kind of place. You can chill out here.'

'Once you've realised the locals aren't going to hit you over the head with a wrench,' said Josh.

'Doh,' said Lucy, striking herself on the forehead as if she was highly amused, yet really quite pissed off.

'It's OK, really, Lucy,' said Sara, patting Lucy's arm. 'We understand. I'm sure Josh isn't offended, are you darling?'

Sara's expression was very like the look the nurses had on *Casualty* when they were telling someone they'd got something embarrassing and/or incurable. Josh didn't reply but Lucy noticed him glancing at his watch. Lucy, too, was longing for them to go so she could find out what Fiona had told them about her. Sara didn't sound Cornish either. Definitely more Cheltenham Ladies College than Penzance Comprehensive.

'More ginseng tea, Sara?' said Fiona.

'No. One's enough for me,' said Sara, tossing back her blond ponytail. 'Good stuff, though. Did you order it over the web?'

'No, it's from ... some little shop near my flat in London.'

'Organic?'

'Yes ... you could say that,' said Fiona. Lucy almost choked on her coffee. Fiona broke out in a rash at the mere thought of healthy eating. Josh downed the last of his drink. 'Fiona, I'll have to shoot off. I need to do some work on Porthcurno before the visitors arrive.'

'And I've got an RYA catamaran course to teach,' trilled Sara.

'Oh, that sounds high-powered,' said Lucy, impressed. Hearing the wind gusting outside she also thought it sounded too uncomfortable and dangerous by half.

'Oh, it's nothing, really. It's just a novice's course, but you do have to lay these courses on for beginners, no matter how boring. And I'm sure capsize drill is nothing compared to the sort of pressure you've been used to dealing with.'

'I've explained to Josh and Sara that you're here for a little rest from your job in the City,' said Fiona.

'My job in the City?' echoed Lucy.

'In merchant banking,' said Josh, making it sound like a disease. He clicked his fingers to summon Tally.

'Oh, Josh, don't bother Lucy with that now. She's come to Tresco Creek to escape from all that,' said Sara, beaming. 'And you know, getting out on the water is one of the best stress relievers there is. Do you sail?'

'Er . . . not often.'

'You should. I'd be happy to put you through your paces. You only have to ask.'

'Thanks,' said Lucy, smiling through gritted teeth.

'It's a pleasure. Anything I can do to help. You too, Fiona. I'm sure Josh would love to get you out on a board. We'll have you planing in no time, won't we, Josh, darling?'

Before he could reply, Fiona gave a broad smile. 'Very

kind of you, Sara, and I'd absolutely love to – if only I could swim.'

Sara stared at Fiona in horror. Josh drained his coffee, by which Lucy guessed he was trying not to sneer. 'You can't swim?' squeaked Sara.

'Not a stroke. Hengist, leave Tally's tail alone, please. She has to be off now.'

Josh tugged his keys from his pocket by way of a hint.

Fiona led the way through the back garden and round to the gate at the front of the cottage. 'Thanks for doing the heating. Put it on my bill,' she said as Josh unlocked the pick-up truck and Tally jumped into the cab.

'No problem,' he said, hand already on the ignition key. Lucy thought he was going to rev up the engine and roar off, he seemed so eager to get away.

Sara climbed deftly into the passenger seat. 'Lucy – hope to see you at the club soon. I presume you can swim?'

'Like a fish,' said Fiona, closing the door before lowering her voice. 'I'll make sure she digs out her cossie.'

Lucy was sure she could hear them laughing as they bumped off down the road. When they were gone, she held her hands up to her head. 'Swim like a fish? Job in the City? Stressed out?'

'It was the best I could do when Sara started asking me who you were. Would you rather I told them the truth? That you're a notorious celebrity bitch whose bare arse was spread all over the *Sun* last week?'

'It was not bare. I had my thong on!'

'Even better. If they do read the *Sun*, they won't

recognise your face. But then again, I don't think Josh or Sara have time for the tabloids or GMTV . . .'

Lucy thought back to Sara's tiny waist, brown legs and toned arms. She looked like she'd stepped straight out of an O'Neill ad. Even Josh had a golden tan and biceps to die for. You didn't get that by an addiction to *Desperate Housewives* and frosted carrot cake.

'Somehow, I don't think they have couch potatoes in Tresco Creek,' she said. 'But, Fiona, do I look like I've a job in the City? Look at my nails, look at my hair. How many merchant bankers buy their jeans from Primark?'

'Ones who've flipped at work and been sent on gardening leave.'

'Oh, Fiona.'

'It's for the best, Lucy. If they think you're slightly bonkers and you've come here to get away from the rat race, you can behave as oddly as you like. It makes sense, you know. They say the only difference between a lunatic and an eccentric is a million or two in the bank.'

'The trouble is, Fiona, that even if I actually enjoyed pretending to be a stressed-out City exec, I'm totally crap at lying. You know I won't be able to keep it up if people start asking questions and then I'll just look even more bonkers . . .'

Fiona was unrepentant. 'Shall I go and put an ad in the *Porthstow Mercury*, then, announcing the arrival of Lucy Gibson in Tresco Creek?'

'You know that's ridiculous but I hate all this deception. It's just not me.'

Fiona pushed open the gate to the cottage. 'Be realistic. They'll leave you alone now. I told them you can't face talking about your past life. It's part of your therapy: Tresco Creek; the simple life, the fresh air, the sea.'

Lucy groaned. 'I don't think a year at RADA would help me carry this off!'

Fiona patted her arm. 'Stop worrying. Aunty Fi will help you. Now, come in and have an almond croissant, Miss Hyde.'

Lucy stopped by the door, hardly able to believe her own ears. '*Miss Hyde*? Oh please. You haven't, have you? Please say you haven't told them that?'

Fiona came the closest to blushing Lucy had ever seen. 'I know, I know. Bit pathetic, but hey, it was the best I could think of on the spur of the moment and I'd just been reading an old Robert Louis Stevenson in the loo and . . .'

That topped it all, thought Lucy, stalking off into the house in disgust and shame. She was now named after a sinister madman with hairy knuckles and it probably served her right.

Chapter Fourteen

Lucy was halfway through *Hanging by a Thread*, Fiona's fourth book, when she knew she had to get out of the cottage or go mad. There wasn't anything wrong with the novel, it was gripping. But then again, so had been books one, two and three. Continuous poisonings, stabbings and stranglings took their toll eventually.

Lolling on the sofa or in the little garden with a coffee and a book had, for about a day, seemed like exactly the therapy she needed. Yet the problem with hiding was that because no one could see you, in a sense, you ceased to exist. She hadn't been forced to run away, she could have taken her leave of absence in the flat. The press interest would have died down eventually. Everyone became yesterday's news at some point; maybe her backside was wrapped around some chips by now.

Fiona had been locked away in her room until late into the night, having been visited by the muse or rather, by a pretty nasty conversation with her editor. Lucy had taken her bagels and coffee at regular intervals and Fiona had waved a hand in thanks, rolled her eyes apologetically, and started typing again.

Lucy had taken the hint. She had been too scared to go out for the first few days in case she met anyone who recognised her, but she was beginning to think that was ridiculous. After all, Josh and Sara hadn't shrieked and pointed their fingers when they'd met her. Well, Josh almost had but not because he recognised her from the TV. In fact, why should anyone recognise her down here? She'd changed her hair. *Hot Shots* had only had ten million viewers – how many of them had come to Tresco Creek on holiday? Very few, she guessed, and on that basis Lucy felt she wasn't likely to bump into any of them in the immediate surroundings of the cottage.

'This is no good, Hengist,' she said to the snoring dinosaur spread over the patio. She could see his lead hanging off the peg on the back door. Through the open window of Fiona's room, she could hear the clatter of a printer as she ran off her latest chapter. Scribbling a note on the back of a council tax demand, she unhooked his lead and prepared to be flattened by ten stone of canine exuberance.

Five minutes later, she was heading along the green lane which (according to the wooden signpost) led down to Tresco Creek. The sun was shining between white clouds scurrying across the sky. Blown by the breeze, they seemed to be bounding along almost as joyously as Hengist.

Several metres ahead of her, he nuzzled the banked-up hedgerows, panting, snorting and snuffling, revelling in the doggy equivalent of an all-you-can-eat buffet. Lucy didn't have to have a snout and a tail to enjoy the scents. She recognised some of them from her childhood; the times when, before they'd split up, her parents had taken her to visit her gran in Shropshire. She had been so young then, she reflected, as she spotted wild garlic, honeysuckle and hawthorn in the hedges.

At the end of the green lane, the high banks opened out into a meadow that sloped down to the creek. Lucy knew that Tresco Farm was about a mile inland from the sea and the creek was tidal, but it was hard to tell, right now, which way the tide was moving, as sandbanks were visible among the pools of water. She could see the eddies and swirls as the sea flowed in – or out – of the narrow inlet. There was bright green seaweed shining on some of the banks, the odd rowing boat wedged on the higher sand bars. The sun came out and, for the first time, she felt the warmth on her arms as the breeze stirred her hair.

'Hengist!' she called, seeing a flash of creamy fur bobbing about on the shore at the edge of the creek. She hoped he could swim and climbed over the stile and into the meadow. After the recent rain, the earth was soggy beneath her feet and her trainers sank in almost to the laces. She knew she should have brought her wellies, but then again, footwear hadn't been a high priority when she'd left London.

Down by the water, Hengist had met up with Tally and she seemed just as interested in him as he was in her. They were doing a lot of highly irregular sniffing; the canine equivalent of foreplay, Lucy guessed. At least Hengist had found love. Lucy also knew that Tally's owner couldn't be far, and when she glanced along the bank out towards the sea, she saw him, striding towards her.

'Tally!' he called. 'Come here, girl!'

Lucy knew it was no use ordering Hengist to do anything. She might have been holding a whole bag of bones and dog chews and he still wouldn't have paid her any attention. He had tastier dishes in mind and Lucy suddenly felt rather sorry for Tally.

'Hey, Tally,' Josh called more sharply this time, as the two dogs bounded into the shallows.

To Lucy's surprise, Tally didn't race back to Josh and lie by his side. In fact, she ignored him and Lucy felt an inexplicable twinge of satisfaction. It was a relief to know that he didn't have everything under control. Too bad, she was going to have to speak to him, at least to exchange pleasantries, although, by his eagerness to escape from the cottage on their previous encounter, she suspected they'd both rather say nothing at all.

'Hello.'

'Hi,' she said as he drew near.

She thought they'd both pass by but the dogs had other ideas. They continued to romp together and Lucy fixed her eyes on the seagulls perched on a rowing boat. Neither of them seemed ready for conversation.

'Tide's on the turn,' said Josh eventually.

'Is it? You can't really tell, can you? I mean, you can probably tell because you see it every day – sometimes twice, of course, but . . . sorry, I must sound like a real klutz.'

Now, in London, thought Lucy, most people, even guys, would have said, *'Not at all. How could you know? Isn't it a glorious day? Have you tried the pasties in the village shop? You must come and share a flagon of scrumpy with Sara and me*', etc. Just for politeness. Even if they did think you were a klutz. But Josh just nodded as if to confirm that yes, indeed, she was the queen of klutziness. Which was a lot easier to deal with than actually being invited to tea and having to pretend she was a stressed-out bond trader.

'Well, I'd better be going,' he added as Tally, tired of flirting, lay down at his feet.

'Fridges to fix?' offered Lucy, flinching as Hengist corkscrewed muddy water from his fur.

'No. My VAT.'

'Fixing your VAT? That's against the law, you know, even in Tresco Creek,' she joked.

He gave her what her mum had always called a 'funny look' which meant the person giving it was the opposite of amused. 'Then I'd better not get caught,' he said, holding her gaze. His eyes, she noted, did not have the look of a criminal. He had no need of mascara, either, she decided, reminded of Nick's tears at the studio.

'Not getting caught is the trick,' she said, looking away first then cursing herself for doing so. 'Hengist, time to go.'

Hengist ignored her and started excavating a rabbit hole. 'Hen-gist!' she called, trying to imitate Fiona in her best mistress mode. 'You villain!'

Hengist lifted his leg, peed on a clump of dandelions, and resumed his excavations.

'Hengisttttt . . .' she hissed, rattling his lead more in hope than expectation.

Josh snapped his fingers. 'Come here, boy,' he said quietly.

Don't do it, begged Lucy silently, but Hengist immediately pulled his nose out of the bank, ran over to Josh, and lay down next to Tally. His eyes had an expression of complete innocence. 'Traitor,' mouthed Lucy behind Josh's back.

Josh was smiling now. 'Thank you,' she said through clenched teeth, bending to snap the lead on to Hengist's collar before he loped off again. 'I'm not a doggy person but then again, he doesn't do what his mistress tells him, either.'

'What bloke does?' said Josh, rubbing Hengist's ears. Hengist was making that satisfied throaty growl he always made when Fiona fed him his absolute favourite treat: fresh tripe.

'I'll be off, then. Sara will be waiting for me,' said Josh.

'And you always do what your mistress tells you?'

She bit her lip but it was too late.

His eyes were sparkling with amusement. 'I've no problem with doing exactly what a woman wants. I've no hang-ups about a woman being in charge, if that's what you're implying. If you want to be boss, that's fine by me and I'm sure you're a very good one.'

She was squirming. 'I didn't mean that. I was just being—'

'Funny?'

'Flippant.'

'I presume you know your way back?'

'You presume right. Up the meadow, along the lane. In fact, the same way I came,' she declared.

'See you later, then,' he said, turning on his heel and

heading off in the direction of Tresco Farm. Lucy watched him as he made his way down the path, his head occasionally bobbing up above the greenery before finally vanishing from sight.

Chapter Fifteen

A few days later, Lucy finally plucked up the courage to make The Phone Call. She'd put it off far too long and she couldn't wait any longer. She'd spent so long sitting on the stone bench staring out to sea that she'd almost become part of the landscape. In a moment, she thought, a seagull might land on her.

The bench, nearly buried beneath the tough gorse bushes that ran riot over the cliff edge, was a haven she'd recently discovered. While it was half hidden from sight, it gave her a magnificent view over the beach. Below her, she could see the sand, washed clean by the outgoing tide. Accessible only by a precarious path from the cliff edge, and a mile from the nearest car park, the beach was never very busy, according to Fiona. On a cool, cloudy day in early June it was virtually deserted.

A handful of walkers, poring over maps or munching sandwiches, had already ambled past Lucy, trying to find the path down to the shore, and hadn't seemed to have noticed her. Now, all she had for company were the gulls wheeling overhead, crying harshly on the wind. And she was still holding the phone, torn in two by indecision.

She wouldn't have been contemplating a further

attempt to contact Nick at all but for the previous day. Feeling the ridiculousness of being holed up at Tresco Farm, she'd finally plucked up the courage to pop into Tresco Creek's one and only commercial establishment: a garage-cum-Spar-cum-post office on the main road that led, after much winding and bending, to Porthstow. Wearing a baseball cap and dark glasses which she'd borrowed from Fiona, and which Fiona claimed made her more conspicuous, she'd hopped into the garage and bought several tabloids and a gossip mag.

Neither the spotty teenage boy behind the till, nor the pensioner buying a white sliced loaf, had so much as tutted mildly let alone thrown eggs at her or asked for her autograph. She was a nobody to them; invisible as she always had been before she'd met Nick.

Back at the cottage, she'd sat down with a swishing stomach to scan the pages but there was no mention of her or of Nick. Her absence from the pages should have filled her with relief and yet . . . the very lack of news was confirmation that what she and Nick had experienced was no more, as far as the world was concerned anyway. The newspapers had wiped her off their pages; their relationship was now over.

So why, she thought, as she punched the speed-dial button on her phone, was she calling Nick again? There was no time to agonise, because the phone was answered almost on the first ring.

'Good afternoon, zees ees Laurentis Event Management. Can I 'elp you?'

Gripped with panic, Lucy couldn't even respond to that simple question. 'Hello, what can I do to help?'

'Is Nick there?' Lucy blurted out.

'Ees Nick 'ere? Who eees Nick?'

'Nick. Nick Laurentis.'

''Old on a moment, I'll see if Mr Laurentis free. Who's calling, please?'

Lucy paused. Who was she to Nick now? A friend? She couldn't call herself that. His ex? She wasn't sure about that. The person who had hurt him so badly he'd so far refused to speak another word to her? 'It's . . .' she murmured, her words caught by a gust blowing across the cliff.

'Excusing me. Could you repeat that?' said the receptionist.

'It's fine. I'll try again later,' said Lucy.

She laid the phone on the bench beside her. Only two weeks had passed and he'd already set up his company and got a receptionist. He was 'Mr Laurentis' now and she was . . . nothing. He'd asked her to be everything and she'd chosen the opposite. Now, to confirm that status, she'd disappeared into thin air. Wasn't that what she wanted – for everything to go back to the way it had been before she and Nick had ever set eyes on each other? It sounded as if he'd moved on from her rather rapidly, which was good, wasn't it? she asked herself as the gulls cried above her head and the wind stung her eyes.

It took a while before she trudged back to Creekside Cottage, hoping Fiona was too embedded in the murky criminal world to notice her tear-stained face.

Fortunately, Fiona had gone out in the Land Rover, leaving a short note on the table to the effect that she was doing some research. Lucy lay in her room staring at the ceiling for what seemed like ages before the door creaked open and a cold, wet nose nudged her leg. Hengist's deep brown eyes were gazing up at her, full of hope. They weren't quite as appealing as Nick's but Lucy knew it was a whole lot easier to give him what he wanted. Minutes later, he was bounding down the green lane towards the sea, Lucy trudging behind.

It had rained that morning and the scent of May, saturated with moisture, was so strong it was almost sickly. Fortunately, Hengist made fewer stops for sniffing and Lucy soon emerged into the meadow. As her feet sank ankle deep into the grass, she was glad of the wellies she'd borrowed from Fiona. Hengist shot off towards the water. Finding a flat rock on the shore, she sat down and gazed out over the estuary. In the distance, the channel opened out to the sea and if she shaded her eyes, she could make out yachts and a tanker heading out towards the Atlantic. She needed a new pair of sunglasses; hers were lurking somewhere in her abandoned flat. Maybe she should venture into Porthstow now the heat had died down.

Hengist paddled happily in the shallows as the gulls cried overhead. Lucy's phoned beeped, startling her. Delving in the pocket of her hoodie, she drew out the phone to find a text from Charlie, asking her if she was OK. She texted back a smiley and a 'yes' and asked him to keep an eye on the flat until she got back.

Going back. That prospect had started lurking like an unwelcome visitor at the back of her mind. Sitting here, at the edge of the ocean, London seemed more than three hundred miles away, it seemed like another planet, and what's more, one that was inhabited by aliens. Hengist didn't seem to be missing the postbox at the end of the road. With a joyous bark, he bounded out of the water and darted into the thick undergrowth that lined the creek. Almost immediately, he emerged from the greenery with Tally at his side. It was inevitable that Josh should follow and Lucy sighed. Her solitude hadn't lasted long.

He managed a gruff 'morning' before jumping down on to the shore and standing next to her, as uncommunicative as the rocks jutting out of the creek. What followed wasn't so much an awkward silence as an excruciating one. She wondered why they both had to be so British, why he couldn't just have stalked off or she couldn't just have beamed Hengist and herself back to the cottage.

'The dogs are enjoying themselves,' she offered at last, as Hengist and Tally romped in the creek.

'They're both going to stink if they stay in that mud too much longer,' said Josh.

Lucy hardly knew how to reply to this so she gave an exaggerated sniff. 'Oh, I see what you mean. The mud is a bit smelly.'

'They'll both be needing a bath, that's for sure.'

Hengist's coat was already thick with grey mud and he had a piece of feathery green weed stuck to his ear. Tally wasn't quite as muddy but her black coat had lost its shiny lustre.

'Fiona won't want Hengist back in the cottage in that state,' she conceded. 'I suppose I'm going to have to give him a bath before he gets home, though goodness knows how. I don't want to bother Fi because she's in the middle of *The Wax Murderer*.'

With most people, thought Lucy, this kind of line would have opened up an interesting conversation. '*So, Fiona's working on a new novel?*' most people would have said.

'*Yes, it's a real winner. She's so-oo talented . . .*'

'*And you're here because of your health . . .*'

And then she would have had to start lying and deceiving but somehow, she knew she was quite safe with this guy. He obviously couldn't give a toss about her or why she was here and that suited her perfectly.

'I'll be off then,' she said.

'If you don't want to go back the way you've come, if you want to walk to Tresco along the creek, I'm going that way,' he said, without taking his eyes from the horizon.

OK. That wasn't what she'd expected. In fact, it was a turn-up. She had been going to say she wanted to spend some time alone but she'd ruined that by telling Hengist it was time to go.

'Thanks, but there's no need.'

'It's up to you, but there's a tap and hosepipe in the yard back at the farm. You can use that to clean up the dog if you like.'

She turned to face him, struck by this open offer not just to help her but also for her to spend more time in his company than was strictly necessary. 'Thanks, but I wouldn't want to put you to any trouble.'

'Why would it be any trouble? I have to go back to the farm; the dogs need a hose down.'

'Yes. Probably a good idea,' she said, suspecting this

was as gracious as an offer from Josh ever got. Though there was more to it than that. She had a strong sense, based on no concrete evidence whatsoever, that a refusal definitely would offend.

'I'll follow you, then. The path's a bit overgrown for two,' he said, stepping aside so that she could climb on to the bank ahead of him. Tally was already on her way, Hengist tugging at the lead in anxiety to be with her. Lucy gripped the lead with both hands, trying to restrain the dog.

'You're trying to hold back the tide there. I should let him go. He won't come to any harm,' remarked Josh as she struggled. Because he was smiling and she didn't think he was laughing at her, she unclipped Hengist's lead and gave him his freedom.

Ten minutes or so later, they were in the farmyard, Lucy holding the dog's collar while Josh scrubbed his thick coat with an old brush. He ran his hands over the dog's back and haunches, pushing his fingers through the matted fur, teasing out the mud from his coat. If Hengist had been a cat, she decided, he'd have arched his back and purred in ecstasy. Instead, he kept giving little growls of pleasure as Josh rubbed him clean. Lucy was glad when it was over; Hengist in love was not a pretty sight.

'Can you wash him down while I brush Tally?' he asked, handing Lucy the hose.

This should have been a simple task but the writhing Hengist had suddenly developed an aversion to water. He twisted away from Lucy, whipping the hose from her arm and spraying Josh.

'Jeez!'

Lucy stared at Josh's soaked combats in horror. A huge wet patch was spreading right across his crotch. 'Oh. God. I'm really sorry!'

She was squirming with embarrassment. Tally cocked her head on one side and gave him a look of puzzlement. Hengist was shivering by the wall, well out of reach. 'I didn't mean it. The hose just slipped out of my hand.'

Josh threw her a very stern look.

'It was an accident, honestly.'

'Hmm,' he said, looking down at his trousers which were clinging to his thighs.

'You wouldn't think a bit of water could make such a mess,' she said, trying to lighten the atmosphere.

His face, terribly serious, made her suddenly want to giggle.

Josh still didn't smile.

'You think it's funny, do you?'

'Well . . .'

'You know, when I was a lad, I used to have water fights all the time.'

'There you are, then,' said Lucy airily. 'Just a bit of fun. Ha-ha.'

He picked up the still-running hose. 'But they were *serious* water fights. We played dirty.'

Her skin prickled. 'Dirty?'

'No holds barred,' he said, taking a step towards her. 'In fact, there wouldn't be an inch of us dry when we'd finished. My favourite tactic was to shove the hose down the neck of anyone I could catch.'

Lucy's skin prickled but she refused to back away.

She stood up straighter and said, through a dry throat, 'You wouldn't dare.'

He raised his eyebrows and, before she could move, he'd flicked his wrist, sending a stream of water spurting over her.

'Ow! You—' shouted Lucy as the icy water soaked through her top and bra.

Josh grinned. 'I let you off lightly,' he said. 'Seeing as you're new here.'

The wet patch was spreading upwards towards her breasts, and she tried to suppress a shiver. As Lucy quickly turned off the tap, she realised her heart was banging away. He curled up the hosepipe and stood up, hands on his hips, watching the dogs playing tag.

'You know,' said Lucy, now that the hose was safely packed away. 'I was going to thank you for helping me to clean him, but I'm not sure I will be nice now.'

'Suit yourself, but he'd have stunk out the cottage if we hadn't washed that stuff off him. Creekside is a very small cottage and Hengist is a very large dog.'

'Yes, he's far too large for London, but I can't see Fiona with one of those little dogs you can fit in a handbag. She totally adores him. Sometimes, I worry that she's too attached to him but then, he's so much easier to fathom than men.'

The instant the words were out of her mouth, she regretted them but he didn't seem to take offence.

'I don't think people are easy to fathom, full stop. Being hard to understand isn't confined to one sex.'

'Really?' asked Lucy, turning to him, surprised he'd even responded to such a topic.

'So I don't even try to work them out these days. All I ask is that someone's straight with me. If they don't like what I do or who I am, they should say it straight out.'

'Oh, absolutely,' she said, suddenly feeling she was being X-rayed by Josh's blue eyes and uncompromising ideals. Any moment now he was going to fix her with a laser gaze and tell her he knew not only exactly what she'd done, but exactly what she was thinking.

'Honesty is the best policy and all that.'

Josh smiled. 'I don't mind what somebody's done, what kind of past they have, as long as they don't try to hide it. The one thing I don't have time for is lying and deception.'

She swallowed hard. 'Awful. Totally awful. Terrible, in fact,' she murmured. 'Wouldn't stand for it at all . . . you know, Tresco Farm is a really beautiful place, the stonework is so um . . . pretty and the roof tiles, they have lots of character . . . is it very old?'

He gave her another un-funny funny look, obviously confused by the sudden twist in the conversation, but then his gaze lingered on the grey stone walls, as if he was sizing the building up for the first time. 'I guess it's about three hundred and fifty years old, as far as we can tell. It was owned by an old Cornish family for generations. They made their money from tin mining.'

Lucy took in the dour farmhouse with its stone lintels and solid walls, imagining it as the focal point of a small community, rather than a holiday home. 'There was probably a medieval manor house here even before this was built but Marnie never got round to digging out the records,' Josh went on. 'The local history people have been round and they've said it goes back to the Doomsday book. 'It's picturesque enough; or so the visitors tell me and I'm supposed to be "guarding it for future generations", according to the heritage people. But at the end of the day, it's just four walls and a roof. It's a home and that's all that matters.'

This was the longest speech he'd ever made to her and Lucy was almost too taken aback to reply. 'Has your family lived here long?' she offered eventually.

He laughed out loud. 'God, no. I only came to live here in my teens. Marnie, my foster mum, inherited the place from some distant relatives before I was even born.'

'So Marnie isn't here now?'

'She died six years ago. She was only fifty-three.'

'I'm sorry. That's way too young.'

'Shit happens,' he said, thrusting his hands into his damp pockets. Lucy didn't know how to reply and when Josh didn't elaborate, she tried a change of subject. 'Do you mind Fiona having Creekside Cottage? After all, it's the only one out of the four that you don't own.'

'It was Marnie's decision and I respected it. These cottages were hers and I was away at college at the time. She left the place to us when she died.'

'So Tresco belongs to you and Sara?'

The sun burst out from behind a cloud, making Lucy squint painfully. 'No. Not to Sara and me. Sara has her own place in Porthstow. I live here alone.'

He'd said 'us' clearly but didn't elaborate on who the other owner, or owners, of Tresco Farm were. Instead, he bent down to pick up the muddy scrubbing brush. When he straightened, he was facing the sun, shading his forehead with his free hand. 'Here's Sara,' he said, tossing the brush into an old metal bucket with a clatter.

On the opposite side of the yard, Sara was emerging from the farmhouse door. She was wearing board shorts, a tiny pink tank top and Animal flip-flops, even though the wind was cool and clouds were gathering. Lucy felt a wimp, wrapped up in jeans, a hoodie and Fiona's leopard-print wellies. As soon as she reached them, Sara linked her arm through Josh's and Lucy saw his hand slide to the small of her back. Lucy wasn't sure who was protecting whom; she only knew she was definitely the gooseberry.

'Getting a bit of country air and exercise, were we?' said Sara, her eyes taking in the wellies and wet clothes.

'I took Hengist for a walk. It's such a lovely day,' Lucy said cheerfully, hoping to fend off any sympathy. It was bad enough being patronised when you really were in need of TLC, let alone when you were only pretending to be.

'That will do you good. You're looking better, by the way. You've almost lost that city pallor, and the dark circles under your eyes are almost gone. I'm guessing you're eating more healthily, too. Not so many cappuccinos and doughnuts in Porthstow, I suspect.'

Her gaze travelled to Lucy's wet top, which she knew was now clinging to her stomach and breasts. Restrain yourself, Lucy told herself. Sara was probably only trying to be *nice* and she had to admit she probably did look tired and unhealthy to a gilded surf babe. But the doughnuts remark was pushing it. A lot.

'The dogs took a dip in the tidal mud by Hannaford beach,' said Josh, pulling his hand away from Sara's waist and signalling to Tally with a snap of his fingers.

'Ah-ha. So you went for a walk together?' said Sara, her eyes lighting up with interest. 'Via the creek probably, looking at how wet you are.'

'I met Josh when I was out,' said Lucy quickly, sensing an atmosphere that had nothing to do with weather conditions. 'And he showed me a new way back to Tresco.'

'Of course! Josh was on his way to the club to meet me. I wondered where he'd got to.'

'I was on my way but I had to walk back to Tresco for the course schedules,' cut in Josh.

'Then it's a good job I came over to fetch you or we might have been late. Are you ready now?'

Josh had a worried expression on his face. 'Well, I really ought to touch up my make-up and slip into something more comfortable first.'

Lucy let out a giggle but Sara's lips were set in a tight line.

'Yes, perhaps you should change out of those wet things. I see someone's been having some fun with the hose!'

'A bit of cold water never did anyone any harm, Sara. Now, I'll just fetch the schedules from the farmhouse and wait for you by the Land Rover.'

As he headed over the yard towards the house, Sara shot Lucy a mega-watt smile. 'Josh is *such* a lovely guy, isn't he? Escorting you back here with the dogs was so sweet of him even though he knew he was keeping me waiting. Still, he never can resist a damsel in distress.'

Lucy smiled back, but not quite so luminously. 'Well, I wouldn't call myself a damsel. I was fine, really. I'm sure Josh was just being—' She was going to say nice, but decided against it. 'Neighbourly.'

'Neighbourly? Oh, you are so funny! Well, we are neighbourly down here, Lucy; we help out everyone, friends and strangers alike. I'm sure you're not used to that where you come from. I should think it takes a real ruthless streak to get where you have in your job.'

'I'm not sure that ruthless quite describes me,' replied Lucy, congratulating herself on keeping on the right side of the truth. Ruthless was a word she'd have thought far more suited to Sara.

'Hmm. I think you're underestimating yourself, but of course, you're here to forget the cut-throat world of banking, aren't you?' She paused before adding, 'Do you think you can find your way back safely to Fiona's cottage from here or would you like Josh or me to take you home?'

Lucy couldn't think of a single reason why she shouldn't respond as if the offer was genuine, even if Sara was being about as genuine as a nine-pound note. 'You know, I think I'll just about be able to manage it, thank you.'

Sara gave a shrill little laugh. 'Of course you will. Just my little joke. We'll see you soon, then. Maybe you and Fiona would like to come along to the sailing-club barbecue the weekend after next, if you feel up to it and you're still here, of course.'

'I'm here for a month, actually,' said Lucy.

'Really? How lovely for you! Anyway, we're having a

regatta during the day and the social afterwards. It will all be very informal, of course. Nothing to compare with the high-powered events you're used to in London, but we do our best to have fun down here in the sticks, simple folk though we are.'

This girl was *really* beginning to grate. 'I don't mind,' she began and was going to add that high-powered events are vastly overrated, but she stopped. She hated been drawn into Sara's spiteful game but the sneering comments were seriously winding her up. So she smiled in what she hoped was a gracious way and said, 'Actually, Sara, high-powered events become rather a bore after a time. I much prefer a relaxed affair myself. You know the sort of thing: a few hundred close business acquaintances and a couple of sophisticated canapés.'

Sara's eyes grew wider. 'Canapés? I must ask the club president to throw a few on the barbie for you.'

Don't worry about me, Lucy was going to say but, seeing Sara's eyes glittering with delight, said, 'Well, I wouldn't want to put you to any trouble, naturally, but if you insist . . .'

'No trouble. We'll get something special in for you. Monkfish, scallops, really healthy stuff like that. And', she added, almost gleefully, 'perhaps you'll feel up to telling me more about London. My father's a director with Metrobank. He's called Roland Pentire – perhaps you've met him? He's quite well known.'

Lucy feigned a puzzled look. 'Hmm. You know, Sara, I really don't think I've heard that name.'

'Maybe that's because he's too senior. I must give him your card, ready for when you go back to London. But of course, you don't want to be reminded of all that horrible corporate stuff now. I'll tell Josh you're coming to the barbecue. I'm sure he'll be delighted to see you rejoining the real world.'

All Lucy could do was simmer inside, smile politely and kick herself for being goaded into embroidering her tale. As for rejoining the real world, after six months with Nick and a couple of weeks in Tresco Creek, she wasn't quite sure what 'real' was any more.

Chapter Sixteen

'You did what?' said Fiona, pulling off her designer glasses and blinking as Lucy hovered in the doorway to the bedroom later that day. It was past six, and Fiona had a large G&T perched on top of her manuscript.

'I got trapped by Sara into going to a barbecue at the sailing club the Saturday after next,' replied Lucy.

'No one gets trapped into going to a barbecue, not even by Sara Pentire.'

'I kind of provoked her into it.'

Fiona laid her glasses on the keyboard. 'Provoked?'

'Well, she was going on about how I must be used to the high life in London and that I'd be too snooty to attend a humble barbecue and so I told her I didn't mind slumming it and now they're ordering in special food to suit my refined palate.'

Fiona covered her face with her hands and groaned.

'Oh Fi, don't go all holier-than-thou on me. It was your idea to make me a stressed out high-flier. All I've done is act in character. It's not my fault that Sara Pentire doesn't like me.'

Fiona frowned. 'What makes you think she doesn't

like you? I don't think the fact that she asked you to a party counts. Sorry, Miss Hyde, but the jury isn't convinced by that explanation.'

Lucy hesitated, unsure how to describe her encounter with Josh. 'She caught me – saw me – with Josh in the yard today and she didn't seem too pleased. And by the way, I am not Miss Hyde.'

Fiona's ears pricked up and Lucy thought that she was starting to look a tiny bit like Hengist. 'What do you mean, "caught"? What were you doing with Josh?' she said.

'I went for a walk by the estuary and Hengist and Tally ended up snogging on Hannaford Beach. They were both covered in that smelly mud so Josh suggested we clean them up in the farmyard.'

Fiona wrinkled her nose. 'My God, Hengist must pong. He's not in the cottage, is he?'

'He did whiff a bit, but he's beautifully laundered now. Josh helped me rub him and Tally down. That's when Sara came along.'

'Oh, is that all? Then I can't see the problem. Hosing down a Great Dane doesn't constitute infidelity, does it?'

'Not in my book, but Sara might see it differently. She seems very attached to him.'

Fiona nodded. 'They've been going out quite a while, and I'm surprised she hasn't moved in with him yet. Then again, maybe he's running scared. Sara's a tad possessive, in my opinion.'

'She's welcome to him,' said Lucy, thinking of the way Josh's hand had slid to Sara's waist the moment she'd reached his side. He'd evidently been very relieved not to be alone with Lucy any longer.

'So you're on speaking terms with Josh now?' asked Fiona.

'We're not hurling central-heating wrenches at each other, but I wouldn't call it speaking. He is a man of few words, if you hadn't noticed.'

'He doesn't need to say much,' said Fiona, her eyes lighting up mischievously.

Lucy hesitated, hearing the whirr of a reel as Fiona prepared to do some fishing. 'I don't know what you mean,' she said.

Fiona poked a finger in the direction of the window and lowered her voice. 'Who needs to talk when they've got assets like that?'

Pushing herself out of her chair, Fiona beckoned Lucy to the bedroom window. The old panes were warped and smeary but still gave a clear view of the front garden of the cottage. Through the glass, Lucy saw Josh crouched down by the gate. 'I saw him on his way back from the sailing club and asked him if he'd mind mending the gate. After all, I can't have Hengist escaping and being shot for sheep rustling, can I?'

When Lucy saw Josh, it was all she could do to stop from letting out a little gasp.

Stripped to the waist, his back was dappled alternately with evening sunlight and shade. His combats had slipped partway down his lean hips and she could see the hard curve where his spine met his buttocks. There was a definite line between the tanned skin and paler flesh.

Fiona gave a long, drawn-out sigh. 'Absolutely criminal, isn't it?'

'What?' murmured Lucy, her eyes still fixed on Josh's body.

'Having a bod like that and showing it off so blatantly. It's like Abercrombie & Fitch meets *Prison Break*. I tried, you know, a few summers ago, but I think Sara had already got him moored in her berth. You never know, he might be open to offers.'

Lucy twisted round. 'When I said I never wanted to look at another man after Nick, I meant it.'

'Well, a girl's got to live. You can't be a nun for ever.'

'Even if I was single . . .'

'Which you are.'

That struck deep. Fi was right. She was single now. She wasn't a fiancée, which had been her decision, and now, she wasn't even a girlfriend.

'Even if I am single, I'm not looking. It's only been a few weeks since Nick. It's still too' . . . She struggled for the word. 'Too soon.'

'Ah, but that's just where you're going wrong. What you need is a no-strings one-night stand with a hot guy. Someone uncomplicated who's only interested in your body, not your mind.'

'I'm not sure Josh is as uncomplicated as he looks and I'm not in the market for a guy right now. I need more time . . .'

Fiona snorted in derision. 'You need a shag.'

Lucy shook her head firmly. 'OK. I admit I like sex, but it's sex with Nick *specifically* I miss, and even if I was looking, I wouldn't go for a guy like Josh.'

'Come on! You have to be joking. The man is hotter than a hundred suns.'

Lucy couldn't help peeping out of the window again. Josh was still kneeling on the flagstones beside the gate. Where the setting sun's rays slid over the curve of his spine, his bare skin glistened with perspiration.

'He's too . . . blond for a start. From what I can see of his hair, that is, it's so short.'

Fiona rolled her eyes. 'Hmm. The Wentworth Miller buzz cut. A pity, in my opinion. Last summer, he had hair to die for, thick toffee-blond and almost down to his shoulders. God knows why he cut it short like that, unless he's making some sort of statement.'

'He's just not my type,' said Lucy, yet unable to banish the image of a bronzed Josh with golden hair.

'He has beautiful eyes,' teased Fiona.

Lucy couldn't help thinking back to their conversation in the farmyard. Josh *did* have stunning eyes and not just because of their colour, which reminded her of the sea off Tresco Cove on a calm day. They were eyes that didn't seem to belong with the hard jaw, the cheekbones, the 'come and have a go if you think you're hard enough' buzz cut. Then she thought of Nick, with his sculptor's hands, his caramel-latte skin, his dark espresso eyes.

'Nick was beautiful.'

'Why didn't you marry him, then?'

Lucy caught her breath.

'If he's so wonderful, why didn't you say yes?' repeated Fiona.

'That's not fair, Fi, and you know it.'

'I think it's fair, hon. You've had a couple of weeks to think about it now. If you want to change your mind, you still could. All you have to do is pick up the phone and ask him to take you back.'

'And this is the woman who reckons the word marriage should be deleted from the dictionary,' she laughed.

'I'm talking about you not me. I've tasted marriage and I didn't like the taste but you're a romantic. You need that fairy-tale ending.'

'You're wrong. I don't want a fairy tale, I want a real-life story. Just straightforward honesty.'

Fiona raised her eyebrows and Lucy remembered Josh's uncompromising views.

'Well, honesty on his part, anyway. And actually, I have phoned Nick,' she said.

'And?'

'His PA answered and I chickened out.'

Fiona gave a knowing look. 'So he's got an entourage already?'

'I expect he's got a complete army of staff and advisers by now. Sir Denby and the TV people would have taken care of all that.'

'So why did you phone if you didn't really want to talk to him?'

'I just wanted to make sure that he's OK. I can't bear to think of him being in the same world as me and hating me.'

'You mean you want him to let you off the hook?'

'He didn't do anything wrong. Not technically. But I did wonder why he asked me then. Right at that moment in front of everyone, almost as if he wanted the maximum impact, almost as if he was playing to the crowd. It's that part of the whole thing that stung me the most: the fact that I might have just been part of one huge drama.' Lucy halted, expecting a smart comment from Fiona but instead, her friend just waited patiently. 'Oh God, Fi, I just wish we could have carried on as we did before! You know, getting to know each other, having a normal life. Or something.'

'Maybe that's too much to ask. Too easy.'

Lucy nodded. 'Yes. Probably.' Because she had to admit, life had never been simple with Nick. There had always been doubt in her mind, even when things had been going well between them: his flashes of temper, his unreliability, his need to control every situation, a nagging feeling that she was being used. The suspicion that he was a player had always been hovering at the edge of her mind. After all, she hadn't known him very long and certainly didn't know him well enough to make a lifelong commitment to him. In fact, she had to admit, a large part of their time together had been spent in bed. They'd both seemed content to just enjoy the drama and the sex as far as she'd been concerned. Even the bust-ups had led to some spectacular making-up sessions, but nothing that had happened between them had ever seemed to be leading to 'for ever'. Even if, in a moment of madness, she had said yes to his proposal, she doubted very much if they would have lasted beyond a year's subscription to *Cosmopolitan*.

Glancing out of the window again, she saw Josh had straightened up and had a bottle to his lips. She imagined rather than saw his Adam's apple bobbing as he drained the water. She strained her eyes, trying to make out the tattoo on his neck. Just as she moved her nose perilously closer towards the pane, he looked directly up at her. She scooted back into the room, breathing hard.

'Oh God, I think he saw me. He must think I'm a total pervert!'

'He already thinks you're a sad nutter, so why worry?' said Fiona, laughing.

'I can't see a way of wriggling out of this barbecue unless I can think of a very good reason,' said Lucy, rapidly changing the subject.

'Well, I can come with you – I presume I'm invited too.'

'Of course.'

'Or maybe you can have an executive relapse.'

Lucy shook her head. 'No way. It would play into Sara Pentire's hands. I'll have to bite the bullet and go.'

'So you're not worried about someone recognising you?'

'Do you think they might?'

Fiona chewed her lip thoughtfully. 'Not really. From what I know of the sailing-club crowd, they're mostly locals who live and breathe sand and salt. I shouldn't think many of them spend their time flopped in front of the TV.'

'Isn't there a yachty set? They might read the gossip mags.'

'Not the low-life papers and you didn't make the quality mags.'

'Well, I can't stay in here for ever. Hengist will be worn down to a chihuahua; he's getting so many walks. I have to face people sometime so maybe this can be a trial run for when I go back to the real world.'

Fiona smiled in a knowing way. 'The real world? Are you sure you want to go back to that?'

Lucy smiled back, but her stomach flipped at the thought of going back to London. 'I'm not sure about anything right now.'

As she carried a book and a glass of wine into the garden later that afternoon Lucy found she couldn't relax.

She was disturbed more than she cared to admit by the warm, tingling sensation that had flooded her limbs as she'd watched Josh in the garden. She tried to tell herself that her response was merely a natural reaction to the sight of a very fit and half-dressed guy. She'd need to be made of granite not to heat up with so much naked provocation.

Chapter Seventeen

The rest of the week passed by uneventfully which Lucy ought to have been grateful for. However, all that time to herself also made her think way too much. After three weeks in Tresco, she was beginning to wonder if she was getting too fond of hiding away.

She hated pretending to be someone else but spending her days walking on the beach and the cliffs was deliciously addictive. *Too* addictive, and that's why one Friday morning, she found herself wedging the Land Rover into a space in one of Porthstow's few car parks. Fiona was at the cottage, having a phone conference with her editor, and Lucy had decided that a trial run at the 'real world' was necessary. Besides, she needed some sunglasses.

Once a humble fishing village, Porthstow had outgrown its grey harbour a few centuries before, its stone houses, shops and pubs now crawling inland from the sea wall. On one side of the harbour, a small beach of buttery sand stretched along the coast to the headland. It was a warm day, almost exactly midsummer, and plenty of people had been tempted to shed their clothes and grab a spot on the beach.

In the harbour, fishing boats rode at anchor on the full tide and the smell of fish and diesel mingled in her nose. Gulls squabbled outside the fish and chip shop on the quay. Lucy spotted a booth by the harbour wall and couldn't resist buying a Flake 99 cone. It was like being eight again, wandering along with her mum and dad before he'd started having affairs with half the girls in the South East – or at least, before she knew about it. The memories back then were still cloudless and sunny just like the sky today and Lucy was going to enjoy her first taste of freedom in four weeks.

Her ice cream finished, she stopped at the first likely shop she came to: a quaint little pharmacy with a bow window bearing faded samples of sun cream, perfume and support stockings. Inside the shadowy interior, she managed to find a large and very dark pair of shades and went up to the counter, the exact cash ready in order to minimise any delay.

The girl at the counter was ringing up a purchase from a red-faced teenage boy.

'Miss Wycliffe? How much are these bumper packs of Ribbed Ticklers?' she called as the boy flushed scarlet. After what seemed an age, a woman of about eighty shuffled out from a small door behind the counter. Almost bent double, she hooked her specs from a chain on to her nose and squinted at the packet.

'Nine pounds forty, if I remember right,' said Miss Wycliffe.

The red-faced teenager looked as if he was going to self-combust as Miss Wycliffe peered at him disapprovingly over her specs.

'You do know, dear, that the Ribbed Super Sensitive are BOGOF? Much better value. Shall I get Calendula to fetch you two of those instead?'

The boy made a strangled sound, threw a tenner on the counter, snatched up the box and fled.

'Oh dear,' said Miss Wycliffe as Calendula giggled. 'I've frightened him away. Now, what can I do for you, dear? Any Ribbed Ticklers?'

Lucy handed over the glasses and the cash. 'No, thanks. Just these, please.'

Miss Wycliffe took the glasses and tutted. 'Young people these days. They don't know how to appreciate a bargain.' She squinted at the bar code on the label. 'On holiday, are you, my lover?'

'Yes,' said Lucy, gritting her teeth.

'On your own?'

No one in London made small talk at the checkout which suddenly seemed like a cast iron reason for going back there. 'With a friend,' she said.

Miss Wycliffe turned to her assistant. 'Calendula, can you come and read this bar code for me? I need a new prescription for my spectacles.'

'Boyfriend?' said Miss Wycliffe as Calendula punched the bar code into the till.

'No, a girlfriend,' said Lucy politely, almost hopping from one foot to the other in her haste to get out of the shop.

'Oh, so you're a lesbian, then? Well, you'll love Porthstow. We've got a hot gay scene here, you know. Calendula, get me one of those little pink gay networking cards from the drawer for this lady. My arthritis is playing me up something terrible.'

Lucy almost choked. 'It's OK, really. Fiona is just my friend, not a partner.'

Calendula handed Lucy a paper bag and a sympathetic look.

'No need to hide it here, dear. Porthstow's a very liberal place. No one has any secrets,' said Miss Wycliffe, patting Lucy's arm.

'I've put the card in the bag,' smirked Calendula.

'Thanks,' muttered Lucy, realising resistance was futile. And besides, she thought as she hurried out of the shop and down the cobbled street to the harbour, she had the last laugh. It was obvious, to her enormous relief, that neither Miss Wycliffe, nor even Calendula, had the faintest clue who she was.

A few days later, Lucy decided to venture further afield. Hengist had been dragged to the vet's by Fiona who'd found him limping with a thorn in his paw and Lucy had a bizarre feeling of nakedness without his lead in her hand. Walking the dog gave you an excuse to wander about all over the place without anyone thinking you were a pervert or a burglar.

Her route took her down the green lane and along the creek as usual but this time she turned in the opposite direction, further along the shore towards the mouth of the estuary. It was further than she'd ever ventured before. The sun was a white ball in a powder-blue sky; almost bikini weather, she thought, as she wandered along the estuary, the sea glittering in the distance. Lucy felt more at peace than she had done for days. Out here, a speck against a huge ocean, she felt insignificant, unnoticed, and that was comforting. As she rounded a spit of land, masts came into view, pointing upwards towards the sky. Then she saw a stone building, a line of flags fluttering in the breeze from its roof.

Tresco Sailing Club was situated on a low bluff, slightly elevated from the beach; a broad expanse of sand and shingle. Catamarans, dinghies and sailboards lay in rows on the shingle. The clubhouse surprised her; it was larger than she'd expected, a two-storey building with a terrace overlooking the beach. In front of it, a couple of girls were dragging windsurf boards down to the water. A gaggle of small sailboats were bobbing about at the edge of the shore, manned by kids who couldn't have been more than ten or eleven. Lucy heard the chugging of a tractor as it towed a trailer down the slipway into the estuary.

She found a spot on the wall in front of the clubhouse and sat down, revelling in the sensation of warm stone beneath her and hot sun on her face. A sudden gust whipped her hair across her eyes and she tucked it behind her ear. She licked her lips and tasted salt.

On the water, a lone windsurfer was bouncing across the white caps, leaning back in what looked like a harness, his arms straining.

'Fucking awesome, eh?'

Interesting way of opening a conversation, thought Lucy. She twisted her head to find a stocky, dark-haired guy in a wetsuit standing next to her.

'Damn nuisance I have to get back to work, but what

can you do? Companies don't run themselves. Are you going out today?'

Lucy laughed politely. 'No. I don't sail.'

The man's expression was even more horrified than Sara's when Fiona had claimed she couldn't swim. '*You don't sail?* Are you out of your mind? With all this on your doorstep?'

'I don't live here. I'm from London.'

'So? That's no excuse. I'm from Wimbledon and it doesn't stop me spending every spare weekend and holiday down here. Just tank down the M4 to my apartment, whip off the kit, pull on the neoprene, and I'm in ecstasy.'

'I get sick on a cross-Channel ferry,' said Lucy, which wasn't strictly true. Or even slightly true. She had crewed once on a small catamaran. She'd been on holiday in Formentera and some local boys had invited her on a trip to an uninhabited island. However, sailing instruction had not been the main aim of the trip and she certainly didn't want to let this guy know the details.

He snorted. 'You won't feel sick, believe me. In the right hands, sailing can be positively orgasmic. I'm Gideon Southall, by the way.'

He held out a hairy hand and Lucy took it limply. 'Lucy um . . . Hyde,' she said, and then winced. Gideon had one of those 'phallic substitute' handshakes. He obviously thought that by crushing her fingers to a pulp, he was telling her he had a big dick. Lucy managed to wriggle her hand free before she got permanent tendon damage.

'It does look exhilarating,' she said, imagining the salt water on her face, skipping over the waves.

'You have absolutely no idea,' he said, deepening his voice in a slightly worrying way. 'You just need experienced instruction.' Gideon shifted so that he was silhouetted against the sun. Lucy had to shade her eyes to make him out and even then his face was a dark blob. 'So what's a gorgeous girl like you doing here, all alone, if you're not going out on the water? Maybe I can try and persuade you into a wetsuit? Or out of it. Haw!' He gave a low growling sound that reminded her of Hengist after a curry.

She jumped to her feet. 'Oh, look! I think I've seen someone I know,' she cried, waving a hand in the vague direction of the shore.

Gideon whipped round and squinted. 'Who? I got the impression you were new round here.' Then his face fell. 'Oh. Him.'

Emerging from the knot of junior sailors by the shore was Josh, and Lucy could honestly say she had never been happier to see him; in fact, she'd never been happy to see him before. However, today her heart did a little skip which she put down to relief at being rescued from Gideon and not to the fact that Josh also had a wetsuit on. Well, he almost had a wetsuit on because it was peeled down, the arms and top half hanging down in front of his waist. Rivulets of water were trickling down his chest and over the hollows of a genuine *Men's Health*-style six-pack.

She had no idea how Josh felt about finding her chatting to Gideon because he was wearing mirror sunglasses. All she could see was her own reflection, distorted into someone resembling a Tellytubby. Which was unfair seeing as how she was only a size twelve.

'You finally decided to join us, then?' he said.

Gideon snorted again. 'No chance, mate! I've been trying to persuade her but there's no moving the lady. She's allergic to water.'

'I'm not so sure. I've seen her when she's wet,' said Josh. Lucy had to stop her mouth from dropping open.

'Gideon, Mack Harris has been asking if you still want to get rid of your Osprey. He's over in the changing rooms right now if you want to talk to him.'

'Right. Yes. Suppose I'd better catch him while I can, then. Strike while the iron's hot and all that. Goodbye, Miss Hyde. Hope we get to see your wilder side at the barbecue, eh? Haw.'

For a moment, Lucy thought he was going to dig her in the ribs and chortle but he just swaggered off, still laughing at his own joke.

'Actually, I did crew a catamaran once. I'm not allergic to water,' she said, eager to show Josh she wasn't a total wimp.

'Only to Gideon?'

Josh pushed back his shades. His eyes were teasing and this time, when Lucy's stomach flipped, she had no excuse beyond pure lust. 'I thought you seemed to be getting on pretty well.'

'No. I mean, he's probably very nice, but . . .'

He raised his eyebrows and his eyes sparkled. In that moment, she realised that since Josh was perfectly capable of teasing her about Gideon, he was also capable of outrageous innuendo. She crossed her arms over her breasts, alarmed that, through her thin T-shirt, he'd notice the effect he was having on her.

'So now you've checked out the club and the locals, I guess you won't be coming to the barbecue?'

He was definitely testing her out and she wasn't about to give him what he wanted. 'On the contrary, I'm really looking forward to meeting everyone. If Gideon is anything to go by, it will be a very entertaining evening. Besides, Sara says you're getting in some special BBQ food just for me so how could I not come along?'

'Then I'm glad you're coming, Lucy.'

That was it? No sarcastic remark? No dour comment? 'I'm looking forward to it,' she murmured. 'Really.'

He covered his eyes with his shades again. 'Good. That's . . . good. I'm sure Sara's looking forward to it too.'

Lucy felt he'd just turned the hose on her again. He turned away slightly so that he was facing the clubhouse. Sara was standing on the terrace watching them. She lifted a hand in a wave and Lucy raised hers back.

'I've got to go. I'm late for a committee meeting,' he said, rolling his eyes.

Lucy smiled and nodded. 'I'm going to Porthstow Library to help Fiona do some research into public hangings.'

'Enjoy.'

Then he was gone, his bare feet crunching on the shingle as he made his way up the beach to the clubhouse. Wasting no time, Lucy turned round and headed back in the direction of Tresco Creek. At the last moment, as she reached the corner of the headland, she couldn't resist a glance behind. On the terrace she could just make out the twin figures of Josh and Sara, although they were so closely entwined, they might as well have been one.

Chapter Eighteen

The evening of the barbecue was gorgeous. Even at eight o'clock, the sun was still bright in the evening sky. Tresco Creek had also heated up considerably in the past few days and Lucy had taken the chance to catch some sun on the beach. Even Fiona had been lured out a few times. At least, reasoned Lucy, if she had to go back to London, she decided she was going to take a tan with her. She felt the sun's warmth even now on her bare shoulders, tempering the cool breeze blowing in from the sea.

'You're very quiet,' said Fiona, as they made their way along the estuary towards the sailing club. 'Aren't you looking forward to your special treats from Sara?'

'Oh, absolutely. Can't wait.'

'Really?'

'Not quite true. There's still a slim chance of being recognised I suppose, especially if I'm feeling "tired and emotional" and let something slip.'

'You'll have to stick to water, then,' said Fiona grimly, picking her way over a discarded bikini top.

'Of course,' said Lucy. 'I'll be as blameless as a saint.'

What she didn't tell Fiona was the way her stomach fluttered; she might have been a teenager again, heading off to a party knowing – hoping – that one particular guy would be there. Even though he probably wouldn't notice her, even though he was with another girl, she couldn't stop the bubble of excitement rising in her throat at the thought of him. Which was why she was going to do her very best to keep out of his way.

The flags on the sailing club came into view. Figures were milling about on the terrace. The breeze carried snatches of laughter, the thud of a bass line and the smell of herbs and charcoal.

'Smells promising,' said Fiona, sniffing the air.

'Definitely scallops and canapés,' replied Lucy firmly as they reached the concrete slipway that led from the car park to the sea. 'Shall we get into our heels?'

Dropping her straw beach bag on the slipway, she delved inside and hooked her shoes: a pair of black wedges with ties that criss-crossed her calves. Back in the cottage, the wedges had seemed the perfect partner to the halter-neck maxi dress she'd picked up on a trip to Naxos almost exactly twelve months before.

Fiona was slipping on a pair of red PVC forties-style open-toed shoes that matched her low cut, clingy dress. She'd piled her auburn hair on her head and fixed it with a fake gardenia. Lucy had left her black hair long and natural but had gone for a dusting of bronzing powder and a rosy lip gloss. As she wound the ties of her wedges around her legs, a group of partygoers spilled out of the sailing club, almost all of them wearing shorts and T-shirts.

'Fi . . .'

'Hmm,' said Fiona, applying an extra coat of cerise lipstick without the benefit of a mirror.

'You don't think we're just a tiny bit . . . overdressed for a beach barbecue, do you?'

Fiona glanced up at the other partygoers spilling out of the entrance to the clubhouse. 'So what if we are? The day you catch me in board shorts and Birkenstocks is the day you can take me out and shoot me.'

'I'll remember that.'

Fiona led the way in and they teetered up the stairs to the top floor. Lucy didn't recognise the music, some Latino dance rhythm. There were tables piled up at one end of the room – to create a makeshift dance floor, she guessed, but right now, no one was dancing. Everyone was, however, talking, shouting, laughing and drinking. Heads didn't exactly turn when they entered the room but there were definite sidelong glances and smiles of amusement. Most people were in casual stuff: flowery shirts, oversize T-shirts, sailing shoes. There were a few girls in sundresses but no one looking quite as flamboyant as Lucy and Fiona. Apart, perhaps, from Gideon, lighting up the room in a startling Hawaiian shirt and matching shorts.

'My God, it's Austin bloody Powers,' hissed Fiona as Gideon made a beeline for them.

'And he hasn't lost any of his mojo,' groaned Lucy. 'I met him the other day when I walked down to the club.'

'Really? You failed to mention you'd been down to the club. Funny, that.'

'Ah ha, but it wasn't that funny in the end. I think Gideon might like me. Brace yourself.'

Gideon bounded up, bearing two plastic half-pint glasses with drink that looked like pink lemonade sloshing over the rims.

'The Lovely Lucy! And an equally lovely friend. This is my lucky night. Two for the price of one and all that. Have a drink!'

'Thanks, Gideon. Um, what is it?' said Lucy, relieving him of the glasses.

He tapped his nose. 'The house special. We call it a "Three Sheets".'

Lucy sniffed. 'Smells like lighter fuel.'

'Or meths,' said Fi. 'I had to try some once for research purposes. It's not as bad as you'd expect.'

'I can assure you this is one hell of a lot feistier than meths, ladies.'

Lucy and Fiona both took a gulp.

Gideon glowed. 'Bottoms up, eh? And may I say what lovely ones they are?'

'Holy Mary . . .' spluttered Fiona.

'What's in it?' coughed Lucy, wiping tears from her eyes.

'That'd be telling,' said Gideon in delight as Lucy and Fiona waited for the fire in their throats to subside. 'It's an old club recipe. Lots of rum, a generous helping of moonshine, and a secret ingredient. Amos Penhaligon brews it in his net loft.'

'Why is it called Three Sheets?' gasped Lucy, her lips tingling.

'Because it gets you Three Sheets to The Wind, of

course. Absolutely rat-arsed, bladdered, pissed as the proverbial—'

'Thank you, Gideon, I get the picture.'

He slapped her back, spilling drink on her dress in the process. 'Don't go away, baby. I'm just going to point Percy at the porcelain,' he growled.

'Is he from this century?' asked Fiona as he headed off towards the gents.

'Not even from this planet,' said Lucy, steering her towards the open doors. 'Quick, out here.'

Out on the terrace, the crowd was slightly thinner. Lucy caught her breath. Across the sea, the sun was slowly dropping towards the horizon, turning pink, a single cloud drifting across its face. Below on the beach, the barbecue was in full swing, with a queue of hungry people snaking back from the makeshift grill suspended over two drums.

'Lucy! Fiona! Woo-hoo!'

Sara was making her way over. Her lithe body was poured into an itsy-bitsy teeny-weeny white shorts and bikini top. She wore no make-up yet still managed to look glowing, groomed and fit yet ever-so-slightly fragile all at once. Lucy was suddenly self-conscious about her height. She usually considered her five feet nine inches an asset: it got you noticed in bars, maxi dresses didn't swamp you, flat boots didn't make you look like a Hobbit, yet against Sara, she just felt clumpy.

'Oh my, don't you two city girls scrub up well?' she said with just the right amount of incredulity. 'Lucy, I adore your dress, how I wish I was that brave and Fiona, shocking crimson really suits you. Goes with your hair and eyes.'

Lucy heard choking sounds from Fiona as she drained half of her punch.

'Are you all right?' asked Sara, her face concerned. 'Or will I need to perform the Heimlich manoeuvre on you?'

'She's fine,' said Lucy, banging Fiona none too gently between her shoulder blades. 'Just a little something stuck in her throat.'

Sara lowered her voice. 'Are you sure? I can fetch Josh if you need him. We keep a full first-aid kit at the club and he's a First Responder.'

Lucy tried not to think of Josh giving mouth-to-mouth.

'Need me for what?'

Turning to face him, she wondered if she should change her mind about accepting medical intervention. Josh was wearing a filmy white shirt, with the sleeves rolled up to midway between his wrists and elbows. The top buttons were undone, he had springy little blond hairs visible in the 'V', and there was a tantalising glimpse of male nipple through the fine lawn of his shirt. At least he wasn't wet.

'Who needs me?' he repeated, his eyes almost turquoise in the bronze evening light. 'And to do what?'

'Fiona was choking,' said Sara.

'I'm f-fine,' blurted Fiona between coughs. 'I blame the Three Sheets.'

Sara gave a tinkling laugh. 'Oh, you girls are so funny!'

'Yes, we're available as a double act for weddings and funerals,' said Lucy.

Sara frowned. 'And how much do you charge? Or do you come as a job lot?'

'I'm sure they're way too expensive for Tresco Sailing Club,' said Josh, his hand slipping behind Sara's waist and drawing her closer to him. He smiled, presumably to show he was joking, but Lucy saw the bob of his Adam's apple betraying his discomfort.

'Have you tried the House Special?' he asked.

'Gideon made sure of that,' said Lucy, hardly trusting herself to meet his eyes.

'Good. Getting drunk on Three Sheets is compulsory for all new visitors to Tresco. I suppose you could call it an initiation.'

'An initiation?'

'Oh, yes. Didn't Sara tell you about the ritual?'

'No, she missed that part out,' said Fiona. 'What ritual?'

'Josh, don't be silly,' said Sara, pulling her arm out of his. 'He's teasing you both. We don't do anything of the kind; it's against the club constitution.'

'That's a relief, I thought you were going to make us walk the plank,' said Lucy.

'We do – after we've thrown you naked in the brig to sober up.'

Lucy's breasts prickled and reminded her she had no bra on.

Beside him Sara's lips were clamped together tightly. 'Why don't you get something to eat, Lucy? Better still, I'll take you down to the barbecue myself and see what our chef Rob has rustled up. Although I think I have an idea.'

Lucy could feel her face heating up. 'Please, it's fine. I wouldn't want to drag you away from your guests.'

'No, *really*. Rob will be terribly disappointed if you don't try it now. Josh went into Porthstow specially to fetch the main ingredient for you.'

'Not specially, Sara. I happened to be going into town and I was passing the quay,' he said firmly.

'Now, Josh, don't tell fibs. You know you needn't have gone into the village today.'

His eyes glinting dangerously, Josh had his mouth open when a man in little yellow wellies and a smock pushed his way over.

'Josh, there's a bit of a fracas going on in the dinghy pen. Can you come and sort it out?'

Fiona's eyes lit up. 'Oh! A fight. How exciting. Can I come and watch?'

'No,' said Josh brusquely. 'You girls stay out of it. I'll be back in a minute.'

Handing his drink to Sara, he stalked off towards the bar. Sara let out a sigh of admiration that made Lucy want to barf. 'It's so useful having Josh around to sort out these incidents.'

'A bit like a bouncer?' said Lucy.

'Or a pit bull?' put in Fiona.

'You really are very amusing,' Sara said, smiling. 'Now, Lucy, come with me and let's get some food for you and Fiona.'

She pulled Lucy by the arm towards the steps to the beach. 'Oh, I don't know what to do with Josh sometimes. He'd put himself out for anyone on the slightest whim,' she said as they walked down the steps from the terrace on to the sand.

'I didn't ask him to put himself out for me, Sara,' said Lucy firmly.

'Of course not, but he's so nice, even a hint is enough to have him at your beck and call. You see,' she added as Lucy almost stumbled on a large clump of seaweed, 'he's such an open, straightforward kind of guy, people get the wrong idea, particularly women, but they know *nothing*.'

'I can't imagine anyone taking advantage of Josh if he didn't want them to,' declared Lucy, her hackles rising.

'Really? Oh, you'd be surprised how many try. The thing is Josh Standring has left a trail of broken hearts in his wake. Misguided women who thought he cared about them in a' – she bracketed her fingers to make her point – ' "special" way when really he was just being *Josh*.'

'But you're not in any danger of a broken heart?' Lucy couldn't resist saying as they reached the queue for the barbecue.

Sara gave her a look of total incredulity. 'Why would I be in danger? Oh Lucy, you don't get it, do you? Josh and I . . . well, I think you can see that we're just so right for each other.'

Lucy was feeling slightly nauseous and put it down to the smell of burning burgers.

Sara bypassed the people in the queue and called to the chef, a red-faced man of about forty who was piling burgers and sausages on to plates. 'Ah, Rob! What a star you are! Have you got those grilled scallops ready for Lucy yet?'

Rob wiped a hand over a sweaty forehead and scowled. He produced a plastic plate from under the barbecue and thrust it at Lucy. 'So you're the one who wanted the scallops, are you? Well, they're a bugger to get right and I'm sorry, but I've overcooked them just a tad.'

Dying with embarrassment, Lucy took the plate which contained three blackened scallops on a sad-looking piece of lettuce. 'Thanks, Rob. I really appreciate the trouble you've gone to.'

He nodded then stabbed viciously at a ring of charred sausage. Everyone else in the queue was craning their necks to get a look at her. Faces were distinctly pissed off and she didn't blame them, yet Sara appeared to be overcome by delight. 'See how we try and make you feel at home, Lucy?'

Chapter Nineteen

Much later, as the punch bowl was down to the dregs *again* and Rob the chef had cremated his last burger, Lucy found herself in the clubhouse, her head spinning. It was almost dark; meshes sprinkled with fairy lights were twinkling from every nook and cranny of the building. The Latin beat had changed to a bizarre version of Scottish reeling. Lucy had been twirled by Gideon, a South African property magnate, and an ocean-going catamaran crew. The room was whizzing round long after she's actually stopped moving.

Fiona was still being whirled by a rugged young guy wearing a red-spotted bandana, a designer kilt and no shirt. The music stopped, Mr Hot-in-a-Kilt disappeared towards the bar, and Fiona lurched over to Lucy, grinning fit to burst.

'You look like you're having fun,' said Lucy, holding on to a chair for support.

'I've been pole dancing and it's wonderful!'

'He's fit,' whispered Lucy. 'And very young.'

'Twenty-one yesterday. I've offered to help him celebrate in style,' she said, lowering her voice. 'Piotrek knows a quiet place in the dunes.'

'He's gorgeous, Fi, but have you checked his IQ?'

'Hmm, that's the trouble. He's a medical student but never mind, I'm in Cornwall so I can make an exception.'

'*Cześć skarbie,*' growled Piotrek, handing over another glass of Three Sheets with a wicked grin. Fiona was visibly melting.

''Scuse me. I need the loo,' said Lucy, not wanting to be a gooseberry. She hadn't even made it to the door before Gideon lurched over.

'I've been watching you all night,' he declared.

'Really? Are you seeing two of me yet?'

He roared with laughter, blasting her with the smell of cigars and whisky. 'By God, I love a feisty female!'

'You'll have to excuse me, Gideon. I have to go to the little girls' room.'

'Not right now, surely?' He leaned closer and she almost passed out with the fumes. 'You know, Lucy, I don't say this to all the girls, but as soon as I met you I felt as if I'd known you for years. Spooky, eh?'

Her heart beat a little faster. 'Very.'

'It must be that de-jay, dee-ja vue whatsit.'

'*Déjà-vu?*'

'That's it.' *Hic.* 'Definitely seen you somewhere before.'

Lucy edged towards the staircase down to the ground floor, keeping her voice light. 'You met me on the beach after you'd been sailing that day. Remember?'

'Oh, no! No, it's more, much more than that. I feel a connection with you. Ever since I saw you, it's been bugging me like a thorn up my arse.'

'I guess I just have one of those faces.'

'That launched a thousand ships! Haw!' He squinted hard at her and then looked down. 'And the view looks bloody good from here.'

His pint glass wobbled, sending Guinness sloshing down her cleavage. He reached out a hand to wipe her clean and she smacked him away.

'Gideon,' said Lucy sweetly, trying to close her nostrils, 'I can assure you we've never met before last week and I'm afraid that if you don't take your nose out of my tits, I'm going to have to slap you very hard.'

Pulling back an inch, he tried to focus on her face, his eyes crossing. Then to her horror he winked and gave a little growl, almost Hengist-like but not half so appealing.

'Slap me very hard? Why, Lucy, I didn't know you were that kind of girl but *ding-dong*, your place or mine?'

'Gideon, will you just bugger off!'

'Even better. Haw.'

'You know, I'm going to get some fresh air,' she said, lifting her chin. 'There's a nasty smell in here.'

She headed down the steps, her wedges clumping on the wooden treads. She half ran, half stumbled down the slipway and on to the sand, then stopped, gulping in breaths of air, her heart pounding like surf. She wasn't sure which had spooked her more, Gideon's lecherousness or the fact that, even though he was completely out of his tree, he'd thought he recognised her. Had recognised her, in fact. Bugger . . .

On the beach, a half-naked couple was snogging in a catamaran and the smell of weed drifted into her nose from the dinghy pen. Lucy made for the white frill of surf breaking ahead of her. Just where the powdery sand turned damp, at the outer limit of the lights of the clubhouse, she sat down. Unlacing her wedges, she stretched out her legs, revelling in the feel of cool, damp sand between her toes.

'Hey.'

'Oh. You,' she said as Josh sat down beside her.

'Pleased to meet you too.'

'Sorry, I just needed some fresh air. There was a bad smell inside.'

'I know. I saw you with Gideon.'

'You saw?' So he'd watched and done nothing.

'Yeah, but you seemed to be handling it fine. I guessed you wouldn't have thanked me if I'd stepped in.'

'I can fight my own battles,' she said perversely.

'I'm sure you can.'

Josh spread his legs wide. His Levis were so soft and worn that the knees had split, exposing slivers of golden skin.

'Where's Sara?' asked Lucy, mentally trying to pour cold water on herself.

'I'm not sure where she is but, at a guess, I'd say schmoozing some financier bloke from Truro. He wants to invest some money in the club.'

'And you don't approve?'

'I want what's best for the club but it's Sara's call. I only have a part share in the place and if Sara wants to deal with it, it's fine by me.'

She nodded vigrously. 'I agree. All that finance and negotiating must be terribly boring.'

He allowed himself a smile. 'Sorry, but I don't buy that. You're taking the piss out of me, aren't you?'

'No.'

'Lucy, don't bullshit me. I know when I'm being taken for a ride.'

Her pulse quickened. She really didn't want to lie to Josh. In fact, she had a horrible compulsion to tell him the whole truth right now, get the whole charade over with. And she wanted him to know her name; her real name, her real reason for being here, but she felt way too stupid to tell him. Either that or she was enjoying the attention too much to spoil it.

'I might know a thing or two about business but, right now, funnily enough, none of it seems relevant.' Not bad, she thought proudly, not bad at all.

'Why not?'

'Who cares about profit and loss, bears and bonds and um . . . bulls when they've got all this.' *Bulls? Bonds?* Surely he'd know she was talking twaddle, thought Lucy, but Josh seemed to be busy squiggling in the sand between his legs. 'At the end of the day you don't really need that much.'

'Nope. Not much at all. I've got a place to live, the sailing, friends, the cottages. That's enough for me. I've got all I need, more than I need, in fact.'

'And Sara?'

'Yes, and Sara.' Then he turned his eyes on her and smiled. 'And Tally of course.'

Lucy laughed. 'Now you're taking the piss out of *me.*'

'No.'

'My incisive business brain tells me you are, in fact, winding me up.'

'If your incisive business brain tells you, then it must

be right. When are you planning on going back to London?'

'Oh, I'm not sure . . .' She stopped. 'Actually, that's not quite true. I'm supposed to be back in the office next Monday. They gave me a month. My time is up on Friday.'

'Right.'

Lucy swallowed, waiting for more. Then cursed herself. What was it to Josh if she stayed or went?

'Are you ready to go back to your job in London? Are you . . . er, sure you're well enough?'

She squirmed with guilt. What had at first seemed a harmless lie was now developing into a very big one. Almost without realising it, she had woven a tangled web of deceit that was going to be very difficult to unravel.

'Yes. I'm well enough,' she said.

'But not ready?' replied Josh, twisting the beer bottle from the sand and bringing it to his lips.

Lucy thought about her answer, but not for more than a second or two, and when it came, it was as honest as anything she'd ever said. 'I don't know. But who can say they're ever ready for anything? I can only do my best and if it's the wrong choice, then I'll have to live with it. I have to go back to my old life sometime. I can't stay here for ever.'

He lowered the bottle and rested it casually against his inner thigh. The wear on his jeans was visible here, too, and between his legs, around the seam that stretched taut over the patently obvious bulge.

Lucy's throat was dry. 'I've got things to do, places to go . . .'

He turned and she snapped her eyes away from his impressive assets and on to his face.

'People to meet?' he offered. 'Maybe one person in particular?'

'No. No one person in particular. Not now.'

'Mortgage to pay on the loft apartment in Canary Wharf?'

She thought of her rented ex-council flat in Kentish Town and bit her lip. 'Slightly further north. And . . . um . . . a little further west.'

'Ah, but what about the Ferrari in the underground garage?'

'Think smaller and you'd be warm . . . oh, there's no point keeping a flashy car in London, as you know, if you're from the Big Smoke,' she said, desperately trying to switch the conversation round to him.

'Yes, but it's been a long time since I lived in London.'

'How long?'

'Twenty years, give or take.'

'So that makes you?'

'Thirty-two.'

Lucy laughed. 'Really? I'd have put you at all of thirty-three.'

The few tiny lines he did have crinkled his eyes at the corners. 'I've had a hard life and spent a lot of it outside.'

'I've had an easy life and spent most of it in Starbucks.'

'I can think of worse places to spend your time, but not much,' laughed Josh, then stopped and frowned. Lucy held her breath. 'What's the matter?' she asked.

His face slid from puzzlement to mild amusement

again. 'Nothing. Just for a moment there, you reminded me of someone, but I must be imagining things.'

She clamped her legs together and hugged her knees, feeling the chill of the night air. 'Tell me more about when you used to live in London,' she said quickly.

'Well, there's not that much to tell, really, and most of it is stuff I'm not proud of.'

'It can't be that bad. I've done things that I'm not proud of, too.'

He gave a wry smile and shook his head. 'Like what? Fiddling your income tax? Parking on a double yellow line? Lucy, I don't think you understand.'

'I could try,' said Lucy softly.

Chapter Twenty

As they sat on the beach, a firework exploded above the clubhouse, arcing upwards in a shower of magnesium-white sparks.

'What have you done? Confess,' said Lucy, looking at Josh intently, relieved that the focus of the conversation was back on him again.

'Enough,' he said. A rocket crackling above made her flinch.

'Enough to have a record. Petty theft, a bit of criminal damage, assorted bad stuff with cars that weren't mine.'

'Oh. I see. Well . . .'

'So it's a bit more serious than parking on a double yellow, but it was a long time ago. My mother couldn't look after us and we never had a dad, so we ended up in kids' homes until I was eleven and Luke was thirteen. We tried a couple of foster homes but didn't get on with the people.'

'So how did you end up down here in Cornwall?'

'Marnie saw us in a fostering newspaper – one of those papers where kids in care are advertised to people wanting families. We must have represented the worst proposition in the whole of social services but for some reason, she was insane enough to take us on.'

'Had she got her own family?'

He shook his head. 'No. She was already widowed by then. Her husband died in a trawler accident. She was on her own but they'd fostered teenagers before. I guess social services probably couldn't believe their luck when she brought us down here to Tresco.'

'That must have been a culture shock after London.'

'I don't think either of us would know what culture was if we'd been hit over the head with it, but Marnie must have hoped we'd change our ways once we were out of the reach of bad influences.'

'But it didn't work?'

'For a while, it did. Until Luke found his feet with the locals and decided to make a name for himself. I tagged along a few times, so I can't blame him; I knew what I was doing. We got caught a few times – got away with a lot more. Petty vandalism, graffiti, shoplifting, that kind of stuff. I got into a couple of fights with local lads. God knows what we put Marnie through.'

'Drugs?'

He shook his head. 'A bit of weed, once or twice.'

She raised her eyebrows and he smiled wryly.

'OK, maybe slightly more than once or twice but it usually made me puke and I looked a right twat so I didn't bother after that. I don't know whether Luke did stuff. No, that's wrong. I guess I know he did, but I just don't want to admit it.'

'So how come you ended up as a fully paid-up

member of the community? Youth clubs, bird watching, sailing club . . . you seem to be a good boy now.'

'Then you don't know me, Lucy. And as for the bird watching, I'll admit it. I don't really do any. Remember that morning when you chucked me out of the cottage because you thought I was a pervert?'

'Well, you might have been. I was only being careful being from London and all that.'

He shot her a stern look then shrugged his shoulders. 'Fair enough. Let's agree to disagree that you're paranoid.'

'You were saying about the birds . . . ' hinted Lucy, before they started another argument.

'Oh. Right. I'd been having a quiet word with some blokes trying to steal chough eggs from the cliffs. They're endangered, you see.'

'What, the guys trying to steal the eggs or the birds?'

He smiled, drained his beer. 'Maybe both for a while but after a little gentle persuasion, the humans were persuaded to see the error of their ways.'

Lucy dreaded to think what Josh had done – or threatened to do – to the egg stealers. 'But I thought you said you'd reformed from your days as a bad boy.'

'I have, largely, but it took a shock. After a few too many cautions, and a couple of fines which Marnie paid, of course, we finally took it into our heads to take a couple of the local farmer's quad bikes for a test drive round the village. We ended up in the local magistrate's front garden, having demolished his wishing well and crushed his gnomes.'

Lucy was glad it was dark. She was trying not to smile

at the idea of a teenage Josh and his brother, lying amidst a gaggle of gnomes, the irate JP shaking his fist over them. Yet it wasn't funny because it had earned Josh a record that must have made his tough life even harder.

'Sounds funny now, eh? I suppose we thought it was at the time. I was fifteen by then and threatened with detention myself if I did anything again. I kidded myself I didn't give a toss and I certainly told everyone I didn't give a toss. Underneath I was scared shitless. When Marnie took me back again, I didn't exactly turn into a model student but I sorted myself out, and eventually went away to college. When she fell ill I came back to help with the business.'

'What about Luke?'

'He chose his own way. He was already growing out of me by then and ready to move into the big league. He got into trouble a few more times, ended up inside and then he disappeared to London. I haven't seen him since.'

'So he didn't know about Marnie dying?'

'He might, but if he does, he didn't bother showing for the funeral. And yes, I've tried to find him, God knows. The police, the Salvation Army, Missing People. I've been up to London a dozen times over the years. I don't even know if he's alive or dead.'

'If he were still alive,' she said gently, 'wouldn't he want his share of the cottages if nothing else?'

'Marnie left them to me, she didn't trust him even though she said she loved him, but I want to help him out. He's my brother. What can you do? I often wonder if I should have tried harder to stop him but what could

I have done? Sometimes you just have to walk away from people. You have to cut the ties or they'll drag your whole life away sure as a rip tide.' He said it with such passion but without bitterness. Lucy stared over the water at a distant light that blinked then faded on and off.

'I walked away from someone too.'

'Who?'

Her heart thudded and she wished it unsaid immediately. She scribbled frantically in the sand.

'Lucy? Who did you walk away from?'

It was hard to look at Josh and lie so she pushed herself to her feet and picked up her shoes. High above a firework burst apart, leaving a screaming trail across the sky above the clubhouse.

'Forget I said anything. It doesn't matter any more.'

Chapter Twenty-one

The week after the party whizzed by and it was almost time to go home. Fiona had got writer's block and decided to cure herself by interviewing the lifeguards at Perranporth beach for 'research' into near-death experiences.

Lucy decided to make one last farewell trip to look at the sailing club. 'Look at' being the words; she wasn't going inside, not even to accidentally on purpose bump into Josh. In fact, she'd done her best to avoid him after their conversation on the beach. She felt she'd opened up far too much for comfort.

Spotting the flags flying, she found a sheltered spot in the dunes and stretched out, staring up at the clouds scudding across the sky. She'd phoned Charlie and her mum weekly since she'd 'run away' to Cornwall; a couple of reporters had hung about for the first week or so but no one had bothered her mum again. Even Nick was out of the papers now, so it seemed safe to go home.

Funny how safe didn't sound as appealing as it once had.

'Yuk!' Lucy's eyes flew open. Someone was licking her toe. 'Hello, Tally.' The dog circled round her, making snuffling noises. 'Your boyfriend's not here, I'm afraid. I had to leave him behind today.'

Tally stared up at her out of soulful eyes, as if Lucy held all the power in the world to make her happy. She reached out a hand and stroked her muzzle. 'I'm sure Fiona will bring him to see you when she's down here again.'

A few seconds later, Josh emerged from dunes, doing a double take to find her there. Lucy did a double take too. He was barefoot, bare chested, and wearing dark blue Gul board shorts that showed his six-pack off to perfection.

'Hi there.'

'Hello. Tally gave me a fright. I think I'd dozed off and she woke me up by licking my toe.'

'I know, she's a real tart. She does it to me, too.'

Tally started nuzzling Josh's bare leg and panting with excitement and Lucy didn't blame her.

'Hengist not here?'

'No. Fiona had to take him to the vet's in Porthstow. Well, dragged him is more accurate. He has a sixth sense about medical matters. It took two of us and a bowl of tripe to load him into the Land Rover.'

'The vet's? Is he OK?'

'Oh, he's absolutely fine and that's the trouble. She wanted to get something to calm him down on the way home. He gets a bit agitated and it's liable to be a long, hot journey.'

'Probably a good idea. It's getting towards high season. This weather will bring out a lot of weekenders and the roads will be hell on earth.' Bending down, he tugged a piece of driftwood from the sand. As he raised it above his head Tally skittered to her feet, pink tongue lolling in excitement.

'When are you planning on leaving?' he said, hurling the stick high into the air which was Tally's cue to shoot off over the sand like a furry black cannonball.

'Tomorrow. We thought we'd get up at dawn and try and get a head start.'

Tally hurtled back, stick in mouth, bounding up the short slope to the dune, sand spraying behind her. Crouching down, Josh patted his thighs and she stopped, the stick clamped between her teeth. Her eyes flickered from Josh to Lucy and back again. She edged forward and raised a paw, seemingly about to drop the stick at Lucy's feet. Just as she was about to relinquish the driftwood, she changed her mind, trotted over to Josh and deposited her prize at his feet.

'There, you see. You are special,' said Lucy, smiling.

His eyes crinkled in a smile. 'I'm afraid it's just cupboard love, not my magnetic personality.'

Pushing herself to her feet, Lucy brushed sand off her legs. 'I'd better be going,' she said, tearing her eyes away from Josh's hand caressing Tally's silky head. 'I'm having a bugger of a job, getting all my stuff back in the same suitcase. No idea how it all fitted before and I was in a hell of a hurry. Now I have all the time in the world and it won't go back inside.'

'Why the big rush?'

'Oh! I don't know. I guess I just needed to get away as fast as possible at the time. The pressure and all that.'

His face was puzzled. 'No, I meant why the hurry *now*?'

Her heart did a fair imitation of Tally's tail. 'Sorry? Oh, none, I suppose. You know how it is when it's time to leave; you get twitchy to be home. Come in, Lucy Gibson, your time is up and all that.'

He looked at her strangely. 'Gibson?'

'I meant Hyde. Gibson is . . . someone else's name.'

He folded his arms. 'Who else's? For some reason, simple Cornish bloke that I am, I don't think I'm getting the full story here.'

'You're not really Cornish, you're a Londoner,' replied Lucy, floundering.

'True, but I'm sure I've heard Gibson somewhere before recently. Maybe Fiona's mentioned it. Or was it Sara?' He frowned.

'Maybe you're going senile . . .' said Lucy lightly, her heart rate rocketing. Josh laughed gently. 'There's always that possibility but it's going to bug me all day now until I remember. I'll ask Sara, she's got a memory like an elephant.'

'Good job she doesn't look like one!' laughed Lucy.

She was struggling even more now, almost ready to hit the rocks. 'However, back to the original question. In answer to me not being ready to plunge back into the rat-race, name me the person who wants to go back home after a holiday?' she tried.

'I don't know. I've seen plenty of people who can't wait to see the back of Tresco Creek after a wet fortnight with the kids,' he said wryly. 'But that won't work, I'm afraid. I still don't think you're being straight with me.'

He had her wriggling like a worm on a hook and he wasn't the kind of man who'd let go easily.

'OK, Josh. I *am* going to be straight with you,' she said in what she hoped was best assertive executive mode. 'I've had a great time here. Staying at Tresco has meant a lot to me,' she felt a catch in her voice. She wasn't pretending. 'An awful lot, but now, I have to go back.'

'Give me three good reasons why?'

'I could give you a hundred. My job, my flat, commitments . . .'

'That's two and a half. Who are you committed to? Those, excuse me, those bastards you work for? No job that's driven you to run away down here is worth suffering like that. I don't think anyone should have you in their power like that, no matter how much money they're paying you.'

Lucy felt almost weak with guilt. Letitia's requests for carrot cake hardly represented the heights of corporate bullying. 'I wouldn't say that I'm in their power, not *as such*. The people aren't that bad and the money isn't, um . . . as significant a factor as you might think.'

Josh's eyes were making her feel as transparent as the sea off the cove. 'So if it's not the money and they're not that bad, what made you race off down here?' he said. 'Because, call me suspicious, but you know what it looks like from here?'

No, but I've a feeling you're going to tell me, she thought.

'It looks like a man.'

'Why should it have to be anything to do with a guy?' she said lightly.

'Because there has to be a very good reason for a

woman in your position, with your capabilities, to just run away and, I have to be honest with you, I've never completely bought the stressed-out executive story. I've seen ruthless and you just don't seem the ruthless type.'

'Thanks for the vote of confidence.'

He shook his head. 'I'm only being honest. I generally know when someone's being economical with the truth, mainly because I've done it myself in the past.'

Her silence told him everything and he went on. 'I thought so. Well, you can tell me to mind my own business, but if it was me, if somebody fucked me up like that, hurt me so much I felt like quitting, you know what I'd do? I'd cut them out.' She flinched as he smacked his hands together hard. 'No one messes me around, I don't give second chances and I never waste tears over people who aren't worth it. I save them for the people who are,' he said, his expression hardening.

No tears. Ever. Apart from Marnie and, perhaps, his brother Luke, she wondered who else had ever made the grown-up Josh cry. Perhaps no one. She was careful when she replied, feeling she was treading on eggshells. 'No second chances? That's one hell of a high standard to live up to, Josh. I'm not sure many people could live with it.'

'Maybe, but I told myself a long time ago that I wouldn't take any shit off anyone. But that's just me. What you do is none of my business, but I can see how he's messed you up and I can see you don't want to go back even now, do you?'

'It's not that simple.'

'Are you denying that some bloke's the cause of you being here? What you said the other night about running away from someone, was it him?'

If only his version of the truth wasn't so tempting, she thought. Being crossed in love by some two-timing git was so much nobler than having humiliated the nation's favourite bagel-maker on live TV.

'OK. You're right. I don't want to go back. I don't want to go back to London or to work but I can't stay here. What about my job, for a start? I'd have to throw that in. Who'd pay the mortgage if I stayed? I'd have to find tenants, sub-let the flat and find somewhere to live down here.'

'There's always Creekside Cottage.'

'That would be asking a lot of Fiona's generosity.'

'True, but she strikes me as a generous woman.'

'She's a good friend, but I couldn't impose on her to that extent. Then there's my mum . . .' and Charlie, she thought, picturing both of them on the beach, drinking Twinings herbal tea and eyeing up surfers in wetsuits. 'Although I suppose she could visit. It's only a couple of hundred miles and Mum could have a break.'

She let her eyes rest on the sea, where the water glittered seductively. 'What have you got me saying? People are always running off to start a new life in the country on TV, but you can't actually give up everything and do it, can you? This isn't actually *real*.'

'Ah, that's the problem, is it? I don't actually exist. I'm a figment of the tourist board's imagination. You know, it always amazes me that people from cities think that their world is the "real" one. As if we vanish after their two weeks of sun and sand. This is *real*, Lucy, to me it's the only real there is.'

'I didn't mean to be patronising. I know this is your home,' she said softly.

'And I shouldn't be so narrow-minded,' he replied with a sigh. 'I know I shouldn't stick my nose in, but I have to say this, just in case. Mrs Sennen, our housekeeper, has finally decided she's had enough. This means I'm going to need someone to do the preparation and changeovers on the cottages. It's time I concentrated on the maintenance and marketing the place properly before I end up re-mortgaging again.'

'Josh . . .'

Lucy could see he was even more awkward now. 'I know it's menial work, nothing like you're used to and the money won't keep you, but it would be a start.'

'Josh, are you actually offering me a job as your cleaner?'

He stared at her. 'Well, yes. Yes, I am.'

She couldn't help but smile. 'It's a kind offer.'

'I just thought if you wanted to stay, I could help. A bit but, oh bollocks. Ignore me. I've had too much sun.'

'No, I'm touched. Really, I am.'

'I was just trying to make you see that it's possible to change your life if you really want to, but I can see I'm way off the mark. If you do change your mind, come round to the farmhouse after supper. I'll be in until seven-ish. If you want the job, it's yours,' he said gruffly.

Clicking his fingers to Tally, he left her, too stunned to move. Too shocked at being offered a choice that made her life ten times more complicated than it already was.

Because Josh had just made staying in Tresco Creek seem not only possible, but more tempting than she could ever have imagined.

Chapter Twenty-two

After leaving Lucy in the dunes, Josh still couldn't believe what he'd just done even as he saw the familiar chimneys of Tresco Farmhouse come into view. He couldn't believe he had asked – make that *tried to persuade* – this girl to stay on in Cornwall when she had a well-paid job to return to in London. Hell, he'd gone and offered her a job as a cleaner.

'Tally!' he called as the dog sniffed the length of the farmhouse wall, searching for familiar smells.

'Are you denying that some bloke's the cause of you being here? What you said the other night about running away from someone, was it him?'

He cringed as he recalled his words to Lucy, wondering if he'd done the right thing by making his job offer. Back there in the dunes, it had seemed exactly the right thing to do. When he'd seen her standing there against the sea and sky, trying to pretend she was happy to go home to London, he'd hadn't been able to stop himself throwing her a lifeline. There was surely nothing wrong with that, he decided, but what if . . . what if he hadn't had Lucy's welfare at heart when he'd asked her to stay? He wasn't normally given to navel gazing or analysing his motives but this was one feeling he couldn't ignore. What if he'd been so insistent that she stay not to help her – but because he couldn't bear her to leave?

Lucy was still telling herself it was impossible that she could stay, as she walked back along the beach to Creekside Cottage later that afternoon. *Still* telling herself as she squashed clothes into her bulging suitcase while Fiona clicked away manically in the main bedroom.

Her own little room was stuffy. The mercury in the old thermometer in the hall had nudged its way past thirty that afternoon, and even now it was stifling. She'd thrown open the window to get some air but found the air as thick as porridge.

She'd already stripped to her bra and knickers to try and keep cool and was thinking of going the whole hog when she caught sight of herself in the mirror and held her breath. She'd changed. Her hair was brushing her shoulders, wild and curly. She'd given up on her straightening irons after a week in Tresco, the moist sea air defeating every attempt to tame her hair into submission. Only now did she realise that she'd given up caring, too. Why spend her life trying to iron out crinkles that were natural?

The 'office pallor' Sara had kindly pointed out had been replaced by a glow that wasn't Josh's deep gold, but was pale straw or clear honey. She must have lost a few pounds too, which she had Hengist to thank for. She found herself smiling, for once, quite liking what she saw in the mirror, at least on the outside.

Inside, she had to admit, she'd changed too. She'd learned how to lie pretty well for a start.

A bloke, Josh had said, that's what brought you running away down here, and he was right. But Josh obviously thought that it was Nick who'd been doing the hurting, the 'fucking around', when in fact it was her.

Downstairs in the hall, the long-case clock chimed a quarter to seven. She wondered if Josh was waiting for her answer or if he'd forgotten he'd even asked. She stood a minute longer then snatched up the nearest piece of clothing from the rug. Shrugging on a pair of flip-flops, she headed down the stairs past an overheated Hengist who was dozing in the hall. As she stepped over him, his ears pricked and he gave a small howl of expectation.

'Not now, boy. Tomorrow.'

'Luce! Is that you?' came Fiona's voice from up above.

'Back later, Fi! Just off for a walk.'

'If you're going to the garage, can you please get some more red wine?'

But Lucy was already through the door. Hurrying down the path and out of the gate, she crossed the yard to Tresco Farmhouse, its grey façade lit by the coppery sunset. The pick-up wasn't outside and her heart sank. Josh must have left already, forgetting his offer – or perhaps, regretting it? Hands on her hips, she stopped outside the gate. To her surprise, she was breathing quite hard.

The farmhouse door opened and Tally ran out, followed by Josh, keys jingling in his hand. When he saw her, he waited. She made her legs move and walked over to him. He said nothing as she drew near then, as she reached the back door, she was sure he was frowning at her.

'What's the matter?'

'Nothing. Only . . .'

'Yes?' she panted, slightly worried by his expression. She was sure he seemed about to say something serious. Maybe he *was* regretting the invitation . . .

His expression suddenly softened. 'I was just wondering if that was your idea of an interview suit?'

She glanced down at her sequined clubbing top, her office pencil skirt, and her little heeled flip-flops with the faded flower between the toes. 'I was halfway through packing,' she said.

'Halfway? That close?'

'Yes. That close. I thought you'd gone out. The truck wasn't here.'

'It's at the sailing club. I was on my way there now, in fact.' He held open the door. 'But it can wait. Come in.'

Lucy stepped through the doorway into the farmhouse. It took a moment for her eyes to adjust to the deep shadows of the room. A few stray shafts of evening sunlight managed to penetrate the thick panes, sliding along the quarry tiles and over the scrubbed wood of the farmhouse table. Box files, official-looking envelopes and a windsurfing magazine were scattered on the table. Washing-up was piled on the draining board next to a Belfast sink. The room smelled of lemon, old age and something vaguely herby.

'Well, this is me,' said Josh, resting his jean-clad backside against the worktop as Lucy hovered in front of the kitchen range.

'It's nice. Cosy,' said Lucy, really meaning it. 'What's that lovely smell?'

'Probably coriander, possibly mint.' He pointed to a casserole on the worktop. 'I've been making a lamb tagine.'

'Oh. You cook then?'

'Yes. And wash up, make beds and clean toilets. In fact, I'm almost half civilised. Are you that surprised?'

'No, of course not,' said Lucy, embarrassed. 'You'll have to give me the recipe for the tagine.'

'Do you cook, then?'

'Occasionally . . . sometimes . . . OK, I admit, I barely know my way around an Indian menu, but I don't want to sound like a complete stranger to domesticity.'

'Then you can relax because no cooking is required for this job. Why don't you sit down?'

'Thanks.'

Lucy settled awkwardly into the wooden chair but Josh stayed where he was. Over in the corner, Tally lapped at a bowl of water, her chain clinking against the enamel.

'Can I get you a drink? Tea? Beer?'

'No, but thanks for the offer.'

He folded his arms, his grey T-shirt tautening across his chest. 'OK. You haven't come here to share recipes or for a nice cup of Earl Grey, so let's not mess about any more. Have you made a decision?'

'Yes, I have. I've been thinking about it carefully, and I'd like to stay in Tresco, at least for a few months. If you don't mind having me on that basis, I'd like to take the job.'

A narrow shaft of sunlight skimmed one side of his body from feet to face, leaving the rest in darkness, so that she couldn't quite see whether he was pleased or sorry that she'd said yes.

Then he levered himself off the worktop and stepped into the light. 'Then it's yours, but I meant what I said about it being menial stuff. Cleaning bathrooms, emptying rubbish, making beds. Clearing up after people and doing the key changeovers. Are you sure it's what you really want?'

'To be honest, I'm not sure about anything any more, but I promise to stay until the end of the season, then I'll decide. Is that any good to you?'

He hesitated a moment then nodded. 'Fair enough. You do know I can only pay you just over the minimum wage, don't you? It'll be a shock after what you're used to.'

'What? You mean there won't be a fat bonus? No stock options?'

'And no company car, either, but I could loan you a board and sail.' He smiled. 'Where are you going to stay?'

'In Creekside, if Fi will have me.'

'What about your place in London? Your job?'

'I've got it sorted,' replied Lucy, which wasn't *strictly* true, but it was a very skinny fib compared to previous big fat lies. 'There's no need to feel guilty for having suggested I stay here, if that's what's worrying you,' she added.

'I'm not worried. You seem like a woman who knows her own mind. I can't imagine you dithering over any decision.'

'Dither? Me? I don't know the meaning of the word.'

'You know, I have to be honest. When we first met I thought you were a bit, um . . . dippy, but since you've been here, I've seen you change. Become more determined. Oh shit, tell me to mind my own business.'

'Josh, it's fine. I appreciate it. After all, I'm hardly a domestic goddess.'

He hesitated and seemed to be looking her up and down as if trying to work out whether she bore any resemblance to Nigella Lawson. I should be so lucky, she thought, her cheeks heating gently under his appraisal.

'I'm glad about that, because I don't need a goddess, just a cleaner and someone to be friendly to the guests. I'm not doing you a favour, Lucy, you're doing me one. Now I can concentrate on getting the place into shape and making it pay. It's high time I took it seriously, for Marnie's sake.'

He stepped forward into a beam of soft light. He held out his hand and she took it. It wasn't a Gideon handshake, her fingers weren't being crushed, yet it was thrillingly firm, all the same. The air in the kitchen was hot and still, dust motes dancing in the beam of light as Josh gently relinquished her hand. 'There's one more thing I need to say before we start,' he said, rather too ominously for her liking.

'Oh gosh, that sounds serious.'

He gave her that look; and she knew exactly what he was going to say and that it would sound really nice but would, actually, be something quite humiliating. He was going to say something about them being friends, that he was only doing this to help her out because *he felt sorry for her*. If he did, she thought, she was off back to London in a flash.

'Yes, what is it?' she said.

'Just . . .' he raked a hand over his head. 'I wouldn't want you to think that I meant . . . anything by offering you the job. I wouldn't want you to think I'm trying to make you beholden to me, or that I'd try to take advantage or anything.'

'Josh, I know you've just offered me a job and I should be polite, but please, just shut up. I needed a job, you needed a cleaner. That's it,' she said.

'Yeah. Sure. Sorry. I'm better if I keep my mouth shut.'

'On this occasion, yes you are.' She hoisted her bag on to her shoulder. 'I'm going to London to sort out a few – um, minor details, but shall I see you next weekend?'

'Yes. Yes, of course.'

She crossed to the door.

'Lucy, could you hold on a minute. There's just one more thing . . .'

Just one more thing? Lucy's blood ran, if not cold, then less than lukewarm. Because that's just what TV detectives always said. *Just* as the villain had his or her handle on the door, congratulating themselves that they'd got away after all. *Just* before the detective moved with the killer question that was going to get them sent down for good.

She turned with a smile. 'Yes, Josh?'

'I'll need all that boring crap for the tax. Your personal details . . .'

'My personal details?'

'I'm afraid so. You know, address, NI number – for the paperwork.'

'You already know my name.'

'Yes, but I need you to fill in some forms. I'm a clean-living lad these days and I want to make it all official with the tax.'

Bugger, bugger, bugger. Why hadn't she thought of that before? He'd have to know her real name, of course, and if he did he might recognise it, Google her, anything, or even tell Sara.

'I know it would be more money for you if I just gave you cash in hand but I play by the rules, even if they are a load of crap.'

'Of course you must do everything by the book. I wouldn't expect anything else. You're self-employed and there are rules and . . . oh Josh, can't we do all of this another time? I've only just got used to the idea of changing my entire life and I need to go back to the cottage and make Fiona speechless for the first time in her life.'

'I'd like to see that, and you're right. The boring crap can wait. Let me know when you're ready to start and I'll show you the ropes.'

'You've done *what*?'

Fiona wasn't speechless when Lucy told her she was staying on in Tresco Creek, but she did spill half a glass of red wine over herself. A ruby stain started spreading over the crotch of her diamond-white skinny jeans. 'Hell's bells, these jeans cost a fortune!'

'I'll fetch a cloth.'

'No, that'll make it worse. Lucy, what in the name of the saints has possessed you to do this? Chuck in a perfectly good job?'

'A perfectly *boring* job, Fiona.'

'A perfectly boring job that kept you in clean knickers and takeaways. And what about the flat?'

'They have knickers and takeaways down here, too, and what's more they're a lot cheaper. I've got a strategy . . . oh, and keep on raising your eyebrows like that and you'll end up like Joan Rivers.'

'B-but—'

'No goldfish impressions either, please, Fi. I have made a decision.' said Lucy dramatically, half enjoying Fiona's stunned reaction. 'Everything is sorted. Well, kind of sorted. I phoned Charlie tonight. He knows a couple of Australian students who want a place for the summer so I can sub-let the flat.'

'Students? Holy Mary, the place will need Rentokil when you get back.'

'That's very narrow-minded of you, not to mention "studentist",' said Lucy, following Fiona into the kitchen. She opened the door of the fridge and fetched out a bottle of white wine.

Fiona's eyes narrowed. 'Don't try and put me off the scent by plying me with alcohol. I want to know how living a lie really has finally driven you bonkers.'

'The wine is for your jeans. And I'm not bonkers. In fact, I think I just made the most rational decision ever. It's time I did something slightly reckless for a change.'

'*Slightly reckless?* Jesus, shacking up with a megalomaniac and turning down his offer of marriage on live telly wasn't reckless? I'd hate to see you do something completely reckless. What about Nick? Does he know?'

'It's none of his business and I don't think he'll be giving me a second chance.'

'Do you want one?'

'I don't know what I want. All I know is that for the first time in my life I need to take a risk.'

Fiona shimmied out of her jeans, laid them on the tiles, and started pouring white wine on them. 'What about your job? What will Able & Lawson say?'

'I've left a message and I'm going up next week to hand in my resignation.'

'Can't they sue you if you don't work out your notice?'

'I'll have to see what they say but I'll go sick if I have to. I've made up my mind, Fiona, and if you or anyone else doesn't like my decision, I'm afraid it's tough.'

Hengist wedged himself between them and started licking the wine off the jeans. Fiona snatched them up off the floor. 'Hengist, I don't mind you having the odd curry, but I draw the line at sampling my D&G's.'

She opened the door of the washing machine and shoved them inside, then turned to Lucy. 'OK. I know I should mind my own business, it's your life, and I love you to bits, Luce, but how are you going to keep yourself? Have you any idea where you're going to stay?'

Lucy grabbed the half-empty wine bottle. 'That's what I've got to talk to you about. Come into the lounge, I think you should sit down.'

Chapter Twenty-three

'Lucy, you can't be serious?'

Oh dear, thought Lucy, that was exactly what Fiona had said when she'd asked if she could move into Creekside Cottage for the summer. Now Letitia, sitting opposite her in the flat in London, was staring at her saucer eyes. The tiny table had been dragged into the sitting room and an assortment of chairs laid round it.

'I am serious, Letitia, I went in to see Mr Lawson this afternoon and explained that I'm leaving,' said Lucy.

'But I thought this was a "welcome home" dinner. You can't actually go! I'll be bereft! Who'll fetch my carrot cake? They're doing a low-carb version now, you know, for fatties like *moi*.'

Letitia patted her almost non-existent tummy. After giving birth to little Crispin, Lucy thought she was as slender as if she'd never been pregnant at all.

'I'm sure you'll find someone else to visit the deli – or you could go yourself?'

'Lord, no. I can't be seen in there myself. Oh, Lucy, the plants have suffered since you left, you know. Your spike wilted and we had to throw it out.'

'Perhaps that was for the best,' murmured Lucy.

Letitia tried her most winning smile. 'We'll miss you so much. We've got a temp, you know, and she tries terribly hard but all she talks about is *EastEnders* and her holidays with the caravan club. Can you believe it?'

Letitia made *EastEnders* sound like hard-core porn and the caravan club like a demonic sect and Lucy, unable to stop smiling, realised she was going to miss Able & Lawson more than she thought.

'She has that awful Ross Kemp pinned on the filing cabinet and she is nowhere near as good at managing the website as you. Oh, do say you'll stay!'

It was almost tempting but Lucy was prepared. 'No, I've promised to take this housekeeping job now. I want a fresh start after all the' – she thought of Mr Lawson's face when she had handed in her resignation – 'unpleasantness.'

'Wasn't Hugo very disappointed to lose you?'

In truth, Lucy wasn't sure Hugo Lawson had been disappointed or just plain annoyed when she'd asked to be let go from her job without working her notice. She suspected he was the type of man who'd go a long way to avoid confrontation of any kind.

'I wasn't in there long, but he did mutter something about "the situation being damned inconvenient".'

Letitia's mouth opened wide. 'Oh gosh, he must be devastated. Hugo never uses profanities. Didn't he try and persuade you to stay?'

'He said they'd be happy to have me back when I'd got over this particular episode of my life.'

'Well, that's something . . .'

'*If* there was a vacancy.'

The door buzzed and Lucy jumped to her feet with a degree of relief. She wasn't enjoying having to justify her move to a chorus of largely sceptical friends, not to mention her mother. 'That'll be Charlie and Fi.' A small earth tremor also appeared to be shaking the building. 'And Hengist too.'

After kisses all round, Hengist was settled in the corner with a bumper pack of Bonio and Charlie handed over a miniature Elvis suit for baby Crispin which had Letitia in ecstasy for a full five minutes. Lucy went to check on dinner. When she got back, Fiona had opened a bottle of Blush Zinfandel and serious glugging had begun. She'd barely taken a sip when three pairs of eyes were focused on her like cats staring at a goldfish bowl. What was coming next was as predictable as rain on a Bank Holiday.

'OK. What? Have I got spinach in my teeth or something?'

Charlie shot a glance at Fiona. Fiona slurped her wine. Letitia reached out and patted her hand as if she were a patient in a rest home. 'We're only thinking of you. We don't want you to go, you see.'

'Thanks, but I've made my decision. I know it seems like I'm bonkers.'

Fiona snorted but Lucy ignored her. 'I guess you think I'm nuts to give up my job, but, like I told Mr Lawson, you have to take risks sometime in life. This thing with, well, with Nick has made me think about what I really want from life.'

'But is cleaning cottages what you really want?' asked Letitia.

'I only do the changeovers part of the week. I'm hoping to build up a small marketing business in my spare time.'

Charlie took a drag of his Gauloise and puffed out smoke in a perfect ring. 'But why Cornwall, darling? You could set up your own empire here and get a better-paid job.'

Lucy felt uncomfortably warm. 'I don't want an empire and a fresh start means just that. Totally fresh.'

'Very fresh,' said Fiona with what she obviously thought was an enigmatic leer.

Lucy aimed a kick at her leg under the table.

'Have you heard from Nick yet?' said Letitia.

Lucy kept her voice level. 'No. Not yet. I tried to phone him while I was in Tresco but his PA answered so I rang off.'

'Coward,' said Charlie then leaned over and kissed Lucy's cheek to show he didn't mean it. 'Actually, I saw him in the *Standard* last week. The bugger must be making a fortune. He's already won a contract for his events management thing from a bank. All those Hooray hedge-fund managers getting shit faced at Wimbledon while Nick plies them with strawberries at a grand a pop. They all deserve each other.'

'That's very bitter, Charlie,' said Lucy. 'Making lots of money isn't necessarily evil.'

'My Henry's a hedge-fund manager,' said Letitia, obviously miffed.

'Partners of present company excepted,' said Charlie, flashing her a generous smile. 'So there's no new man in Cornwall? No rugged surfer or wickedly handsome smuggler?' he offered, stubbing out his cigarette.

Lucy smiled. 'Smuggling ended a couple of hundred years ago, Charlie.'

Letitia sighed dreamily. 'I know, but the whole thing sounds so romantic, don't you think? All that Daphne du Maurier-style swashbuckling?'

'Being carried off against your will by a brooding pirate in tight breeches.' Charlie grinned.

'They wear wetsuits these days,' said Fiona.

Charlie licked his lips. 'I still wouldn't mind having my buckle swashed by a nice taut blond.'

Lucy had a horrible feeling her face now matched the Zinfandel. 'I'm going to be a housekeeper. I won't have a chance to be swashed or swept away by anyone.'

Letitia smiled sympathetically. 'Of course you won't, and I suppose there's an upside to a manual job. I must admit, you do look fit and you've done your hair purply again. I quite like it now.'

'Yes, she's positively blooming,' said Fi, eking out the dregs into her glass. 'Charles, petal, can I have one of your vile French fags before we open another bottle?'

He handed over the packet but Lucy got there first. 'No. You promised Hengist you'd give up,' said Lucy, snatching the packet from Fiona's fingers before the flat was engulfed in a blue fug. She stood up, determined to be assertive.

'Guys, I have something to say. I love you all and I'm grateful for your advice, concern and general barking madness over the years. But this time, I'm on my own. If I get things wrong, it's down to me. You can say I told you so when I slink back here with my tail between my legs.'

As if on cue, Hengist gave a whimper.

'On Monday, I'm going to Cornwall, at least until the end of September, maybe for longer. I'm going to clean toilets and work on my tan. I might also eat my own weight in pasties and sign up with a pilchard fishing crew.'

Letitia looked horror-struck and Lucy treated them all to an indulgent smile.

'The point is, I won't *have* to do anything or *be* anyone. I won't be the marketing assistant, I won't be the girl who waters the plants and I won't be that bitch from the telly who dumped Nick Laurentis. I can just be *me*.'

Three pairs of eyes stared back at her, three tongues twitched but didn't move. Charlie ran his hands exaggeratedly through his hair and gave a knowing smile. Fiona sat back in her chair, her eyes narrowed like a cat's.

'But you always have been just Lucy,' said Letitia, the only genuinely innocent one among the trio.

Lucy was sure that Fiona had been talking to Charlie about Josh. In fact, it would be a miracle if she hadn't been making up stories. Well, they could think what they liked. *She* knew why she was going back to Cornwall and it had nothing whatsoever to do with a man this time. She snatched up a tea towel.

'Thank you, Letty, but I'm still leaving. Now, anyone for some lamb tagine? It's a new recipe I got from a friend and I hope you'll like the taste.'

Chapter Twenty-four

A week later, Lucy was back in Cornwall, knocking on the door of Tresco Farmhouse, ready to run through the procedure for cleaning and preparing the cottages with Josh. She'd brought her car down this time, cramming every corner of it with her stuff. Having decided to move into the main bedroom at Creekside Cottage, after Fiona had returned to London, the solitary cupboard was stuffed full of clothes. Far more had been packed away and stored in the attic at her London flat. She guessed Charlie's student friends had already started trashing the place, but at least they were paying enough to cover the bills so that was all that mattered. After she'd got over the shock, Fiona had refused point-blank to accept a penny in rent but Lucy was determined to pay her back sometime, if only by keeping the cottage clean and cared for.

She banged on the door of the farmhouse again. Josh was taking a long time to answer, so she bent her head to the letterbox, pushed it open and called in a chirpy, Cockney cleaning-lady voice: 'Hell-oo, Mr Standring, it's your new cleaning lady come to do for you! Can you let me in?'

She almost fell inside as the door was suddenly pulled open. When she straightened up, she found herself face to face with a woman in her late sixties, with her wrist in a blue sling and a blue-rinse hairdo to match. Opening the farmhouse door with a scowl, she could have passed for the forbidding Mrs Danvers from *Rebecca*, except that she was wearing a pink velour tracksuit with 'Party Babe' embroidered on the breast pocket.

'You must be the new woman,' she said.

Lucy treated her to a chirpy cleaning-lady smile. 'Yes, that's me. Just trying to make Josh hear. Sorry about rattling the letterbox.'

'That letterbox has been here longer than you or me, young lady. And Mr Standring has gone to Truro on business. He asked me to show you round, tell you what's what. I'm Hannah Sennen.'

Lucy wondered if Josh had gone out to avoid her but couldn't think why. 'Pleased to meet you, Mrs Sennen.'

Mrs Sennen didn't ask Lucy to use her first name and instead, treated Lucy to a look that would have withered even the hardiest house plant. 'Where's your tabard?'

Lucy had a vague idea that tabards were worn by medieval squires or Rainbow Brownies. She hadn't expected them to be essential for dusting knick-knacks.

'Um . . . I don't seem to have one but these clothes are quite old.'

The older woman eyed Lucy's shorts and T-shirt as if they were a see-through body stocking. 'You should have a tabard. You'll have bleach, dust and worse all over you in no time.'

'Really, I'm fine.'

'It's just not professional,' said Mrs Sennen sharply. 'Here, you can have mine.' She opened a cupboard under the stairs and pulled out a flowery tabard of the school-dinner lady variety. As she handed it over, her face suddenly crumpled and she let out a sob. To Lucy's dismay, a big fat tear rolled down her cheek.

'Oh, I'm sorry, I know I'm being silly, but, you see, I won't be needing this any more, will I?' Mrs Sennen said, screwing up the tabard in her reddened hands.

Lucy was horrified. 'Don't cry, Mrs Sennen. I'm sorry you've had to give up your job,' she said, guiding her into the sitting room.

'I ought to be hardened to it but I shall miss the cottages and working for Josh. He's a good lad.' Lucy smiled at the very grown-up, tough-looking Josh being described as a lad. 'He hasn't always been, of course, but what's done is done. I don't think he'll mind me telling you he was heading straight for a spell at Her Majesty's Pleasure for a while, but he sorted himself out and pulled himself up by his bootstraps.'

Lucy handed over a clean piece of loo roll, wondering what a boot strap looked like.

'And he was golden to Marnie. Gol-*den*. Not many youngsters would have looked after a woman as ill as Marnie Trewellan. No, most young lads I know would have run a country mile from sickness but Josh stayed with her to the end.'

'What did she die of?'

Mrs Sennen lowered her voice as if imparting a great secret. 'Cancer. You know,' she murmured, pointing at her chest.

'Oh, I'm so sorry,' said Lucy, realising it was no help saying sorry to Mrs Sennen. It was Josh who deserved the sympathy, although she suspected he'd rather die himself than accept it.

Mrs Sennen blew her nose noisily. 'So I shouldn't complain because I've got my health.'

Lucy nodded, feeling slightly guilty that she had ever coveted more; like a fortnight in Barbados or a glimpse of Josh completely naked.

'I should have retired ages ago but I'm a stubborn old bird and I made Josh keep me on long after I should have stopped. He made me cut my hours but wouldn't hear of cutting my wages, the daft young devil.'

'I'm sure he thinks very highly of you,' said Lucy, trying to be reassuring while bracing herself to wear the tabard. After what Josh and his mum had gone through, wearing a tabard didn't seem that bad.

Mrs Sennen's face brightened. 'Like I said, I mustn't grumble and,' she added proudly, 'I'm off to that Faliraki place in Rhodes with Irma Wycliffe next week.'

'Is that the Mrs Wycliffe who works in the chemist's in Porthstow?'

'Worked, dear. She's retiring, too. Poor old thing can't read the packets these days. Nearly gave some woman nipple shields instead of Durex.'

'Faliraki should be fun,' said Lucy, hiding a giggle while picturing the two ladies at a topless foam party.

'Yes. Irma says she's hoping to spot some talent but I hope it won't be too hot, because my ankles swell up something terrible in the sun. But this won't do. I'm keeping you from the toilets.'

Two hours later, after cleaning her third bathroom and kitchen, Lucy was ready to drop. Having persuaded Mrs Sennen to go home, she wondered how she'd ever coped with the cleaning by herself. She suspected Josh had been secretly running around afterwards.

'Still, mustn't grumble, only one more bog to go,' she murmured, hauling her bucket into the downstairs cloakroom at Porthcurno Cottage. As she squirted green bleach into the bowl, the front door opened. It was Sara and her eyes lit up at the sight of Lucy's yellow Marigolds and flowery apron. 'My, haven't you been a busy bee?' she said.

'Actually, I've nearly finished,' said Lucy cheerfully. 'If I don't get high on pine disinfectant fumes first.'

'Hmm. I suppose it's a bit of a comedown after London, but then again, Josh tells me you're going back there at the end of the season.'

'Probably. I haven't decided yet but I'll let Josh know in good time.'

'You know, I think I can hear the boss now,' said Sara.

Lucy heard the pick-up grinding to a halt outside. 'He's not my boss, Sara. He's a customer. I'm self-employed now.'

There was a difference, she wanted to add, and setting up a holiday services business had, she thought, been one of her better decisions of late. Webs & Dusters (cringeworthy but the best she could come up with at short notice) had its own bank account in its own name. The money went straight into W&D from Josh's business account. More importantly, the fact that Josh wasn't her boss, but a customer, made her feel far better about the arrangement. She was independent; free to take on new customers, expand if she wanted to, or end the arrangement any time she liked.

Sara's eyes narrowed. 'You're still his cleaner.'

'I don't mind,' said Lucy, determined not to get drawn into Sara's spiteful game. 'I'm doing what I want and I'm planning to branch out.'

'Well, in that case, maybe you'll have time to come and do the farmhouse. It will need a good clean before I move in. You'll find this hard to believe, but I'm a bit of a control freak. I like everything perfect, you see, and Tresco is just that bit too authentic for me.'

Move in. Well, it was inevitable, thought Lucy.

'Ah, Josh! Lucy's doing a marvellous job, isn't she? Quite indispensable.'

Josh's face was impassive. 'Quite.'

Sara giggled and Lucy's fingers tightened around the loo brush in her hand. She was on the edge of doing something very childish involving heads down toilets.

'If she doesn't mind, I need her help elsewhere, too.'

Sara's eyes shone in delight. 'Cleaning the farmhouse?'

'No. I want some business advice.'

Sara's face fell. 'But she's far too busy here, aren't you, Lucy?'

'I'll be finished up in half an hour,' said Lucy mutinously. 'But I'm not sure how I can help you, Josh.'

'I thought you'd been a business manager,' said Sara sharply.

'More on the marketing side,' she replied, aware that the toilet brush in her hand wasn't adding to her image.

'Good, because that's exactly what I need. And Sara, I want a word with you as well.'

'You go ahead. I'll be along in a moment.'

'Suit yourself, but if you don't come now I'll be tied up with Lucy for the rest of the morning.'

His tone left neither Sara nor Lucy in any doubt that he meant business. Sara pouted, reminding Lucy of a little girl about to have a tantrum.

'Of course, Josh,' she said, eyes downcast and meek and Lucy suddenly realised how desperate she was for his attention, how much power he held over her. Lucy almost felt sorry for her. She was certain that Josh would never be pushed around by anyone, and woe betide the woman who thought she could push him. She guessed his tolerance went so far and no more; that if he was backed into a corner, he would be ruthless in protecting himself and anyone he loved. He opened the front door for Sara then turned back to Lucy. 'I'll see you in about half an hour, then?'

She nodded, dragged her bucket back into the cloakroom, and was about to shove the brush down the loo, when she overheard Sara hissing in the porch. 'I expect she'll want to charge you extra for marketing advice.'

As the front door slammed, Lucy thrust the brush down the toilet and flushed it hard.

Chapter Twenty-five

June was long gone and a warm July slid into a sizzling August. A tropical heatwave held Cornwall in its grip and the pavements, let alone the ice creams, were melting. Preparing the cottages and greeting guests was hotter and harder work than Lucy had ever imagined, but she was determined to make a go of it. In fact, she picked up some more work with a caravan park near Porthstow. Then, Mrs Sennen, back from Faliraki with a tan and a twinkle in her eye, suggested she do some shifts in the chemist's, much to the delight of Calendula, who had been trying to manage with only the spotty young pharmacist, who had a crush on her, for company.

As Lucy arrived at the pharmacy, admitting she'd never worked in retail, Calendula had dismissed her worries. 'Oh, whatever! I hadn't got a clue when I started either. I can't let you help with the dispensing, of course,' she said importantly. 'But I really need someone to help out with the general stuff on the till. And for God's sake, call me Cally. Calendula makes me sound like something breastfeeding women use when their tits are sore.'

So began her new life in Cornwall. If she'd counted the pennies in London, she had even fewer to count now, but she didn't care as much as she'd thought. Working for herself had given her a motivation and sense of satisfaction she'd never known before.

Besides, she didn't need many clothes in Tresco Creek. When Fiona wasn't visiting, she spent her evenings hanging out at the beach or the harbour pub with Cally and her surf buddies. She let her hair grow long and wild, she stopped working on her tan and just let it happen.

As for Josh, she would have hardly spoken to him at all, had she not agreed to help out with the marketing of the cottages. When she'd seen what passed for the website she'd decided to be honest with him. She was no web wizard but she knew enough to see that the state of the existing site might well put people off, rather than tempt them to visit.

'Both the website and the cottages themselves need a complete makeover,' she said as they'd sat in the farm-house kitchen, scrolling through the pages of other complexes. 'Tresco Farm Cottages are pretty and they've got wonderful views but, inside, they're looking a bit tired.'

'You mean they need gutting.'

'Not gutting, exactly, but redecorating, some new furniture, styling, dressing . . .'

From Josh's expression, you'd think she'd asked him to dress up in tulle and fairy wings. 'Do I look like Laurence Llewelyn-Bowen?'

She burst out laughing. 'Perhaps not, no.'

'I know the place needs help and I'm grateful to you for not sugaring the pill. Bookings are down on last year, way below what they used to be when Marnie was alive. I've let things slide. Maybe I've spent too much time on the water instead of focusing on this place. Tresco Creek is a bit out of the way, takes a bit of effort to reach.'

'And that's just why your visitors love it,' said Lucy, thinking of how she'd grown to feel safe here too.

'In the past, I'll admit, maybe I haven't been that keen to share the place with strangers, but the bank manager's telling me different now.'

'I know what you mean. This place seduces you . . .' she bit her lip. 'When we get a funky website up and running, we can offer a PDF brochure, set up online bookings. Then, over the winter, you need to spend some time doing them up.'

He pulled a face and Lucy glimpsed, for the first time, a hint of the boy he had once been. It made him so much more human, that hint of vulnerability.

'Do you want me to get a designer to put some ideas together for the interiors too?'

His obvious relief made her smile. 'Do you mind? I'll pay you for your time, of course.'

'Thanks for the offer. I'd do it for free if I have to, just to save you from the agony of having to choose paint colours. You need saving from yourself, Josh, before your business fades away to nothing.'

A couple of weeks later, Josh found himself sitting at the farmhouse table, running through the ideas Lucy asked Porthstow Interiors to draw up. He'd found himself thinking about her more and more as the days passed but had rationalised that this was hardly surprising since she now worked for him. Yet he couldn't deny how much he enjoyed having her buzz about the place on changeover days. Her dedication to her new job both touched and amused him. He now knew why she'd risen so far in her high-powered job in London: she was obviously one of those people who threw themselves into whatever they did with a real passion.

'I've bought some mood boards from the designers,' she said, spreading folders on the table. Each held sample material, magazine photographs and paint charts. She glanced up at him hopefully, her eyes sparkling with enthusiasm.

'They look fine to me,' he said, desperately trying to sound equally enthusiastic over the nautical theme she'd suggested. He was fascinated by her eyes. Were they brown or green or that weird 'hazel thing' Marnie always used to go on about?

'Josh?'

'Sorry. I was miles away.'

'I hope not. This is important,' she said, but he could see she was laughing quietly at him.

Folding his arms, he sat up straight in his chair. 'You have my undivided attention.'

'Good. Now – what do you think about this Cath Kidston theme for the end cottage? I really like it. It's country but not chintzy. Slightly Glastonbury, but if we're aiming for up-market ... Josh, are you paying attention?'

Yes, he was paying attention, but not to the swatches of fabric she'd pushed in front of him. Not even to her passion for the job. No. His eyes were drawn to her cleavage: the way, as she leaned over the table, her breasts were pressed firmly together, straining the fabric of her pink camisole.

'Josh? Have you heard a word I said or did you tune out at the part about chintz?'

He picked up one of mood boards and nodded sagely, though it might have shown the design for a bondage den for all he'd taken in. 'The Cath thing sounds great to me. Go for it and let me know the cost.'

He saw her hesitate. 'That's the marine-themed board you're looking at.'

'Is it? It's fine.'

Lucy was frowning and he wondered if she'd noticed his trip into top-shelf fantasy.

'Wouldn't it be a good idea to ask Sara?' she said.

No, it would not, he thought. Sara would definitely have an opinion but mainly on turning the farmhouse into a home and he didn't want that. 'She wouldn't be interested,' he said, knowing that he was being economical with the truth. 'She's too busy and she's in Poole on a leisure management course all week.'

'I should still show her your ideas or she might feel left out. I think the cottages will be great when you've finished them and the new websites are getting plenty of hits. You've already got some bookings for next spring.'

'I appreciate it.'

'You're paying me, Josh. It's a job.'

He flinched. He'd found employing Lucy to do the cottage changeovers more awkward than he'd imagined it would be. At first, having laid his cards on the table about the limits of their relationship, it hadn't been too difficult to keep her at arm's length. But now, she'd carved out a niche for herself in Tresco and he suspected it wouldn't be long before she could do without his help at all.

'So how's things at Creekside?' he asked, pushing the sample boards aside. 'I don't see so much of you these days. You seem to have settled in here like a local.'

Her smile, which held both pride and pleasure, made his stomach do a tiny flip.

'I'm fine. I've made friends with Cally and her crowd. Fiona's been back here a couple of times, as you know, and Charlie and my mum came to stay while you were away at the Boat Show.'

Josh's stomach flipped again, not so gently. 'Charlie?'

'He lives in the flat below mine at home. He's an actor. Absolutely gorgeous.'

'I'm impressed,' he replied, meaning exactly the opposite. Though he didn't want to admit it, he was bloody jealous.

'He's making quite a name for himself in musical theatre,' she went on, her eyes shining with pride, completely unaware of how she was turning the screw on him. 'He's just finished an all-male production of the *Sound of Music* and now he's starring in *La Cage aux Folles* in six-inch heels.'

As the penny dropped Josh let out a laugh that was way out of proportion to her gentle teasing. 'Six-inch heels, eh?'

'He's a lovely man, one of my best mates,' said Lucy.

It was a bright afternoon and the kitchen was about as sunny as it ever got. She sat back in her chair, her hands round a mug of tea. Her long, curly dark hair was caressing her bare shoulders in places he desperately wanted to touch.

She put her mug down on the table and crossed to the worktop, turning her back on him to gather up her bag and some magazines. 'I'll leave the mood boards with you, then, just in case you do want to show Sara.'

As she bent over the worktop, her high-cut denim shorts rode up, showing off long, shapely legs that were topped by a round and luscious bottom. Josh very much wanted to slip her camisole over her head and free her breasts. Then he very much wanted to pull down her shorts and knickers and make love to her on the table.

He felt his jeans tighten painfully around him. She was all voluptuous curves, her skin a pale golden brown. *Golden brown . . .* she reminded him of the Stranglers song, even though he knew they weren't singing about a woman but a temptation far more dangerous. Just then, she twisted round, the wad of brochures in her arms covering up her lovely breasts. She must have known he'd been staring at her because her cheeks were flushed, so he swallowed hard and then the words just came tumbling out.

'Lucy, do you fancy a trip to the beach?'

Chapter Twenty-six

Lucy was as surprised as Josh seemed to be when she said yes to his invitation.

'I'm not sure . . .' she said, hesitating at first.

'It's just a few beers on the beach with some mates from the sailing club. Cally and her brother might be there,' he said in his gruff fashion.

'If it's a party, I'd love to come, but I just need to nip back to the cottage for my swimsuit and a towel.'

'I'll meet you by the cliff path, then. Ten minutes enough?'

He shoved his hands in his pockets and Lucy wondered if he was already regretting asking her. She would never have agreed to go if it hadn't been a gang of them, but then again, she was pretty sure he would never have asked her otherwise. Anything else would have felt like cheating on Sara, and even though Lucy sometimes wanted to flush the woman's sun-streaked head down the loo, she drew the line at doing anything that might be construed as stealing her boyfriend. Which was ridiculous, of course, considering Josh had made his feelings about her quite plain at the outset of their 'arrangement'. She wondered if he'd asked her just to be polite.

Josh led the way as they zigzagged their way down the cliff path to the beach. Lucy had a cool bag full of Red Bull over her shoulder, while Josh manhandled the cool box.

'OK?' he asked halfway down.

'Uh-huh.'

Actually, she was more than OK. She was having a very nice time indeed, thank you very much, watching the way the muscles and tendons tautened in his arm as he carried the heavy box down the path. Sweat ran down the small of her back, down her shorts. Josh's spine and shoulder blades were glistening as they neared the foot of the cliff. At the bottom, they headed for the end of the beach towards a knot of people. Lucy tried to keep her eyes on the view and not on the way Josh's shorts were slipping down his lean lips.

'Yay! Lucy!'

Lucy waved and mouthed a 'hello'. Cally, her brother, Nathan, and assorted people she vaguely recognised from the sailing club were throwing towels down on the beach.

'Thank God for that. The beer wagon. What's kept you, mate? Thought we'd have to send out the coastguard for you,' said Byrne, an Australian Lucy recognised from their 'research' trip to Perranporth.

'As long as it wasn't a lifeguard, otherwise I wouldn't have been found by Christmas,' said Josh wryly.

Behind Byrne's back, Cally pointed to the Australian, licked her lips, and mouthed a 'yum'.

Lucy winked at her.

'Where's Sara?' asked Cally as Lucy unfurled a towel.

'On a course in Poole, apparently.'

Cally shook her head. 'She'll kill you if she finds out you're here with Josh.'

'No, she won't,' said Lucy optimistically. 'I'm not here with Josh. I'm here with you and Nathan and Byrne.'

'Hmm. Byrne. Come on, baby, light my fi-re . . .' giggled Cally.

Around them, the girls were wiggling out of their shorts, flipping open bottles and slathering tanned bodies with cream. Byrne, wearing a floppy cricket hat and tight Speedos, was talking to Josh. He thumped him on the arm so Josh whacked Byrne on the back.

'Why do guys have to beat each other up to show they like one another?' said Lucy, as Cally pulled a well-thumbed copy of Katie Price's new novel from her beach bag.

'I don't know. I suppose it's all to do with testosterone. We did have a leaflet on it at the pharmacy but Mrs W took it home. Nathan says the lads were always playing about at school. You know, flicking each other with wet towels, giving each other Chinese burns and running around naked in the locker room. It's pathetic really.'

'Yes, all very *Top Gun*,' said Lucy, stuffing her shorts in her beach bag and stretching out on her towel. Lucy tried to erase a vision of Josh standing under a shower. She wondered if Cally was thinking the same about Byrne.

'Aren't you going to take your top off, then?'

Lucy shaded her eyes with her hand. Cally, minus her bikini top, was rubbing sun cream into her boobs. In fact, all the girls, some with help from the boys, were in the process of untying strings, whipping off tops and generally getting them out. Only Lucy, slightly older and ten times more self conscious, still had her top on.

Cally giggled. 'You need to get rid of your white bits or you'll look like a real tourist.'

Lucy hugged her knees to her chest.

'You're not shy, are you? It's not because the guys are here?' said Cally, grinning.

She let out a laugh. 'God, no!'

Cally lay back on the sand with a sigh and closed her eyes. 'Do I look OK? Tell me if Byrne the Babe comes over.'

The ritual fighting over, Josh was laughing and drinking beer with Byrne, Nathan and the other guys. Lucy knew she was going to seem old fashioned if she didn't strip off soon. It wasn't as if she hadn't gone topless on holiday. It was just that *Josh was here*.

All she had to do was reach behind her, elegantly loosen the string, pull her top over her head and turn over on to her tummy, pretending to do her back. Yet she was fumbling and struggling with the knot of her bikini like a two year old. She considered pulling the halter over her head, strangling herself in the process and untying the strap from the front but that would have made her look like a granny.

Just when she thought the embarrassment factor couldn't get any higher, it did. Josh, can in hand, was looking directly at her. The next thing she knew, he was crossing the beach, crouching behind her and touching her. She felt the pressure of his fingers against her skin, heard him whisper gruffly, 'Keep still', then felt him pull the knot loose.

Then, just as quickly, he was back with the boys, laughing and chatting. Lucy pulled the halter strap over her head and felt the cool sea breeze whisper across her now bare breasts.

She lay back on the sand trying to focus on cleaning toilets, decorating cottages or anything to take her mind off Josh. Finally, she hit on the marketing plan she'd worked out for Tresco Farm Cottages. She'd really enjoyed researching what other companies did to maximise bookings, and she was quite proud of what she'd come up with: website, a brochure, maybe some PR. She wondered whether the owners of the caravan site she worked for might be interested. Their website and brochure was looking a bit tired too.

'Is Byrne looking at me?'

She turned her head to see Cally, eyes still clamped shut.

'Um. Hold on.'

She risked a quick glance at the cluster of guys round the beer box. Someone was hammering a piece of driftwood in the sand, ready for a makeshift game of cricket. 'No. I think he's still talking to Josh. Oh . . .'

'*Is he? Is he?*' hissed Cally, wiggling her toes.

'Stay calm but I think they're coming over with a drink.'

As he approached, Byrne put a finger to his lips and mouthed: 'Shhh.'

'If he speaks to me, I think I'm going to wet my knickers,' said Cally.

Seeing Josh right behind Byrne, Lucy felt ready to do the same. Quietly, Byrne took a step forward, bent down and touched the ice-cold can to Cally's stomach.

She let out a shriek that had everyone on the beach craning their necks to look at them. 'Arghh! You git! You evil rat bag!'

Byrne roared with laughter as she scrambled to her feet and pummelled his chest. Then he swept her up in his arms and dashed towards the sea, Cally squealing in delight and shock.

'I think Byrne is in trouble,' said Josh.

'No, I think he just made her day,' replied Lucy, laughing.

Josh held out a can. 'Drink?'

'Thanks.'

He sat down on the towel next to Lucy just as the sea breeze gusted, setting goose bumps running down her arms and stiffening her nipples. She really thought she might die of embarrassment. The wind blew a little harder, and white-tipped breakers began to pound up the sand.

'Do you fancy a walk around the headland while the tide's out?' he asked.

Walking couldn't be worse than lying here like a wax model from Madame Tussauds. 'Sure, why not?' She smiled.

When Josh held out a hand to help her to her feet, she felt like a gauche teenager being asked to the dance by the hunky boy in the year above. Grabbing her top, she hurriedly shrugged it on as Josh waited.

They walked level with the waves where Byrne was

showing Cally some pretty unconventional lifesaving techniques. The wind was whipping Lucy's hair into her eyes, making them water. With each step, her feet sank a little into the damp sand. They walked towards the headland, past rock pools smelling of seaweed and hard-packed ripples of wave-washed sand. Her small footprints almost perfectly matched his large ones. When he turned to her and smiled, and her stomach twisted with a sharp pang of desire, she knew she was in real trouble.

'You like it here, don't you, Lucy?' he asked.

'Of course. What's not to love? Wall to wall pasties and cream teas, not to mention the lifeguards. Not, clearly, that you've had many of them. I mean the pasties and the cream teas.'

Josh eyed her curiously. 'I don't know, I've had my share of local delicacies,' he said, picking up a stone and throwing it high over the sea. 'What I meant was, I've seen you change down here, Lucy. It suits you. I hope it's helped you get over him.'

'*Him?*'

'The guy you came here to forget.'

A pang of guilt stabbed at her heart. Even now, when they were so far away from the past and London, there was no escape from the fact she was living a lie. She'd run away from her life and now she was deceiving Josh.

'Josh.'

He stopped. 'Yes?'

'Remember at the boat-club party when I told you I'd run away from someone?'

His eyes were encouraging and Lucy was melting from the core outwards. 'Are you ready to tell me who?'

'I want to tell you, yes.'

'Then say it. Tell me.'

Her heart was in her mouth. Could she explain what had happened, all the lies she had told? She could be excused the initial deception, surely. After all, she'd been desperate not to be recognised. But to carry on and on lying to him, when she'd had so many opportunities to tell him the truth – how would he react now, if she came clean? He'd been so kind to her, so welcoming, and she'd never forgotten what he'd said outside the farm that day, months before. '*All I ask is that someone's straight with me.*'

She gave him a smile, though inside her stomach was turning over. 'It was my dad. I pushed him away, locked him out of my life.'

It was true. She hadn't lied, just given Josh another version of the truth. 'And you regret it now?'

'I don't know. That's the funny part. I always thought that if there was one thing in life I was sure of, it was that I never wanted to see him again. He didn't treat us very well, you see.'

'He didn't hit you, did he? Je-sus . . .' his voice was rough and Lucy was afraid he might rush off in search of her dad there and then.

'No. Not hit. The opposite, in fact. He was always buying us things, treating us to holidays, presents and dinners out for my mum, a trip to Disneyland for me, but it was all guilt. He had other women, you see. A whole harem, as it happens. Every time Mum threw him out, he swore he wouldn't let us down again but he always did. Mum kept giving him one last chance until she snapped. She left him when I was fifteen and we haven't seen him since.'

'Has he tried to contact you since then?'

'Yes, but Mum was having none of it.'

'What about you?'

She looked incredulous. 'I haven't seen him either.'

'Why not?'

'Out of loyalty to Mum, of course. He did try and come round to the house a couple of times. Sent cards, a few gifts, but after that, he gave up.'

'Why have you never forgiven him?'

'You said yourself you don't give people second chances, Josh. You must understand. I value loyalty and honesty in my relationships too.' Then she realised how hypocritical that statement was. 'And you've given up trying to find Luke,' she said.

'Yeah, I have, but not because of what he's done to me or Marnie. Because, after all this effort, I reckon that if he wanted to speak to me he would. He doesn't want to be found. Either that or he's dead.'

'Oh, Josh, I hope not.'

'After all this time, I'll have to face that fact, Lucy. Now please, come with me . . .' he held out his hand and she took it and they rounded the rocky outcrop to where the sand changed to shingle and then, in the distance, to boulders and rocks as big as cars. On the main beach, it had been windy but the sun had been gentle and warming. Here, the wind cannoned in off the sea, snatching her breath away and making her shiver. The giant shadow of the rock also dropped the temperature by several degrees.

Josh led her to a small cleft in the rock. 'There's some shelter here. Let me go inside, the rock's a bit rough.'

He slipped inside the cleft, pushing his bare back against the rock.

'Doesn't that hurt?' she asked.

'I'm fine.'

The gap that was left was Lucy-shaped and so she filled it. Josh's body was warm, and her breasts were crushed against his chest. His skin was smooth and radiating heat.

'I don't think this was such a good idea,' she said, looking up into his eyes.

'Probably not, but there's no going back now,' he said.

Lucy wasn't sure who made the decision but as Josh lowered his mouth, she stretched up to meet it. As he kissed her, she almost tore into his mouth and he responded with his tongue, tasting her. The waves thundered and the wind keened above their heads. The roar was so loud that neither of them could hear. His hands shifted lower on to her bottom and she longed for him to push them inside her bikini bottoms and see how wet she was. Her own hands ranged over the muscles of his back, as hard packed and honed as the sand ripples.

Then it was over. He took his hands from her waist, started to pull away and gently push her back out of the rock. As she stepped out on to the shore, the warmth of his body melted instantly and it was then she felt the full force of the cold wind buffeting her. Clambering out, he wrapped his arms tightly around his chest, as if he was trying to protect himself. 'Tide's coming in. We have to get back to the beach.'

He set off, faster now, and from behind she could see where his back was grazed from the rock face. 'You've cut your back,' she said, wanting to cry for him and herself.

'It's nothing,' he said roughly. 'And what happened back there shouldn't have. I'm a bloody fool.'

Lucy felt tears of misery and of anger stinging her eyes. 'I never asked for anything to happen, Josh, remember that? We just took a walk and got carried away. That's all it was, a bit of fun after a hard day's work.'

She smiled to make light of their kiss. If she didn't, she'd be thinking that it meant a whole lot more and that would hurt so much, she couldn't bear it.

'A bit of fun?'

'Yes. It was inevitable, really. We're both half-naked, if you hadn't noticed.'

'You don't say?' he said, looking her up and down in a way that made her feel like her face had caught fire.

'There you are, then. It's hardly surprising we were carried away,' she said lightly. 'Now that's over with we can forget it.'

'Forget it. Yes. That's what we'll do. Just pretend we didn't nearly screw each other senseless on the beach. Lucy, I'm with someone. I'm ...' he hesitated for a moment. 'I'm committed to Sara.'

The way he said committed sounded like a jail sentence to Lucy but she was too angry that he'd implied she'd led the way to feel sorry for him.

'Then we should never have walked off on our own. I

should never have agreed to come down to the beach with you.'

'And I shouldn't have asked. You're right, and it won't happen again, I promise.'

Chapter Twenty-seven

Too right it wouldn't happen again, thought Lucy, sitting in the dark in the sitting room of Creekside Cottage. She could barely see the words on the page of Fiona's seventh book, *Cut like a Knife*; she'd been staring at that page so long. If she moved to turn the light on she thought she might cry. Then she reached up to touch her damp cheek and found, to her shame, that she already had been. It was ridiculous shedding tears over Josh; over what had been a stupid error of judgement on both their parts.

The phone rang and though she didn't feel like answering it, she went through the motions. It was Nathan and he wondered if she'd like to come and watch him gig rowing. He was a sweet guy, good looking, floppy haired, and she ought to have said yes. He obviously hadn't been put off by seeing her go off for a walk with Josh. In fact, when they'd returned from their walk, even a particularly dim seagull could have guessed that they'd had a row and that Sara had nothing to worry about.

So she told Nathan she'd think about it.

*

The following weekend, she was standing outside the Crab & Lobster in Porthstow, a half of cider in one hand, the other cupping her mouth as she cheered herself hoarse for Nathan's gig-rowing team. Porthstow had managed to pull almost level with the leading crew, a boat from St Martin's and their deadliest rivals.

'Stuff em, Nate!' shrieked Cally, as her brother and his crew edged their boat ahead.

'Sink em!' shouted Lucy, as if her life depended on the boat winning.

'Ye-esss!' screamed Cally, almost perforating Lucy's eardrum. 'What a bunch of girls!'

'Maybe we should be more discreet,' hissed Lucy as a man shaped like a bulldog ran his finger over his throat in a cutting motion. 'That's the St Martin's team mascot.'

'Oh, bollocks to that! We did him a prescription for you-know-what last week. Hello, Septimus, how's your . . .' Cally pointed at his groin and Septimus beat a hasty retreat towards the slipway.

After the races, the guys returned, sweaty, salty and soaked, gasping for cider before they joined in the traditional quayside songs. Lucy thought back to her nights in the West End with Fiona; her trips to see 'classic' musicals with Charlie and she wasn't sure where she really belonged. She slipped round the side of the pub garden to use the loo, and on the way back, came face to chest with Josh, who was carrying a glass of wine and a Coke.

'Hi there,' he said, blocking the way out of the garden.

'Hello. Can you let me past, please? I'll miss the singing.'

'I need to tell you something first.'

'We've nothing to say, Josh. And you'd better get those back to Sara,' she said, nodding at the drinks.

'They aren't for Sara.'

'Fine. Take them to whoever's waiting for them now. Can you let me past, please?'

Setting the glasses down on the wall, he pulled her aside. 'I think I should tell you that Sara and me – well, we're not seeing each other any more.'

Lucy felt like a giant hand had seized her chest. She couldn't speak for a moment.

'When did that happen?' she said at last.

'After she got back from Poole last Sunday night.'

'Josh, I'm genuinely sorry. Please tell me this had nothing to do with me.'

He shook his head. 'No. Things haven't been right for some time but what happened between us did make me realise I had to sort things out with her.'

'How does she feel about that?' said Lucy, wondering how Josh had escaped in one piece. She couldn't stand Sara, there was no use denying it, but she felt she'd arrived in their idyll and overturned their lives. Being dumped by a guy like Josh was enough to make anyone feel sick and Sara was certainly not the accepting type. Lucy hoped he hadn't got any white fluffy bunnies.

He glanced away over the sea, maybe because he was feeling guilty for having led her on.

'Better than I'd thought,' he said, wondering how he'd got off so lightly. He'd sat her down in the sitting room and said it wasn't working out, he needed a break, and he wasn't ready for moving in together. He'd expected tears, tantrums, protests, but there had been none. She'd taken it well, coolly even.

'She acted as if she was expecting it,' he said, voicing his thoughts out loud.

'Maybe she was,' said Lucy.

Maybe. Lucy, I'm sorry about what happened at the beach. It was a crap thing to do. I know you'll be gone at the end of the summer and, let's be honest, with my track record, I'm not a long-term prospect. There'll only be pain in it for both of us if we start a relationship.'

Lucy wasn't sure what she felt; right now, anger and hurt were fighting it out in her mind and heart. Josh's guilty face only made her feel worse and perhaps made her crueller than she ought to have been.

'You're forgetting something, Josh. I never said I wanted to have a relationship with you. Now, I'm going to congratulate Nathan. His boat won, you know.'

'Yeah. I saw.'

The pleasure of wounding him back lasted about a nanosecond before remorse kicked in but she was way too proud to show it. 'Fine. Now can I get back to my friends?'

Pushing past him, she hurried over to the quayside and was soon joining in with an enthusiastic rendition of 'Trelawny', with the rest of the gig racers and their friends. She could see Josh and some girl by the wall. Was she a date? If so, it was a bit soon after Sara, even for Josh, but there was no denying the girl was stunning and very fit looking. Lucy sang even louder, determined to show him she didn't care and to drown out the voices in her head telling her how much she did.

*

Three weeks later, it was clear that Tresco Creek wasn't getting an Indian summer. September had started off damp and got wetter. Already, Lucy had noticed that the roads were quieter and the queues at the beach café much shorter. You could even find a parking space on the quayside in Porthstow. The café staff, the workers at the caravan parks, and even the car-park attendants, all had an air of weariness. You could see they were beginning to long for the end of the season when they could take a break, pull down the shutters, and get out of Cornwall.

If she was honest, she was knackered herself. Not just because of the physical work but from the deception, the not-quite-telling the truth.

And there was worse to contend with. She'd seen Josh with the girl from the gig racing twice over the past few weeks, once at the Smugglers and once in a coffee shop in Porthstow. She'd found out from Cally that the girl's name was Rowena and she was a brilliant young board sailor, probably one of the best in the country.

'I thought Josh quite liked you. I thought you and he might get together now that the Bunny Boiler's gone,' said Cally as she and Lucy headed off to the cinema one evening. 'But he must be shagging Rowena now.'

'We only work together,' Lucy had said. 'And he's not my type.'

'Maybe our Nathan is . . .' said Cally. 'He really likes you, you know.'

So guilt was added to misery but Lucy still summoned up her brightest hostess voice for the new guests who had arrived at the cottages for an early autumn break. 'Here you go. If there's anything you need, please call this number and have a great holiday,' she said, handing over the keys for Seaspray Cottage to a young couple from Birmingham.

'Actually, it's our honeymoon,' said the woman.

'So you won't be seeing much of us,' added her husband.

'Happy honeymoon,' said Lucy and gave the kind of knowing wink that was required. As the man staggered up the garden path to the cottage, his bride giggling in his arms, Lucy collected her cleaning kit from where she had left it by the hedge and headed back home for a glass of wine and a well-earned bath. As she pushed open the garden gate with her backside, her arms full of brushes, bleach and polish, a Land Rover pulled up outside.

'Still got your hands down a toilet, Lucy?'

Oh happy day. 'Hello, Sara.'

'Josh not with you?' said Sara, smirking down from the open window of the car.

'I don't know where he is.' Lucy's heartbeat quickened as she realised where the conversation was heading. 'I don't see that much of him, to be honest.'

'You mean you aren't all snuggled up in the farmhouse? You're wasting time, aren't you? I should have thought you'd have been over there, warming his bed for him.'

'My relationship with Josh is purely professional.'

Sara's eyes glinted dangerously, malice written all over her face. 'Come on, don't be so naïve. You're not telling me that cleaning is the only service you provide for him.'

Simmering inside, Lucy summoned up every ounce of dignity, which was difficult while carrying a bottle of bleach and a broom. 'Sara, I'm sorry you've split up, but it's nothing to do with me and if you have a problem with that, tough.'

'*I* don't have a problem, and we haven't "split up". For your information, *I* dumped Josh. I can do better than him, *much* better, and I'm so-oo glad I realised in time. I'm going to London, Lucy. I've been offered a job by the Yachting Association. You see, Josh was only ever a bit of an amusement. You didn't think I'd ever actually marry a guy like him, did you? Frankly, you're welcome to him.'

'He's a nice guy, Sara. He doesn't deserve to be spoken about like that.'

Sara's eyes widened, then she let out a squeal of laughter. '*A nice guy*? Oh my God. Don't tell me, you're *in love* with him!' she cried, clapping her hands in delight.

'I am not in love with him!'

Sara shook her head in contempt.

'You need help, Sara,' said Lucy softly, angry with herself for reacting.

'Oh, spare me the amateur psychology, please. It's you that needs help. Look at what you've sunk to. Senior executive at a City bank – not that anyone I know has ever heard of you. Now, you're just a glorified skivvy. A toilet cleaner.'

Lucy felt something snap inside her. 'Better than a stuck-up cow!'

Sara raised her eyebrows. 'Oh my, my. Now we're seeing the real Lucy, but I can understand why you're so upset. He'll get tired of you, you know. A man like Josh wouldn't know commitment if you hit him over the head with it. He's a loner and the sooner you realise that, the better for you.' She revved the engine of the Land Rover. 'If you think a loser like you can change him, you're wrong.'

'You're the only loser for driving Josh away,' said Lucy as Sara wound up the window and pulled away. She wished she could think of something cutting, something withering and witty like Fiona would have done but she was way too angry and upset.

And worst of all, she had the sickest feeling that Sara was right about one thing. She was falling for Josh and he would never have a place for her in his life. He was self-contained and he didn't *need* anyone. In frustration, she threw the scrubbing brush at the retreating Land Rover but it only hit the garden wall with a clatter. Smoke billowed from the exhaust as the car disappeared up the lane, the stink of diesel following Sara out of Tresco.

Leaving the scrubbing brush, Lucy stomped up the path, her heart banging fit to burst. She was angry with Josh for having led her on, upset at his coldness since that day at the beach, but Sara's spiteful words about him had hurt her even more. He'd cared deeply for Sara, Lucy was certain of that, and she had just laughed at him when she couldn't get her own way.

Lucy realised in that moment, that to be cared for by Josh would be something very special and being loved by him would be something else entirely.

Chapter Twenty-eight

A week after Sara had left Tresco, Lucy found herself hammering on the door of the farmhouse. A few frizzled leaves had already blown on to the path and the geraniums could really do with taking inside. It was evening and after the rain they'd had, the air held a distinct autumn chill, not helped by the message she'd come to deliver.

'Josh, I'm leaving because I need to go home.'

'Josh, I'm going back to London to get a life.'

'Josh, I'm going home because I've fallen in love with you.'

'I don't think so,' she said under her breath as she waited for him to answer. She'd rehearsed the words a dozen times and, each time, she'd given up trying to make them sound remotely convincing. Maybe she should send him a letter or email him via the new website she'd set up. Since Josh and Sara had split up, the friendship that had begun to develop between them had been crushed. He hardly spoke to her beyond the absolute essentials and she was sure he'd found excuses to avoid discussing the renovations to the cottages.

She rattled the letterbox. 'Josh, if you're in, can you open the door, please? I need to talk to you.'

There was still no answer yet Lucy knew he must be at home. The pick-up truck was parked in the yard and she could hear Tally barking inside the kitchen.

'OK, if you won't even speak to me so be it,' she said and started walking back to the gate.

'Lucy.'

When she turned round Josh was standing at the door, a towel slung low on his hips. 'Sorry. I was in the shower.'

She bit her lip. Water droplets were running down his face and chest and his hair, not quite so short these days, was damp and glistening.

'Do you always have to be wet?'

He frowned. 'What?'

She smiled sadly. 'Nothing.'

'Are you going to come inside or are you going to keep me standing on the doorstep freezing my balls off?'

'I'd like to keep you standing on the doorstep, but on reflection—'

'Lucy, just come in please.'

As she entered the kitchen, Tally jumped out of her basket and padded over, tail wagging in delight.

'Help yourself to a beer or a coffee. I'll just get dressed,' said Josh.

Lucy was glad because the sight of his naked torso was weakening her resolve to tell him she was leaving. After he'd gone, unable to sit still, she filled the kettle and put it on the Aga. She got out two mugs, spooned in the coffee, and waited for the familiar whistle.

She could hear Josh moving about upstairs, the old

boards creaking above her head. Knowing he couldn't be much longer, she filled the mugs with hot water, splashed in some milk from a carton on the table, and sat down to wait for him. She wondered how he'd react to her news: he must be expecting it sooner or later. Would he be relieved? Disappointed? Would he try and disguise one emotion with another?

Tally laid her head on Lucy's knee and stared into her eyes hopefully. Lucy's bare knee was damp with drool but she didn't mind. 'You still miss Hengist, don't you?' she said, stroking the dog's head.

'More to the point, does Hengist miss Tally?' said Josh, reappearing in the doorway in the threadbare Levis he'd worn at the boat club party. A dark blue T-shirt hid his chest away from temptation.

Lucy's heart thudded painfully in her chest. 'Yes, Hengist misses Tally. Fiona phoned last night,' she said, realising Josh had handed her the perfect cue to tell him she was leaving. Yet still she wasn't quite ready to say the words out loud. 'Apparently, he howls every time she puts him in the Land Rover and he goes wild if he sees a suitcase.'

'I think Tally expects to see him every time we go for a walk by the creek,' said Josh, leaning against the worktop. Lucy pressed her thighs together hard under the table, trying not to notice the way the worn denim tautened over his crotch.

'I've left your coffee on the worktop,' she said.

'Thanks.'

When he didn't make any attempt to touch it, she said softly, 'I didn't really want one either.'

'I know you didn't.'

'Josh . . .'

'You're going home, aren't you?'

It hurt her throat to say the words. 'Yes. Yes, I am.'

'Because of him?'

'No, not because of him.' Then she stopped, thinking that if she could face telling Josh she was going away, she could face seeing Nick again and explaining, properly, why she couldn't marry him. She knew exactly why now.

'I can't lie to you, Josh. Not about this. It's true that, partly, I'm going back because of him. You see, I feel that I've run away by coming down here. Taken the coward's way out by staying here.' She couldn't bring herself to say any more. She'd left it way too late to be telling him everything now. She'd felt like she'd wandered so far from the truth that it was impossible to find her way back.

Josh shoved his hands in his jeans pockets and looked away towards the casement window. It was what he did, she now realised, when he was cornered, possibly when he was *hurt*. And the fact he *was* hurt by her leaving made her heart skip in a stupidly hopeful way.

'I know you have to go,' he said. 'It was inevitable, I suppose. You don't belong here.'

'And you do? You're from the city. You didn't ask to come here; I bet you hated it at first.'

'I thought it was a Godforsaken dump full of hicks. I gave Marnie hell for at least a year. Now I feel the whole place has seeped into my blood, if that doesn't sound like a load of psycho-bollocks.'

'Not bollocks, no,' she said, smiling. 'I understand

exactly how you feel and I've only been here a few months. Josh, it's not that I feel I don't belong here or that I don't – absolutely – love Tresco Creek. It's more that I've got unfinished business to sort out and not just in my personal life.'

'Will you go back to your old job?' he asked.

'No, probably not. I've been thinking, you see.'

'That sounds dangerous,' he said with a smile that didn't reach his cool-blue eyes.

'I know, but I like to live dangerously, as you know. I've been doing my research and I might be kidding myself, but I think I could build up a marketing and PR business specialising in travel and tourism clients – having hands-on experience, that is.'

'You aren't kidding yourself,' he said, finally picking up the drink she'd made him. 'And I know you'll make a success of it. You're a fighter, a survivor.'

'Well, I'll give it my best shot and if the whole thing goes pear-shaped then I could always go back to my old firm. They must be missing their plant-care consultant, not to mention their sandwich jockey.'

Josh looked puzzled, then laughed. 'Somehow I can't see you watering plants and fetching sandwiches. I'll bet you had a whole team of assistants to do that.'

'Not as many as you think,' she sighed. 'It was all very egalitarian.'

He sipped his coffee but Lucy still couldn't stomach hers.

'When are you leaving?'

'Next weekend after I've done the final changeover. You only have one booking after that until half-term so you'll manage OK without me. And I've spoken to Cally; she has a friend in Porthstow who's been looking for some Saturday work, maybe you could ask her over and see what you think?'

'Yeah. Maybe I will.'

The old clock above the Aga chimed the hour. It was five o'clock on a dim evening. Time to switch on the lamps, almost. Lucy didn't think she could cope with being seen in the light; in fact, she suddenly had a desperate need to be on her own.

Reaching down, she tangled her fingers in the strap of her bag. 'If you don't mind, I've got some work to do on the computer. I want to do some surfing, maybe draft out a mail shot.'

When she straightened up, he was standing in front of her.

'Don't go.'

The shiver, as he spoke, whispered its way from the roots of her hair, down her spine to the tips of her toes. Reaching down, he took her bag from her hands, walked calmly over to the dresser, opened the cupboard door, and put it inside.

She stayed where she was, palms face down on her thighs, back straight, shaking inside. Then he held out his hand.

'My keys are in that bag. I can't leave without them.'

'I know. Lucy, you're not going anywhere right now.'

She needed his hand to help her to her feet because if she didn't take it, she thought her legs, already turned to jelly, might give way. 'Don't be silly. I have to.'

'Not until I've said what I have to say. Do you

remember the day you came in here to talk about taking this job and I said that I was only offering you a job and that it meant nothing more?'

'Yes, I remember.' She hesitated, then met his eyes. 'In fact, it's etched on my memory.'

'So you *were* upset?'

'Annoyed. It was patronising.'

'Oh, Fu— Sorry.' He raked a hand over his head. 'OK. I'll try again. Would it help to know I lied to you that day?'

She had no answer to that but he'd obviously got into his stride and didn't dare stop now.

'In fact, I lied a lot and I've hated lying, but I did it because I thought it was kinder on Sara and on you. Now I know I was lying because it was easier on me. Easier than having to face up to the fact that things weren't working with Sara and that I had feelings for you. If I had been honest, do you know what I would have said?'

He took a step towards her. Oh God, she thought, if he touches me I'm going to make a fool of myself.

'What I really wanted to say was that I wanted you so much it was hurting me. Just like now. What I really wanted to do then and what I really want to do now is lay you back on the kitchen table and make love to you.'

Smiling tenderly, he kissed her on the lips.

'I want to make love to you too. Very much,' she whispered as he pulled her against him. With that, he lifted her up with one swift movement so that she had to fling her arms round his neck and her legs round his waist for support, the peachy softness of his jeans rubbing against the tender skin on the inside of her thighs. He laid her gently on the table, the oak hard and cool beneath her skin as he pushed up her skirt. Newspapers, cutlery and a biscuit packet flew off the wooden surface as he swept them away with his hand. Something clanged on the tiles, then there was a crash as a mug shattered and the smell of coffee filled the kitchen.

Tally let out a howl and shot out of the kitchen.

Josh was fumbling with the fly of his jeans so Lucy reached forward and helped him, hurting her fingers as she tore at the metal buttons. His eyes followed hers downwards and he grinned wickedly. 'I go commando. Healthier.'

He shoved his jeans over his thighs and she let out a little gasp of delight and shock at the sight of his erection which was very impressive, rather beautiful and a little overwhelming. 'You're quite, um . . .'

He looked hurt. 'Quite what?'

'Ermm. Big. That's the word. Big, but in a nice way.'

His eyes lit up with pride and she forgave him this touch of masculine vanity because she was in love. He kicked off his jeans and stood between her legs as she leaned back on the table on her elbows.

'Hold on.'

'What?'

Rescuing his jeans from the tiles, he pulled a foil packet from the pocket and tore it open. The sound of the packet tearing filled her with relief but also made her so wet, it was all she could do not to scream at him to touch her.

Considering his hands were not quite steady, Josh

rolled on the condom almost flawlessly and then he lowered her gently to the table top. Above her face, his beautiful sea-blue eyes held tenderness and raw, hard-edged desire. Then he was pushing her skirt up above her waist and she vaguely heard herself begging him to rip her knickers off. There was a sound of snapping and fabric tearing, the brief sting of elastic against her skin, and then he was pushing inside her.

Chapter Twenty-nine

When they surfaced some time later, the kitchen looked like a bomb had hit it. Clothes and cutlery were scattered across the tiles and sticky coffee, paper and broken biscuits coated the floor.

Lucy spotted her knickers hanging over the edge of the dog basket.

'I'm going to make love to you on the beach,' said Josh.

'Now?' she asked, her face flushing as he bent over, naked, to pick up his jeans. The paleness of his backside against the tan made him seem more human, more imperfect.

'Yes. Right now,' he said, shrugging into them.

Lucy wasn't sure she could wait until she got to the beach but she didn't dare argue. 'Good. I thought you'd never ask,' she said, pulling on her skirt and tossing her knickers in the bin.

Outside it was almost dark, just a few final shafts of sun piercing the clouds over the sea. They almost ran down the green lane, along the edge of the creek to the dunes. Josh led her into a clearing in the marram grass and they stood together, facing each other. She helped him out of his T-shirt and he helped her out of her top. His jeans were round his ankles in no time and he was unzipping her skirt. When they were both completely naked and shivering in the evening air, he held out his hand and they sank to their knees.

'What happens next?' whispered Lucy, out of breath.

'What do you want to happen next?'

'I don't know. You tell me.'

'Everything.'

His arm shot out and he grabbed her wrist, pulling her down on top of him. He smelled of salt and the clean night air and his body was hard under her breasts, her thighs.

'Your everything can't possibly live up to my everything,' he whispered between kisses. 'Not in a million years. I'll show you what everything is and I won't stop until I have to carry you home to Tresco.'

His mouth was warm, moist. He tasted of coffee and smelled of sex. His tongue slipped inside her mouth, insistent but gentle.

'Your breasts are so beautiful,' he said and as if to show her, he dipped his head and reverentially kissed each nipple, then circled each one in turn with a warm, wet tongue. She had to shut her eyes to avoid coming before he'd even touched her.

Josh wanted to look into Lucy's eyes as he entered her. He wanted to know how she felt, revel in every flicker of sensation and emotion.

'Look at me, Lucy.'

When she did, he pulled her towards him so that she was straddling his legs, and then guided her on to him.

She let out a gasp and he wondered how he was going to hold back long enough to give her the pleasure she deserved. Then he pushed a little harder and she slid down further on top of him. He rocked inside her, touched her lightly with his fingers and rocked again. She gripped his back harder, her fingers digging into his flesh. How he loved that feeling, even though it almost hurt. He loved the way he was making her feel, the way her head was thrown back, her sighs and moans, his power to make her lose control.

But he knew she had just as much power over him and he was losing control too. Any second, in fact. Now . . . the next cry he heard was his own as she started to squeeze him tighter and tighter. Her body shuddered with intense pleasure and then she was throbbing around him and making him come harder than he'd ever come before.

It was virtually dark when they finally gathered up their clothes and wandered back towards the farmhouse, Josh's arm around her waist. Only as they made their way along the green lane in the dusk did Lucy realise how cold she was. Josh must have felt her shiver because he turned to her, his eyes full of concern.

'Do you want my T-shirt on over your top?'

'But you'll be freezing then.'

'I don't care.'

She stopped, and kissed him on the lips. 'But I do and it's not far home now.'

At the end of the lane, the chimneys of the farmhouse came into view and Josh stopped.

'What's the matter?' she asked.

'I need to know what's next.'

Her heart flipped and a tingle ran down her spine. 'We're going back for a hot shower, I hope,' she said. 'And to see if Tally is OK after witnessing us wrecking half the kitchen.'

He stroked her hair as she gazed up at him. 'A shower sounds great, Lucy, but you know I didn't mean that.'

Of course she knew. She knew exactly what he meant.

'I know I said – claimed – I didn't want to get involved after I'd split with Sara, but I was talking crap. I thought it was too soon, but what I know now is that I've thought about you for a long time.'

'I've thought about you too. Night and day.'

'I know we're complete opposites. I'm just a country boy, not a city high-flier, and you're ambitious. You want to leave and go back to London. I understand that but Lucy, you need to know, I'm in big trouble here.'

Her heart nearly leapt out of her chest. She wasn't sure whether what he'd just said – what he seemed to be trying to say – scared or thrilled her. He cared for her, maybe felt something much more than that. He expected something from her and she realised as he kissed her and held her in the cool, dark night, that this time she didn't want to run. She wanted to say yes, as much as she'd ever wanted to say no to Nick.

'Lucy, we need to get things straight between us.'

If he only knew, she thought, coming back down to earth with a painful bump. Seeing his eyes, seeing how he felt about her, she knew that this was the moment. No matter what he thought, she had to unravel the web of deception now. She couldn't carry on lying to him any longer. She smiled at him, though inside she was feeling incredibly nervous about his reaction. 'Straight sounds good to me, Josh. Let's go back to the house.'

With that, she grasped his hand, hoping he wouldn't notice her trembling fingers, and led him back to the farmhouse. As they drew near, they could hear barking, faint but desperate, from inside the kitchen.

'Poor Tally,' said Lucy as they rounded the corner of the building into the farmyard.

'Yeah. She must be crossing her legs for a walk and I don't quite think she can understand why.'

The gate clattered behind them as Josh quickened his step and opened the oak door, letting Lucy in first. Tally almost leapt on them both, barking, tail whirring like a mini-helicopter.

'She must have thought I'd done you in,' said Lucy, laughing as the dog almost licked Josh clean away.

'OK, girl,' he was saying as Tally ran to the front door, pawing it in desperation.

'Lucy, I have to take her out. I'll be five minutes, I promise. Or you can come with me.'

Lucy wanted his full attention when she told him what she'd done; just enough time to think how she was going to tell him but not enough to chicken out. 'Five minutes? Do you promise?'

'Four and a half,' he said, kissing her cheek before the wildly excited Tally shot out into the night.

When he'd shut the door behind him. Lucy surveyed the fall-out from their lovemaking. Then she began to gather up newspapers and packets from the floor. Her fingers shook as she picked up the shards of broken mug off the tiles. The smell of the coffee was making her feel faintly sick but that was nothing to the prospect of trying to unweave her web of lies. She loved him so much it hurt, physically, in her chest, in her stomach. What did he feel for her? Was it a fragile, shallow thing or something more robust and deep? The strength of her feelings for him terrified her. She felt vulnerable in a way that was almost overwhelming. They hadn't known each other that long and what if Sara was right? Now he'd had what he wanted, would he lose interest in her? As she wrapped the pieces of china in some newspaper, she heard the gate clang shut and knew it was time.

Expecting the door to open at any second, the banging of the knocker took her by surprise.

'It's open,' called Lucy, depositing the broken mug in the swing bin.

There was silence and then the knocker rapped again.

'Josh, I didn't lock the door. Just push it.'

As she walked forward, the door swung open on to a dark night that suddenly exploded into day.

'Lucy Gibson? It's the *Gazette*. Give us a smile, love.'

Chapter Thirty

Blinded by flashlights, Lucy tried frantically to shut the door on the photographer but the reporter had stuck his foot in the jamb.

'Go away!'

'Not until we've spoken to you. Miss Gibson, is it true you're living with Josh Standring?'

It was the reporter with the purple Mohican haircut. His breath smelled of garlic and she almost gagged. 'I know you. You were outside my flat in London,' she said.

He grinned, showing yellow teeth. 'Clever girl. Actually, it's Ross Carmody from the *Gazette*. Nice place. Is it your boyfriend's?'

'He's not my boyfriend.'

'But this is Mr Standring's house, isn't it? He does live here? And you're sleeping with him.' He smirked at her tousled hair, the mess in the kitchen. 'Just have, by the looks of it.'

'Get lost,' said Lucy, trying to close the door.

'Now, that's not very hospitable, is it? Wouldn't it be better for everyone if you just let us come in and have a chat?' He smirked. 'We're doing a follow-up story now that Mr Laurentis is doing so well with his business.

Don't you think people would love to know that the girl who rejected him ran off to Cornwall and has already found herself another bloke?'

'You bas—' Lucy was cut off in mid-expletive, as a black bundle of fur hurtled up the path and launched itself on Carmody. He flew backwards and landed in a heap next to the geranium tub. Tally straddled the reporter's chest, snarling and barking.

'Get your dog off me!'

Josh came pounding down the path towards the door. 'Lucy, are you OK? What's happened?'

'Is *she* OK? That's rich! What about me with this bloody dog about to munch my nuts?'

Josh spun round. 'And who the fuck are you?'

'Ross Carmody, *Gazette*,' he panted from the ground. 'We just want to ask you and Miss Gibson a few questions.'

Doubt and confusion flickered across Josh's face as the reporter said Lucy's name. Lucy's stomach turned over. Tally took the cue to give an impressively ferocious snarl. 'Jesus, can you do something about this stupid sodding animal?' snapped Carmody.

'Tally, do something about this stupid sodding animal. Lay off him,' Josh said.

In other circumstances, Lucy would have laughed but Josh was so angry, it really wasn't funny. Reluctantly, Tally slunk away, growling low in her throat.

'Stay there,' said Josh, then he turned his eyes on Lucy, standing in the doorway. 'Lucy, do you know who these wankers are?'

'They're reporters . . .'

A flash fired and Josh lunged for the camera. 'Give me that, you shit-head!'

Lucy thought it would have all been quite thrilling, if it was a scene from a TV drama. Josh was actually rather magnificent, hurtling forward to defend her honour. But, in reality, seeing him about to commit a string of arrestable offences on her behalf was just plain frightening. She tried to grab his arm. 'Josh, no!'

He held the camera high, about to hurl it over the gate.

'Please, no. Don't let these two provoke you. You'll only make things worse.'

'I don't give a toss. I want to know what the hell these bastards are doing in my garden.'

Carmody pushed himself to his feet, keeping a wary eye on Tally. 'So you don't know who Miss Gibson is, then?'

Josh looked like he'd been felled by an axe. He looked at Lucy then at Carmody. Lucy could see that light was dawning on him. That he was torn between anger, confusion and loyalty to her.

'Miss Gibson? I don't know what you're talking about, and if you don't get off my place, I'll throw you out or call the law.'

'With respect,' the reporter sneered, 'it's us who should be calling the police. You've assaulted me and you're about to commit criminal damage. Why don't we all go inside and act like reasonable people?'

Josh looked at him with contempt. 'One problem: you aren't a reasonable person. You're a snivelling little tosser.'

'I realise this may come as a shock, Mr Standring, but—'

'How the hell do you know my name?'

'Actually, I told them.'

Lucy glanced over to the gate to see Sara heading down the path. The expression on Josh's face switched from anger to disbelief.

'Josh, come inside and let me talk to you,' said Lucy, reaching out a hand to touch his arm but he flinched away.

'Oh dear. Lovers' tiff already? You still don't know who Lucy is, do you?'

'Who she is? What the hell are you talking about, Sara?'

Carmody smiled. 'Miss Pentire kindly alerted us to the fact that Lucy's living down here. We're doing a follow-up now her ex, Nick Laurentis, is so successful and we thought it was a nice little twist that she's ended up with you.'

'And we thought it was in your interest to know exactly who she is, of course,' added Sara.

Lucy stood up straight, trying to ignore the sick feeling in her stomach. 'Actually, it's in nobody's interest for any of you to be here. It's no one's business but mine and Josh's' she said.

Sara pouted sweetly. 'You and Josh. Oh, how twee.'

'Lucy . . .' said Josh, shooting Sara a look of anger and disbelief, 'what's going on here? Who the hell's this Nick? What are they talking about?'

'Lucy's famous, didn't you know? Or should I say notorious. She's a national celebrity, you see. It's been in all the papers, especially the cheap ones. She's the woman whose gorgeous and rather famous boyfriend asked her to marry him live on TV. But obviously he wasn't good enough for her and Lucy turned him down. Rather bluntly, allegedly. She does a good job of humiliating her men in public, don't you, Lucy?'

Lucy could see that Josh was fighting a battle between defending her and trying to take in Sara's words. With gut-wrenching loyalty, he stuck up for her.

'I don't know what's the matter with you or what you're talking about. You people are nutters and Sara, I'm sorry for what happened between us, but this won't make any difference.'

He tried to take Lucy's hand but she stepped away.

'Josh, it's no good. They're telling the truth.'

Carmody took a step closer, careful to avoid Tally's teeth. 'Miss Gibson was Nick Laurentis's girlfriend until he asked her to marry him on *Hot Shots*. Poor bloke looked a right twat when she said no. Afterwards, she disappeared down here.'

There was a silence as Josh held Lucy's eyes, looking at her with an intensity that almost scared her.

'You're making it up, mate, and if you don't bugger off, I'm going to throw you over the hedge,' he snarled at Carmody.

'It's true, I'm afraid, Josh,' said Sara sympathetically. She held out a crumpled cutting to him.

As Josh stared at the newspaper, the confusion on his face was painful to see. It gave Lucy a feeling of sickening light-headedness.

'It was Gideon who told you, wasn't it?' she said to Sara, avoiding Josh's eyes. 'He thought he recognised me at the party when he was drunk.'

Sara laughed. 'Oh no, it wasn't Gideon. It was dear old Mrs Sennen, as a matter of fact. She didn't mean to cause you trouble, of course, she thinks the world of you, just like Josh did. I saw her in Porthstow the other day coming out of the doctor's. She'd been reading an old copy of *Chat* and thought the girl in the gossip pages looked just like you, apart from the hair, that is. By the way, I preferred the mousy look.'

'I don't care what you think.'

'But you very much care what Josh thinks.'

Carmody was frantically scribbling away. 'You've done pretty well for yourself considering your family background, Mr Standring. Have you heard from your brother lately? Is it true you both have criminal records?'

Josh took a step towards him, eyes blazing. 'Yes, and I'm just about to add to mine, dickhead.' He screwed the newspaper into a ball, threw it away, and lunged forward. There was another flash.

'Always carry a spare,' said the photographer, shooting off pictures.

Sara cackled in delight. 'A leopard never changes his spots, does he, Josh? You're just a thug at heart.'

'You're sick,' said Lucy.

Josh flipped a thumb in the direction of the gate. 'Right. I'm giving you ten seconds to leave. That includes you, Sara.'

Sara feigned hurt. 'Josh, I'm sorry you're upset, but I had to do it for your sake. I had to tell you who she really was. I couldn't have you deceived like this. You do understand, don't you?'

'I'll never understand you, Sara.'

Then he turned to Lucy, his eyes full, not of the anger and shock she'd expected, but sadness. 'I'm going in the house before I do something I'll regret and I'd appreciate it if you'd come inside and tell me what's going on.'

He clicked his fingers and Tally ran after him, leaving Lucy on the path.

Carmody shrugged his shoulders. 'Come on, we're wasting our time here now. We've got the pics and we can try and unearth some locals to give us a comment. With what we've got from Miss Pentire, we've more than enough to make a page lead. That is, unless you want to give us an exclusive, Lucy. There'll be a few bob in it and Miss Pentire says you could do with the money. Haven't you been working as a cleaner?'

'Better than a parasite scumbag.'

'Suit yourself, sweetheart. Let's go.'

'Josh will never forgive you for the way you've lied and deceived him,' spat Sara as Lucy made for the half-open door of the farmhouse. Lucy looked at her with genuine pity. 'Maybe you're right, but I know for certain he'll never forgive you.'

Chapter Thirty-one

As she walked into the kitchen, Josh was leaning against the sink with his back to her. When he turned round, she could see he was struggling to contain his emotions. She didn't know what they were yet, she didn't even dare guess.

'Do you want me to go first?' she tried when she could bear the silence no longer.

'Some kind of explanation would help.'

'You're angry with me and I don't blame you.'

He shook his head. 'No. You're wrong, Lucy. I'm not angry with you. I'm angry with those parasites out there. I'm angry with . . . I think you know who.'

'But you're hurt. Confused. Disappointed.'

'I didn't say any of those things.'

He scraped back a chair from the table. 'Sit down.'

'I'd rather stand.'

'Sit down,' he ordered, gripping the back of the chair so hard, his knuckles whitened.

She thought she may as well sit down because her legs were slightly shaky. Josh positioned himself opposite her, folding his arms. 'Right. Now, I want to hear how much, if any, of this tale I just heard is true.'

How much? Who could say where the truth had begun. The more she thought about how to start, the more ridiculous, bizarre and just plain stupid the whole story sounded.

'It's true what they said about . . . the TV and Nick,' she faltered. 'He did ask me to marry him. It was on that reality TV show called *Hot Shots*. Maybe you've heard of it.'

'I don't watch TV.'

Lucy sighed. 'I know, and that made things easier . . .'

'*Easier?*'

'Not easier,' she said hastily. 'That was the wrong word to choose. I only meant that the fact that you obviously don't take too much notice of the telly and newspapers, meant that you didn't know who I was when I first arrived and then Fiona made things worse by saying I was a stressed-out City exec and . . .'

He leaned an elbow on the table, rubbing his chin as if he couldn't take it in. 'Carry on.'

'When Nick asked me to marry him and I said "no", I suddenly became public enemy number one. The newspapers waited outside my door, they hid at my mum's house, they followed me to work. You can't imagine what it was like. Nick wouldn't speak to me, everyone hated me, so we thought the best thing to do was to get away for a while.'

'*We?* Who the hell's we?'

'Fiona and me.'

He shook his head. 'I might have known.'

'It's not her fault. She was only trying to help and Josh — have you any idea what it's like to be — well, notorious?'

'No, Lucy, as a matter of fact, I don't. Why don't you tell me?'

She was hurt by his sarcasm but bit back the urge to mention it. 'Can you imagine what it was like to be laughed at on websites and in trashy magazines? To have muck raked up about your family by people who have never met you . . .'

'I think I'm going to find out, aren't I?'

Lucy thought of Carmody's face as he grinned and asked Josh about his past. 'Yes. There'll probably be some stuff in the papers about you. I'm truly sorry. I never thought things would get this far but once I'd started telling you stories, I just couldn't stop. At first I only wanted to hide away and spend some time as Lucy again, not as "that bitch off the telly". I kept meaning to tell you the truth but I just got deeper and deeper in.'

'What about this guy you jilted? This Nick?'

'He isn't speaking to me any more.'

'I can't think why.'

'Don't you dare judge me, Josh. Not like the rest of them. You don't know what it was like.'

'The bloke must have been pretty sure of himself to have asked you in front of thousands of people.'

'Millions, actually. Ten point three million.'

He turned his head and looked away in disbelief, but Lucy wasn't quite sure whether he couldn't believe the numbers involved or what had happened between them.

'Can I ask you something else?'

'Yes.'

'And get an honest answer?'

'That's cruel.'

'Not cruel. I'm just confused. Why did you turn this guy down? Did you even love him?'

She took a deep breath. 'Because I wasn't sure. Because I didn't know him and I wasn't sure why he'd asked then. Because I'm deluded enough to think getting married ought to be for ever and not a smart career move.'

Josh said nothing. He didn't seem impressed by her romanticism and she hardly blamed him.

'So let me get this straight. Just for turning this guy down, you were hounded out of your flat and your job and ended up running down here.'

'I didn't have to leave but it seemed like a good idea at the time, and then I genuinely wanted to stay.'

'So you didn't work for a merchant bank in the City?'

'No.'

'Jesus. So, what *did* you actually do?'

'I did work in London. I was a very junior marketing assistant with a law firm. So you see, I really do fetch the sandwiches and water the plants.'

She smiled gently in the hope that he might smile too, but it wasn't to be. He just looked tired and sad. Any chance that he might understand or forgive her seemed to be ebbing away. She stayed silent until she couldn't bear it any more, then said: 'I think we could both do with some time to ourselves. Do you mind if I go home?'

'I'll come over with you. Those bastards might still be about.'

'No, I'm fine.'

'I said I'd walk with you.'

Having shut the door on the downcast Tally, Josh led

the way across the dark farmyard. The beam of his torch wavered over a broken flower pot and the discarded newspaper showing Lucy in full flight on her doorstep.

When they reached the cottage he walked in first, ignored her protests and turned on all the lights upstairs and down. Then he checked the garden before he was satisfied no one was hanging around. When he'd finished, Lucy was standing in the sitting room, unable to move. She felt ready to cry at any moment but bit her lip, determined not to shed a tear in front of Josh. She suspected that any tears of hers might seem part of the act to Josh. If he only knew how real her misery felt. How much she regretted not being straight with him from the start . . .

As he entered the sitting room, she brushed her face hastily with her sleeve. It was too late. She could see by the expression on his face that he'd seen the gesture and thought the worst.

'You'd better call me if you're worried about anyone hanging around,' he said almost brutally. Then he walked out of the front door, slamming it behind him.

Lucy decided that if the whole of the world's press started hammering on her door, Josh was the last person on earth she'd call.

Waking early after a terrible night, her eyes felt like she'd had all the sand on Tresco beach rubbed in them, so she got up and went for a walk by the shore. It was Sunday and a fine morning, so there were quite a few people up and about, exercising their dogs. At the far end, a tall man was throwing something into the sea for a dark-haired dog. She quickened her step but as she drew closer she could see it wasn't Josh.

The disappointment made her eyes sting so she started to jog, then to run, anything to try and shake off the realisation that she might have lost Josh. By the time she'd climbed back up the cliff path, she still felt terrible and was out of breath too.

Josh was loading up the pick-up truck with wetsuits and buoyancy aids. When he saw her, he shut the door and came towards her. She still cherished a glimmer of hope that he'd calmed down and wanted to talk. Her heart lifted momentarily until she caught sight of his dark, unsmiling face.

'Josh, we have to talk about what's happened. You have to believe that I never meant for things to go this far.'

He swung round to face her. 'You know what, Lucy? I never meant for things to go this far either. Not with Sara, not with you.'

She was shocked but had to persist. 'Why don't you just listen to me?'

'No, I think I've done enough of that. You listen to me. You know what? I don't give a toss that I'm going to be all over the frigging newspapers tomorrow. I don't really care that you chucked some bloke in front of every man and his dog. What I do care about is that you didn't trust me.' He paused and Lucy was going to speak but he carried on before she could open her mouth to protest. 'You know what I think hurts and disappoints me the most?' he said quietly. 'It's the fact that I was so completely straight with you about my past and my family. I trusted you with stuff I don't share with people, Lucy, and yet you just kept on lying. When would you ever have stopped?'

'I had stopped. Long ago.'

'Really? How can I ever know that, now? I trusted you, *believed* you. Everyone did. Jesus, you and Fiona must have been laughing at us all.'

Lucy felt angry and frustrated now. 'We were never laughing at you. Never for a moment! How could you think that?'

'How will I ever know where the truth begins and ends, more like? When we were making love, the things you said to me – how good I made you feel, how much you wanted me . . . how will I know that wasn't part of the act too?'

'Josh. Give me some credit. That was no act. I've never acted with you, not in the things that matter. Touching you, being with you – it was amazing.'

The fleeting spark of tenderness in his eyes made her hope that he was about to throw her a lifeline but his next words stifled any hope.

'Lucy, I lied to you last night and it's been bothering me ever since. I had heard of *Hot Shots*. It's the kind of crap I turn off as soon as it comes on screen. And I know damn well what the newspapers are going to say about me and Luke but that doesn't bother me. It's the way you've betrayed me.'

'Josh, I didn't mean to hurt you—'

He cut her off. 'The way you betrayed me and kept on doing it. I always knew you were from a different world from me but lately, I thought you might be growing to love this place, the people ... Christ, I thought you really cared for me. You know what? I just can't handle this right now.'

She had just enough dignity left to say, 'No. I can see that. It's too soon.'

'Lucy, I don't think soon is ever going to happen for us.'

With that, he opened the door of the truck and got in, leaving her standing in the yard. As he started the engine, she realised the crushing sensation in her chest was Josh trampling on her heart.

Chapter Thirty-two

It hadn't taken a genius to know that not everything she'd brought to Tresco would fit back in the suitcase and boxes, Lucy thought, as she tried to cram yet another pair of flip-flops into her case. It was mid-afternoon and packing up her stuff had taken her nearly all day but she'd been grateful for anything that took her mind off the feature that had appeared in one of the red-top newspapers that morning.

They claimed it was a 'follow-up' feature showing the 'contrasting fortunes of the *Hot Shots* contenders and their 'hangers-on'. '*Nick's business*', said the article, '*was going from strength to strength while his ex, Lucy Gibson, was now forced to work as a cleaner for her new boyfriend, a man with a string of convictions for petty theft, motor offences and criminal damage.*' Funny how they made petty theft sound even worse than the big sort, she thought, hardly daring to imagine how Josh would feel when he read it.

Even after all she'd read in the papers, she thought this article rated as muckraking of the lowest kind. There was a picture of Josh about to hurl the camera at the photographer and one of Lucy herself, her mouth wide open in a shout of what looked like rage. She'd been trying to stop Josh from launching himself on the reporter, of course, but in the photograph, she looked like she was urging him on. She'd come across as a gold-digging bitch. Josh had been portrayed as an aggressive thug and Luke as some sort of criminal.

'It's vicious and it's just not true. God knows how Josh must be feeling,' she told Fiona on the phone after pouring out the whole sorry story.

Fiona gave an audible sigh. 'As far as I can tell, they haven't actually said anything libellous. I mean, this stuff about Josh and his brother – I presume it's based on fact?'

'Based on, just about. From what he's told me, I suppose some of the stuff about his background is true but all that stuff happened years ago. You know what Josh is like now and he was hardly a hardened criminal back then. He'll hate this, Fi, I know that much. He's a private guy. He keeps his business to himself. And when he sees this, I don't know what he'll do.'

'Maybe he'll see it for what it is: vicious tabloid dirt, but I don't know him as well as you do, hon. Why don't you ask him?' said Fiona tentatively. Oh dear, thought Lucy. Fiona treading on eggshells was always a sign that the situation was dire.

'Even if I wanted to ask Josh, I couldn't. The pick-up's not outside the farmhouse and no one at the sailing club seems to know where he's gone, other than "away".'

There was a short silence before Fiona replied, 'I knew I should never have left you down there with him. You needed saving from yourself.'

'It's a bit of a mess, Fi.'

'I'm afraid it is, hon, and I don't have an answer other than giving Josh time to cool down. I suppose there is one consolation. Nick's obviously refused to comment. It says: *"Nick Laurentis maintained a dignified silence when asked for his thoughts on his former girlfriend's new man."* '

'I know. That was big of him.'

'Least he could do,' said Fi. 'Ohh. Stop that . . . I'm talking to Luce.'

'What was that?' asked Lucy, perplexed.

'Um. It's Fergus, my toxicologist. We're doing some research.'

'After office hours?'

'Naturally. Fergus is far too busy during the day. Now, Lucy, do you want me to come down to Cornwall? Just say the word and Aunty Fi will be there with the gin and Kleenex balm.'

'Gin and tissues sounds good,' said Lucy, eyeing the almost-used-up loo roll by the bed. 'And thanks for the offer, but you'll see me soon enough. I'd decided to come home before all this happened and I'm not going to change my plans now. I'll be back on Friday.'

Later, having finally managed to squeeze the flip-flops into her case, Lucy bumped it down the stairs and into the hall. While she was debating whether to take the case to the car or leave it in the hall overnight, there was a knock at the door that made her almost drop the case on her toes. She could see a man's figure through the glass and her stomach did a flip. Without hesitating, she pulled the door open.

'Hello, Bagel Girl.'

Her stomach plummeted as she got a proper view of the handsome man standing on the doorstep. His dark hair was long and floppy; he was paler and, somehow, he seemed slighter than she'd remembered, yet he was still the same old Nick.

'Nick?'

'Yes, Nick. Who did you think it was?'

'No one. It's just such a shock to see you here. I – I don't know what to say.'

He flashed a smile. 'You could ask me in for a start.'

She kept her hand on the door. The very last person she had ever expected to see after all that happened in Cornwall was Nick, least of all a Nick who was now smiling at her gently, apologetically even.

'Look, I can understand you're surprised to see me and that maybe me turning up unannounced isn't a pleasant surprise.'

'Well, I definitely didn't think you'd be coming all this way down here after all that's happened.'

'I won't blame you if you don't want to see me, but I've spent a long time thinking about what happened at the studio. It was very wrong of me to put you on the spot like that. And what went on afterwards was, frankly, shitty.'

'Yes, it was . . . but I appreciate that what the press did wasn't your fault.'

He smiled disarmingly. 'Perhaps not, but I have to share some of the blame for causing it and for not doing anything about it. Now I'm here. Several months too late, maybe, but I'm here.'

Lucy hesitated. 'I don't know what to say. Things have changed so much. I've changed.'

'I can see that,' he said, shooting her an appraising look. 'You look great, Lucy.'

She should have felt flattered but she just felt embarrassed and she certainly didn't feel great. 'What's made you decide to come here?' she repeated, determined not to be sidetracked by his charm.

'I just thought you might need a friend right now after this latest business in the newspaper. I'm sorry the way things have worked out with you and John.'

'His name's Josh. And we never really got started. In fact, I'm just packing to come back to London.'

He raised his eyebrows. 'Not staying to try and make a go of things with him?'

'No. The newspapers had everything out of proportion. He's not my boyfriend or my partner. They made all of that up.'

'Ah. In that case, I really think you should let me come inside.'

When she still hesitated he gave the little-boy pout she'd once found so sexy.

'After all, whatever's happened, it's just me underneath. Just a humble sandwich maker, and he's here asking you to bring him in out of the cold before he collapses on your lawn and is found eaten by crazed sheep,' he said. 'They *do* have crazed sheep here, don't they? Because there were a few over by that wall that seem slightly deranged.'

She followed his gaze to the lane where three woolly faces peered through the fence at a sleek sports car.

'You'll be OK. Most sheep are quite safe unless provoked.'

'Even so, I still don't fancy being left alone in the wilds.' His face became serious. 'Isn't it time we had a proper grown-up conversation about what happened?'

'You're right. It is. More than time.'

She made him a coffee while she tried to calm herself down and make sense of his reappearance. When she walked back into the sitting room, he was stretched out on the sofa, leafing through a copy of *Horse & Hound*. He brushed at his trousers. 'The dog hairs are Fiona's, I take it?'

'Hengist's. I've tried to clean them up but they stick to everything,' she said, handing him a mug. 'Sorry, it's instant coffee and I've no brownies either.'

'Sadly, I haven't brought any with me. No time for hands-on stuff these days, I'm afraid.'

His eyes sparkled briefly and she waited for the flip, the once-familiar twist in her stomach, but there was nothing.

'Nick, you said we should have a proper conversation.'

'Yes. Of course. The thing is, we've both managed to make quite a mess of the past few months.'

'Apart from you winning *Hot Shots*, that is . . .'

'Well, yes, of course,' said Nick, waving his hand dismissively. 'But I've made a mess of *us*. I've been doing a lot of thinking, mainly about what happened in the studio. Now I see that I just got carried away by the moment and that was unforgivable. Lucy, I really cared for you.'

'Then why wouldn't you talk to me afterwards? I was desperate to talk to you.'

He held up his hands. '*Mea culpa*. I was just too hurt, Lucy. Too raw and, let's face it, you made me look like a total jerk in front of millions of people. No man's going to enjoy that kind of humiliation.'

'I just couldn't lie to you, Nick, but I never meant to hurt or embarrass you either. I cared for you, too. In fact, I cared way too much just to say yes for the sake of appearances. I didn't want to lie. I hate lying . . . despite what the world may think. And you did put me in an impossible position.'

'I'd like to,' he said, winking.

Alarm bells rang in her head. He was still gorgeous, and now he was famous and successful too. Most women would fall into his arms. Most would think she was completely raving mad not to have accepted him: not to be melting now.

'How are your family?' she said, changing the subject and not even bothering to be subtle about it.

He frowned but took the hint. 'They're fine. Hattie's engaged to a stockbroker so Mum and Dad are doubly happy. Both their offspring have finally made sensible career choices.'

That brought a smile. Same old Nick.

'Lucy, do you have a bathroom? It's been a long drive from London and I don't have hollow legs.'

'Upstairs on the right through the latch door. Don't bump your head on the beam.'

'A beam and latch door, eh? And there's me thinking this place might have an outside privy.'

'Not quite.'

When she was alone, she sat back in her chair. Nick turning up had knocked her for six. He was genuinely apologetic about the proposal and some of the guilt she'd felt about turning him down crept back into her mind. To come all this way to see how she was, to have finally faced up to talking over what had happened – well, he was a better, braver person than she was in that respect.

She heard the creaking of the floorboards above and the flush of the antiquated cistern. As his footsteps thudded on the stairs, her mobile buzzed. Lucy picked it up from the table and was about to press the answer button when she realised that it wasn't her phone. It was Nick's phone. And she recognised the name on the screen. Just one word but unforgettable all the same: CARMODY.

She pressed answer and held the phone just away from her ear, too afraid to listen too closely, yet hearing the voice loud and clear anyway.

'Nick? It's Ross, mate. Any joy with the great reunion?'

Lucy's throat was dry.

'Nick, are you all right? Not got her into bed already, have you, you jammy bastard?'

She was still holding the phone as Nick entered the lounge. Seeing her expression, his grin melted from his face.

'You've had a call,' she said, holding out the phone to him.

'I'm too busy to take it right now,' he said, almost smiling again.

'Yes, but it looks important. I think you should take it.'

As he reached for the phone and saw the screen, his mouth set into a hard line. He stabbed the 'off' button and glared up at Lucy.

'Won't your mate be expecting an answer?' she said quietly.

'Fuck him.'

Tossing the phone on to the sofa, he stepped forward and gripped her arms with his hands. Lucy flinched but stood firm.

'Things don't have to be over, Lucy. We've made a mess of things, but I think there's a way forward for both of us,' he said soothingly.

Her skin prickled where his fingers pressed into her flesh. '*Forward*?'

'Yeah. Onward and upward. People will understand that you had a fling, that we've both made a mistake. They're desperate for us to get back together, don't you see? It's human nature to want a happy ending.'

Lucy felt faintly sick, unable to believe what he was proposing. 'You can't still want us to get married after all that's happened?'

'Why not? We had a blast together and you know how good the sex was. It wouldn't do either of us any harm. Your profile's high and so is mine. The door is still wide open. What is so wrong with making the most of your opportunities? Why do you have to take everything so seriously?'

The phone buzzed from the sofa and Nick glanced down at the screen. 'Don't you want to answer that? It might be important,' she cut in smoothly.

'No. You're more important.'

'Nick, I'd like you to leave now.'

'If you force me to walk away again you'll be making a big mistake.'

'No. The only mistake I made was in ever letting you chase me down the street with that bagel. I should have carried on walking.'

He shook his head, as if she was a disobedient and rather dim child. 'Oh dear, Lucy. I really like you, but you know what? I'm not so sure you'd fit in my world.'

'I never wanted to fit into your world, Nick. I never want to fit into anyone's world except my own. And now, I think you really should get out.'

Opening the door wide, she held it so that he could pass through. As he strode up the path towards the gate she half expected Josh to appear. If this was a TV drama, he would appear, and then there would be a fight for her honour.

'You really are mad. You won't get another chance,' he called, flicking the remote on his car. The last she saw was him wrenching open the door, throwing his phone on the seat. Then he revved the engine and drove off, leaving a cloud of dust behind him.

No Josh had appeared. Lucy knew he was never going to fight for her again. But she wouldn't cry. She'd wasted too many tears over Nick, then some over Josh. She was still telling herself not to waste any tears at two in the morning when, watching another rerun of *Brief Encounter* on the old TV, they burst forth in great sobs and howls that soaked the cushion Fiona had bought specially for Hengist.

Chapter Thirty-three

Six Months Later

'Lucy, I'm just off to lunch. Can I get you anything?'
Lucy glanced up from the media proposal on her desk and smiled at Lorna, her assistant, hovering by the door of their office. 'I wouldn't mind some soup and a sandwich, but only if it isn't out of your way.'

'I'm going right past. It's no problem. Shouldn't you take a break yourself?'

Lucy shook her head. 'Probably, but I want to make some changes to this proposal for Countryland Holidays.'

'I can stay, you know. I'll just nip out for rations, then I'll come back and help.'

'Thanks for the offer, but take a break and don't worry about me. I'm going out for dinner tonight, so I can't stay too late.'

Lorna raised her eyebrows. She opened her mouth then closed it before disappearing into the corridor. Lucy was amused. Lorna had only been working as her assistant for a few weeks, and Lucy could see that she was not quite sure whether she dared tease her boss yet.

That was fine, thought Lucy, who had hardly got used to being 'boss' to herself yet, let alone to anyone else.

When she'd first moved back to London from Cornwall the previous autumn, Able & Lawson had offered her her job back. She'd been touched but she'd said no. If there was one thing she'd learned after the events of the past year or so, it was that her independence meant more to her than almost anything. In fact, she'd decided that nothing would make her give it up now she'd tasted freedom. One of the holiday parks she'd worked for in Cornwall had given her their PR business and as a result of that, she'd picked up the account for the whole group. Clients were impressed by the fact that she'd had literal 'hands-on' experience of the business, and after three months of running Gibson Marketing from her kitchen table, she'd picked up three more holiday accounts and some freelance bits and bobs from Able & Lawson. It was time to branch out and if that meant a tiny office above a chiropodist's in the suburbs, so be it. Finding Lorna, an ex PR wanting a part-time job, had been a huge stroke of luck but Lucy thought she deserved a little luck right now.

By six thirty, Lorna was still doggedly researching prospects on the web and Lucy's hand was beginning to ache from gripping the mouse. It was also freezing: the central heating in the office had already been switched off by the landlord, even though it was barely March.

'Time to call it a day, I think,' said Lucy, noticing Lorna's red eyes and blue fingers.

'Are you sure? I only have a few more possibles on the list.'

'It's Friday night. It's minus two in here, and I'm sure you must have more interesting places to be than here.'

Lorna's face went slightly pink.

'I can see you do,' said Lucy.

'It's a guy I met at nursery, actually,' said Lorna. 'My mum's offered to babysit for Chloe so we can go for a meal together. To be honest, I haven't been out with a guy for nearly a year and I'm as nervous as hell. What will we talk about? Toilet training? Who's shagging who in the *Fimbles*?'

'Why don't you tell him how you helped your firm win the Countryland Holidays account? On second thoughts . . . just get out of here – and that's an order from the boss.'

Five minutes later, the computer screens were dark. Lucy locked up the office and followed Lorna out into the street. Wrapping her scarf tighter around her neck, she waited as Lorna pulled on woolly gloves.

'Goodnight, Lorna, and thanks for staying late. Hope your date with Mr Mum goes well.'

'No problem. Have a good evening and er . . .' Lorna hesitated then added slyly, 'enjoy your date too. You look great.'

'See you Monday,' said Lucy, smiling yet feeling suddenly overwhelmed with nerves. There was still time to back out of tonight's encounter, she told herself as Lorna headed in the opposite direction, leaving her alone in the shadows. There was still time to save herself from the pain, the awkwardness of the meeting she'd agreed to. No, she told herself as she gripped her briefcase. Been there, done that. She didn't run away any more.

She made her way towards the Tube station, surfacing twenty minutes later into a quiet side street where the door to a bistro beckoned, its lights glowing. She stopped and took in a lungful of the cool night air. Would he be there? she wondered, or had he got cold feet like she almost had?

Would he be bearing gifts? Flowers? Chocolates? An explanation? Suddenly, a whole field of butterflies took flight in her stomach. All she really wanted was his presence.

She was greeted at the door by a wave of warm air and a smiling waitress who asked her if she'd made a reservation.

'Table for two. I've reserved. It's in the name of Gibson,' said Lucy.

'Oh, yes,' replied the waitress, checking the list for the name. 'Your guest's already here.'

He was sitting at a little table over in the corner, his face half in shadow and half in flickering candlelight. He hadn't noticed Lucy yet and she could see from across the room that he was empty-handed, apart from the table napkin he was twisting in his hand. As she drew nearer, he glanced up and his face was such a mixture of guilt and hope that Lucy had to dig her nails in her palms. He looked so different in his smart suit.

It was almost comical how restrained they both were while the waitress was still fussing around taking drink orders. His polite peck on the cheek, her muttered 'hello' – anyone would think they were business acquaintances. Yet inside, Lucy sensed he was going through the same turmoil of expectation as she was.

Finally, the waitress left them.

'I didn't know you drank gin and tonic. That was your mum's favourite,' said her father.

'Gin? Did I say that? God, I meant to order a vodka and tonic.'

'I can't remember what I ordered either.'

'Half a lager.'

'Bugger. I could really do with a pint.'

Lucy started to get up. 'They don't serve draught, but I can try and get the waitress to change it . . .'

Her father laid his hand on her arm. 'No, Lucy, pet. Leave it be.'

At the sound of that endearment, she knew she couldn't take any more. 'Dad, I'm sorry. I need the loo.'

Ten minutes later, she was trying to reapply her mascara with a shaky hand, wondering why they'd plumped for such a public reunion. They hadn't even spoken yet and already she was worried about making a fool of herself in this smart bistro. Maybe they should have met at her flat, but she'd wanted this first encounter to be on neutral territory. She made it back to the table and, some time later, as the waitress cleared away their uneaten steaks, she had the chance to get a good look at her father. She wondered how he felt, seeing her as a woman for the first time, rather than as a teenager. An angry, bitter teenager.

'You look like you're doing well for yourself,' he said as they sat over a coffee. 'But I always knew you would. Where are you working?'

'I run my own marketing business, specialising in the holiday trade. It's nothing grand but I like it.'

'Sounds good to me,' said her dad and the pride in his eyes made her feel light-headed. It was what she'd once craved, what she shouldn't long for: his approval and approbation. Realising she still cared so much about what he thought was scary.

She allowed herself a small smile. 'I love working for myself. There's risk but I like that. Having no one to answer to.'

He nodded. 'And no one to turn to if things go wrong. You know you're really living when you set up on your own.'

'That's it. *Exactly*,' she said, surprised that he understood so well.

'I've got my own business, too. It's nothing so glamorous as yours, of course, just a small builders' merchants,' he said.

'So you don't work for Hudsons any more?'

'Oh Lord, no. They went out of business years ago. I worked for a couple of other firms after that before I decided to have a punt myself. Take control of my own destiny and all that.'

'Yes, I know what you mean.'

His eyes crinkled at the corners as he smiled. He had deep brown eyes and he was still a good-looking man, despite the grey hairs. He was still her dad; the man she'd once been proud to have pick her up at the school gates; the man her mum had fallen in love with and then out of again.

An awkward silence was broken by the waitress asking if they'd finished and both Lucy and her father refusing the dessert menu.

'I agonised for months over whether to try and contact you again. I saw all that terrible stuff in the newspapers. Those parasites made me want to punch their lights out but I thought that if I joined in, I'd only make things worse or you'd think I wanted to jump on the bandwagon.'

Lucy was going to tell him not to be silly but realised he was probably right.

'I phoned your mum, you know,' he said out of the blue.

Lucy fiddled with her teaspoon, trying not to feel defensive over her mum. 'What did she say?' she asked carefully.

'Well, she didn't slam the phone down, which was a start. She told me you'd gone off to the seaside for a while to sort yourself out but that you were back now.'

'Have you seen her?'

'I didn't ask, Lucy. I think we're way past reconciliation. She's got her life and I've got mine. I heard a man's voice in the background. Scottish, I think . . .'

'Hmm. That was probably Big Kev from the gardening club.'

'Lives there, does he?' asked her dad.

'Not officially, but he doesn't seem to go home much.'

'She deserves to be happy.'

'Yes,' said Lucy, draining her drink and feeling uncomfortable. 'Are you with anyone?' she asked.

Her father gave a wry smile. 'I was. A woman from work, actually, but I've just been passed over for one of our suppliers. He's got two things I haven't: a villa in Tenerife and a clean licence as far as his reputation goes.'

Lucy wondered whether or not to say she was sorry he was alone, but she wasn't quite ready to be that generous. Not yet. 'What about you? Has there been anyone else since that Nick bloke?'

She felt her body stiffen. That was one thing that time hadn't healed: the raw wounds left by Josh. She still thought of him every day. Every time she had to write about Cornwall, or cottages or even the seaside in general. Every time Fiona arrived with Hengist. When she woke up in the morning and last thing at night when she went to sleep. How long would it take for him to disappear from her world? Would he ever?

'I'm too busy with the business. I don't need a man to complicate things.'

'No, I shouldn't think you do. We're nothing but trouble, eh?'

Chapter Thirty-four

'Lucy!'

Fiona bounded up the steps to the cinema where Lucy was waiting, stamping her feet to keep out the spring evening chill. *Psycho: The Director's Cut* wasn't really her thing but Fiona had an obsession with Hitchcock movies and afterwards they were going on to a new club in Piccadilly, where Fi was 'on the list'. Lucy was aching for some escapism. The previous evening's reunion with her dad had left her drained and, though it was hard to admit, had also made her realise how much she still missed Josh.

'Lucyyyy! Wait until I tell you what's happened,' called Fiona as Lucy skipped down the steps to meet her friend halfway. Fiona's face was glowing pink in contrast to her emerald-green trench coat.

'Fi! Are you OK?'

'Oh, I'm fine. No, it's Fergus the toxicologist!'

'God, what's happened to him?'

'He's only gone and proposed to me, the mad bugger! Can you believe it?'

Fiona threw her arms around her and hugged her in a most un-Fiona-like way. 'Poor Fergus, he must be heartbroken,' said Lucy sympathetically.

'Heartbroken? What d'you mean? Of course he's not bloody heartbroken, because I've accepted!'

Lucy's jaw dropped towards the pavement.

'Don't give me that look. I said I'm getting married.' Fiona beamed.

'But he's *brilliant*, Fi! You said yourself he was the cleverest man you'd ever met. Even cleverer than you. *And* you told me to have you sectioned if you even so much as contemplated getting married again.'

'Yes, yes, I *know* I did, but the thing is, Fergus makes Simon Cowell look like a pauper. He's got his own moated manor in the Cotswolds and some kind of castle in Bute. Besides,' she lowered her voice, 'you just wouldn't believe what he can do with his tongue.'

Abandoning *Psycho*, they jumped straight into a cab and headed for the nearest champagne bar where Fiona ordered Krug. Then they went on to the club and were joined by Charlie and Fergus who was drop-dead gorgeous in an aristocratic, slightly ravaged kind of way. Lucy wondered how he'd ever cope with Fiona but Fi was deliriously happy and that was all that mattered. It was Fiona's moment so Lucy danced and laughed and tried to think of all the good things she had in her life such as her business, her new relationship with her father and, as Mrs Sennen no doubt would have reminded her, she had her health.

Yet later, as she lay in bed at the flat in the small hours, all she could think of was the one thing she didn't have and how much she longed to be wrapped in his arms right now. She hugged her pillow, longing to be pressed against his warm, big body, safe in the knowledge that he'd be there the next morning and every morning.

She awoke shivering with the kind of hangover that not even intravenous Lucozade could shift. She couldn't hear the comforting sound of Charlie moving about in the flat downstairs. In fact, every little noise she made, from her bare footsteps on the floor to the kettle boiling, seemed to echo off the walls, as if the flat had been emptied by phantom removal men during the night.

Unable to bear the emptiness, she decided to go for a walk and even outside, everywhere seemed muffled and blank under the cloudy London sky. Wrapped in her raincoat, a scarf wound around her face, she was on her way into the gates of the nearby park when there was a squeal of brakes.

'Ow!'

The next thing she knew, she was lying on the pavement. Someone who appeared to be a sailor was peering down at her.

'Charlie?' she said, as her eyes focused and her head throbbed.

Resting his bike against the park railings, he held out a hand. 'So sorry, darling. No bones broken, I trust?'

'No, I'm fine,' said Lucy, hearing him grunt as he hauled her up. 'Have you thought of getting your eyes tested?'

'Often. However, I've never met an optician I liked the look of yet. Besides, I was in a tearing hurry to try and catch you. Lucy, there's a Greek god on the steps to the flat and he's looking for *you*.'

Her heart, already jogging after the collision, went into sprint mode. 'A *Greek god?*'

'You know the kind of thing – tall, blond, chiselled, would look good naked on the walls of the Parthenon. I passed him on my way out.'

She could hardly squeeze out the words. Someone seemed to have botoxed her vocal chords. 'D-did he – did he say anything?'

Charlie looked puzzled. 'That was the *weirdest* thing. He asked if you lived there and if I was Charlie. I have absolutely no idea how he knew who I was.'

'I do,' said Lucy, taking in the vintage sailor boy outfit her neighbour was wearing and guessing that he must be on his way to a *South Pacific* rehearsal. 'Charlie, I think I know who it is. I think it's Josh. You see, I told him about your musical career.'

Charlie's face filled with pride. 'In that case, if I were you, apart from putting on a lot of slap, I'd whizz over to the flat now before Zeus decides to fly back to Mount Olympus.'

In Lucy's wildest dreams, when she'd first returned to London, she'd imagined Josh walking into her workplace, in *Officer and A Gentleman* style. In her fantasies, her document wallet would fall to the floor as he swept her into his arms and carried her down the corridor past a whooping Lorna who'd be shouting, '*Way to go, Lucy!*' All the patients from the chiropodist's on the ground floor would be clapping and cheering as Josh whisked her off towards . . .

She'd never been sure where because she hadn't really known what she wanted to happen next.

'Oh, for heaven's sake, what are you waiting for?' said Charlie as she hesitated.

Lucy was wondering the exact same thing until she realised that the feeling that was keeping her frozen to the pavement was fear. Fear mixed with pride. Josh hadn't been prepared to give her a second chance. She knew that she'd deceived and hurt him but she'd always nurtured that tiny flame of hope that he might have softened.

'I don't know,' she told Charlie. 'It's just that I've worked so hard to get over him. I thought I had got over him, but if he's just turned up to say "hello" or ask me the way to Buckingham Palace or something, I don't know what I'll do.'

Charlie gave an exasperated sigh. 'Lucy, I give up on you. Whatever he has to say, it can't be worse than the agony you've been going through, my lovely. Now, be brave. Go and talk to him.'

Everyone was always giving advice about thinking positive, thought Lucy as she tried very hard not to run back to the flat. Thinking positive might work if you were pushing for a new contract or you'd been shipwrecked on a desert island, but in the case of love, thinking the worst meant you could never be disappointed. Just because Josh was here, in London, waiting for her, she told herself, didn't mean he'd come back to *her* or for her. There could be any number of reasons he was here; he had business in London, he was looking for Luke. Yes, that was it. *Of course*. He'd made one last attempt to find his brother and had decided to see her at the same time. Now that was sorted, she could be calm.

At the corner of her road, she stopped and reminded herself of what he'd said to her that horrible night in Tresco even though the words still cut like a knife. There would never be a 'soon' for them, he'd said, and the words had echoed in her mind like a great oak door clanging shut on a prisoner in a dungeon.

Soon, the flat came into sight and Lucy's emotions went on a Big Dipper ride. There was no Josh outside. He must have already gone. She'd reached the flat before the door of a black cab opened and a man got out, pulling a wallet out of his back pocket.

It was Josh. There was no mistake but it was a Josh she had never seen before. He had thick toffee-blond hair curling against his neck and he was wearing a trench coat over a thick sweater.

And only now, in this instant, as her stomach did an impression of fairground waltzers, did she realise how much she still loved him.

He shoved some notes through the window of the cab before he turned round and saw her. When she saw his expression she knew straightaway he wasn't going to do a Richard Gere and sweep her out of the paper bag factory.

'Have you been looking for Luke?' she said, before he could hurt her by saying it himself.

'Yes, I have.'

'And?'

'I found him.'

'Oh.'

'Or rather he found me, Lucy.'

Just then, the breeze whisked up a leaf and whirled it

past her face and into her hair. She suddenly realised she was too afraid to brush it away, too afraid even to move. Because, she thought, if she actually moved, she might break into little pieces, she felt so brittle and fragile. Maybe Josh would melt away too, if she brushed away the leaf, because maybe he wasn't here at all and she had imagined him because she wanted him so very much. Only the leaf was the charm that kept him here.

'He found me because his girlfriend saw an article in the newspapers about us. He's been trying to pluck up the courage to get in contact with me ever since and last week I got a phone call. Yesterday I went to visit him and I've been staying with him.'

'Where is he?' asked Lucy, shivering beneath her raincoat.

'In Pirbright at the moment. He joined the Army a few years back. He's served in Iraq and Afghanistan but now he's back at the base for a while with Suzy, his partner. They've got a baby on the way.'

'So you're going to be an uncle?'

'Yes.'

'That's great, Josh. I'm really happy for you,' said Lucy, meaning every word, yet weirdly feeling like crying. 'How did you know where I live?' she asked.

'I called Fiona first thing this morning. She didn't seem too pleased.'

'That's because she just got engaged. You probably got her out of bed.'

His wry smile, softening his expression, threatened to have her on her knees. 'I never was one for the social niceties. You know that.' He hesitated before he went on.

'So, Lucy, are you going to let me in or are you going to leave me out here, breathing in all this pollution?'

Her heart beat a slow, painful rhythm against her chest. 'I'm not sure, Josh. Maybe I'll leave you out here. It depends just how much you want to come inside.'

He took a step towards her and reached out his hand. She barely felt his hand touch her hair, but when he uncurled his fingers, the leaf was sitting in his palm. His fingers were blistered and calloused from windsurfing and work yet Lucy wanted to lift them to her mouth and kiss them.

He let the leaf fall to the pavement and gently brushed her cheek with his hand. 'Lucy, sweetheart, I want to come inside with you so much, it hurts. Please let me in. Don't leave me out here.'

The stairs to the flat felt like Everest as she led the way up, hardly able to bear the weight of hope and expectation filling her heart. All the time she'd spent trying to force him from her mind, she'd known that she would survive as long as she never had to see him again. Now that he'd burst back into her life, real flesh and blood, she didn't know how she could cope with another parting.

Inside the flat, the curtains were still drawn so she tugged them open and let in the weak spring sunlight. Even so, Josh seemed too massive for her little sitting room. 'Can I get you a coffee?' she said, bizarrely hoping he wouldn't notice her knickers drying on the radiator.

He smiled gently. 'Not right now, thanks.'

'Will you sit down, then?'

He chose the sofa, carefully pushing a couple of DVDs and an empty packet of Doritos to the end of the seat to make room.

'Are you sure you don't want a biscuit or some breakfast?'

'Lucy, I mean this really nicely, but can you please shut up for a minute? Don't you know I've been dying without you?'

'You don't mean actually *dying*, Josh. You mean hurting. That's how you know you're alive.'

'Hurting, then. Suffering.'

'I've not been very happy either.'

'How "not very happy"?' he asked, shifting forward in the chair, daring her to put into words what she'd been going through. But how could she tell him about the lonely nights, the longing for his body and his quiet, rock-steady presence? The misery she'd felt when she'd locked up the cottage on that last morning and seen Tresco Farm growing further and further away in the rear-view mirror.

'Like the sun got switched off,' she said at last.

He was off that sofa and holding her in his arms in an instant. He was big and warm and golden and she couldn't believe that he was here in her life. Then he brought his mouth to hers and she tasted him again, the heat and sweetness, the Josh-ness of him. His sweater was rough against her wet cheek, his fingers tangled painfully in her morning hair as he kissed her as if he would never let her go.

She didn't know how long they kissed and held each other but eventually she broke the silence. 'I've missed you so much. I'm so sorry for lying to you, letting you down. I've regretted it every day.'

Josh groaned. 'No, I've regretted it every day. I should have trusted you but, Lucy, I don't find it easy to trust people. If it's any consolation, life has been hell. Pure hell. I tried to convince myself I could live without you but I just couldn't do it. And then, when I heard from Luke, and realised just how much of his life I've missed, I knew I couldn't waste another moment without seeing you. I've only been hurting myself and God knows what I've done to you. He smiled gently. 'And I think Tally hates me too.'

'Because Hengist left?'

'Because I drove you away and I wouldn't give you a second chance. Because I'm a stupid, stubborn bloke who didn't know what he had. But I do know now and I love you, Lucy.'

She could no longer stand the pressure of his arms about her waist, the tantalising pressure of his fingers on the bare skin where her T-shirt met her very glamorous jogging bottoms. Too late to worry that she had her oldest knickers on and a bra that she should have thrown out ages ago. Josh only seemed to care about ripping her clothes off as fast as possible. It was cold in the flat and she was shivering by the time he'd unhooked her bra and taken off her knickers. In no time, he was naked too and every bit as hard and magnificent as she'd remembered and dreamed about. She realised it wasn't *that* cold in the flat.

'Kitchen?' he panted, holding out his hand to her.

Lucy gulped. 'Love to, but I don't think my little table will survive.'

He looked downcast until she ordered, quite sternly: 'Bed. Now.'

As he let her lead him into the bedroom, she marvelled at her new assertiveness and wondered if that was what being your own boss did for you.

Much later, glowing and warm, they were walking through pools of spring sunshine in the park. With Josh's arm around her back, Lucy felt as if she owned the whole world. When they reached the café by the lake, he pulled her into his arms.

'Lucy, I want you to come back with me to Tresco. I sold one of the cottages and bought out Sara's share in the club.'

'She let you do that?'

'She told me it was a poxy dump and I was welcome to it and we both know I'm much better at sailing than property owning.'

'Perhaps,' she replied carefully.

'But the point is, Lucy, I don't want to be Josh the island any more. I want to share my life with you.'

Lucy buried her face in his sweater. For so long, she'd longed for those words but now they presented a dilemma. Gradually, she'd moved forward, made plans, set them in motion, entangled herself with other responsibilities. Her business had kept her sane while she'd been trying to forget Josh. She couldn't just abandon it and yet she ached to be with him.

'It's not that I don't want to come with you. I do, so very much, but things have changed, Josh. I have a business, staff—'

He raised his eyebrows in surprise. 'Your own empire?'

'A teeny tiny one, more like a mini-kingdom. There's Lorna, who's my assistant, and my clients. I can't just abandon them. It's not that simple.'

'Life never is,' said Josh. 'And I don't want you to give up everything for me, but I have to try and be with you somehow.' He pulled her to him and kissed her head. 'And I'm not going to stop trying until we're together.'

Chapter Thirty-five

Three Months Later

Lucy spotted Josh standing in the small arrivals area at Newquay Airport before he saw her. He was jingling his keys in his fingers and anxiously scanning the passengers. As he finally caught sight of her, she lifted a hand and he smiled back. She quickened her step, her body tingling in anticipation of the tightening of his arms around her, the gentle sweep of his lips against hers.

'Hello,' she said as she reached him at last, her breath coming in little gasps that had nothing to do with hurrying towards him and everything to do with what she had to say.

'How was your flight?' he asked, taking her bag from her without asking as he always insisted on doing. He kissed her on the lips briefly but there was no 'sweetheart', and certainly no bear hug.

'Oh, fine. We had a bit of a bumpy landing but otherwise it was good. You can see all the boats, you know, as you come in to land,' she said as they walked outside, blinking against the redness of a sinking sun.

Josh flicked his key at the pick-up truck. 'Could you see Tresco?' he asked as he dropped her bag in the cab and waited for her to climb inside.

'Well, I tried to spot it but I couldn't quite—'

'No, of course not. Stupid question.'

He slid into the driver's seat and Lucy touched his hand as he held it over the gear stick. 'Josh? Are you OK?'

'I'm fine,' he said, starting up the engine. 'Absolutely fine.'

'How's Tally?' she tried later, as they rattled along the road towards Tresco Farm.

'She's fine too.'

'Right. That's good, then,' said Lucy, her tingle of anticipation having rapidly changed to genuine anxiety. What was the matter with him? Surely he couldn't have changed his mind about asking her to move down here to Tresco with him? For the past three months, they'd talked of little else. Every weekend, they'd met up either in Cornwall or London, planning how they could be together and now that Lucy had finally decided, now that she was here to tell him she'd actually gone and *done* something, he seemed distant and cold. Her stomach lurched. Oh please, let him not have changed his mind. Not now.

Josh seemed to be concentrating unusually hard on negotiating the twisting high-banked lanes that led to Tresco and by the time they pulled into the yard of the farmhouse, she was feeling almost sick with tension. He got out of the driver's door and unloaded her bag while she climbed down from the truck. Then he went on ahead to unlock, stepping into the kitchen without switching on the light as she hovered half in, half out of the doorway. From the gloom of the kitchen, a furry bundle hurtled towards her, its tail banging softly against her legs. Crouching down, she ruffled Tally's head, grateful to have a moment to compose herself. 'Hi, girl.'

Josh had crossed to the worktop and had his back to her, seemingly intent on the mail that was scattered on the counter. After he hadn't said a word for what seemed like an age, Lucy could stand it no longer. She flicked on the light and crossed the tiles towards Josh.

'Please tell me what the matter is,' she said, reaching out a hand to touch him.

He flinched. 'Nothing. I'm fine.'

'No, you're not. I know you too well now. Tell me . . .'

Lucy almost imagined rather than saw him rub his sleeve over his face before turning to face her and because she loved him and knew he'd die if she let on, she pretended she hadn't seen him crying. And because she loved him she summoned up every ounce of courage and gave him a lifeline, if that was what he needed.

'Josh. Please. If you've changed your mind about me moving down here, it's OK. I mean, it's not OK. Not at all! What I mean is, I'll try to understand.'

His face crumpled in horror. 'I haven't changed my mind.'

She searched his face and he glanced away at the window in shame.

'Then why are you acting like this? All cold and . . . and *stiff*?'

'*Stiff*?'

'Well, yes. Not speaking to me. Distant. You know what I mean!' she cried. 'Josh, I can't keep this up. Tell me that you still want me to move in here, because if you don't, I take back what I say about it being all right. I've given Lorna a full-time job looking after the London office and I've told all the clients I'm going to be working from down here and I've got tenants for the flat and—'

Josh reached out his fingers and lightly stroked her cheek, making her mouth tingle inside, almost unbearably. 'Lucy, my love, I want you with me more than anything in the world. In fact, I want more than that. I'm sick of losing the people I love and I want to make sure, this time, that I don't lose you. You see, I've agonised for a whole damn week, wondering if it was too much to ask you to rearrange your life for me. By the time I saw you get off the plane, looking so . . . bloody corporate, I'd convinced myself that it was too much to ask. I thought you were going to tell me it was all over.'

'All over? Oh Josh, nothing could be further from the truth!'

'I can see that now but you have to understand. Until now, I've lost pretty much everything I've ever loved and I'm scared that having you is too good for me. You see, I want to – God, I don't know how to say this without it sounding cheesy, but I really want you to spend the rest of your life with me. Make it formal. Jeez, what a mess I'm making of this. Look. I want you to marry me.'

What happened next was weird. Lucy felt as if the whole world had begun to turn around her and that neither of them was quite real. But Josh was still talking, running his hand though his hair and stumbling over the words. 'I know it will mean putting up with my moods, my cooking, wetsuits in the kitchen, but I really love you . . .'

It was then that Lucy realised that there are very few moments in life when you knew what you wanted, completely, utterly, and without a single shred of doubt. And this was one of them.

'Josh, I love you. I love the whole messed-up, beautiful package that is you. The answer's yes and just so you understand, I'll keep on telling you until you believe it.'

He seemed so genuinely amazed at her answer that she knew, then, she would love him for ever. Then a smile spread over his face.

'You know, I don't think telling me will be enough,' he said, pulling her towards the farmhouse table. 'I think you'll have to actually show me how much you love me, every day.'

Claws clattered on the tiles as Tally shot out of the kitchen.

'*Every day?*' whispered Lucy as her head bumped softly against the tabletop. 'Three times at least,' said Josh, lowering his mouth to hers.

Discover more gorgeously romantic reads
from Phillipa Ashley . . .

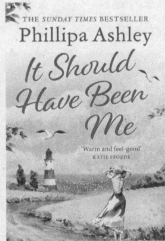